ONE SMART WITCH

The Hollowbeck Paranormal Cozy Mysteries
Book 2

AMELIA ASH

KIM M. WATT

STERLING & STONE

ONE

It started with ferrets

THE DAY BEGAN WITH A FERRET.

The blonde woman stood in the middle of the shop, wearing spotless white jeans, strappy high heels, and a silk blouse that would have cost at least a month's wages in my last job. Currently, I had no wages, so that didn't even come into consideration, a fact that didn't make me feel any better, but at least excused the fact that my own jeans were far from spotless. I wiped my hands on them surreptitiously, as if I might get grimy fingerprints on our visitor by some sort of osmosis. Her complexion was flawless, her makeup perfect, and her hair was doing that *just-so* thing some women seem to have a talent for. A cavernous and distinctly designer-looking handbag hung from one shoulder, somehow not daring to crease her blouse, and her earrings were devastatingly tasteful.

And then there was the ferret.

The little village of Hollowbeck had its share of *eccentric* residents, to put it mildly, but the ferret was definitely clashing with the woman's whole vibe. A chihuahua or one of those little poodle things, likely with ribbons or

1

diamonds or both adorning it, I'd have accepted. The ferret, not so much. I'd have been able to guess it was the problem even if she hadn't been holding it out in front of her, both hands wrapped around its torso just behind its forelegs. It dangled there docilely, staring at me and Starlight with bright eyes, not looking particularly perturbed.

The woman, however, looked distinctly perturbed. "It's a ferret," she said, as if we might not have noticed, and gave it a little shake. The ferret blinked lazily, then yawned.

Starlight clicked her tongue in disapproval. She came out from around the shop counter, long skirts swirling in soft shades of greens and silver-shot blues, and rescued the ferret from the woman, who relinquished it eagerly. Starlight cradled the creature in both arms, making little shushing noises at it, and I hoped it didn't bite her. It seemed relaxed enough, lying there with all four paws in the air, but I wasn't an expert in ferrets. Its teeth looked worryingly sharp, if it decided to use them.

"So, a ferret," I said to the woman, raising my eyebrows at her. "Um ... do you need some help with it or something?" It wasn't like we had a sign saying *Ferret Rescue* over the door.

The woman sighed, a large and exaggerated sound, and took a bottle of hand sanitizer from her bag. She doused her palms, rubbing it in enthusiastically, and I wasn't sure if that was due to the ferret or to the distinctly less than pristine environment of our shop. Well, my shop — The Cosy Cauldron, which had yet to have the spring cleaning I'd promised it when I'd found myself unexpectedly its proprietor. I had a feeling the previous proprietor had never got around to one either, and every time Starlight and I managed to clear one shelf, we seemed to find another five stuffed with acid-etched souvenir seashells, (*why?* We were in the middle of the damn country), bundles of desiccated medicinal herbs with spider colonies in the twigs, or mysterious bones that I hoped were some sort of arcane paraphernalia but which I suspected were actually the remains of small animals that had happily lived out their lives in the shop and whose descendants were probably still doing so. Clearing out was going to take *a lot*, and I'd been otherwise occupied, for the most part.

Largely I'd been dealing with the large ledger that lay open on the counter in front of me, and the old, leather-bound grimoire next to it. I'd acquired both along with the shop, an aging rat called Jacqueline who was currently regarding the ferret with myopic suspicion, and a huge number of dodgy deals that seemed to involve most of the inhabitants of Hollowbeck in one way or another, all of which I was still trying to untangle. All of which had previously belonged to Norma, a woman I'd never met until I found her dead in a cauldron out the back less than a month before.

Like I said, I'd been busy.

Now the woman pointed at me with one perfectly manicured finger. "You said you were going to release everyone from their deals," she said.

"I'm doing it as fast as I can," I replied. "It's quite a complicated process." Understatement of the century. Norma had been the sort of dealmaker that would've made those demons who buy souls at crossroads jealous. Wait, were they real? I'd never considered that possibility, but then I'd never considered the possibility of witches being real until a few weeks ago, either.

"Well, something's gone wrong," the woman said. "I've got ferrets."

I looked at the ferret, then back at her. "I mean, he seems quite nice."

"*Ferrets.* Plural. A whole bloody plague of them." She pushed her hair back with one hand, and I saw a bite mark on the inside of her arm. Okay, so ferrets did bite, it looked like.

"Were ferrets part of your deal?" I asked.

"No," she replied, and waved at the ledger. "I'm in there. Janice Thornbury. I'm the estate agent."

"Right." I started leafing through the pages, squinting at Norma's cramped handwriting. That explained the woman's flawless appearance. I had the vague idea it was part of estate agent training, how to look so immaculate no one wanted to raise any concerns that might slow down a sale or ruffle a seam.

Starlight came to peer over my shoulder, and after a moment she looked at Janice and said, "Was it to do with that big country house you sold? Something about making sure you got the sale, not your partner?"

Janice straightened her blouse. "*Ex*-partner. He didn't deserve that commission. I do all the work in this place. I always have."

Starlight and I carefully didn't look at each other, but I was fairly sure she was wondering the same thing as me — was he "ex" before or after the country house deal?

"What was Norma's fee?" I asked, still searching for Janice's name. There was no system to the damn ledger, nothing alphabetised, just written as the deals occurred, and half of them didn't even make sense. Norma had had her own codes and shorthand, and so far, Starlight and I hadn't been able to find the key. I had hoped Starlight would have some insight on the matter, as she had worked with Norma, but the old witch (that's literal, not an insult — she was an actual witch) hadn't let her apprentice deal

4

with anything more exciting than mixing up tinctures and salves. As a result, we were still figuring things out, and not always entirely successfully, as evidenced by the ferret.

"I just had to deliver a couple of items," Janice said, heavy bracelets clinking on her wrist as she folded her arms. "That was all. Nothing particularly excessive."

"Right," I said. "So where do the ferrets come in?"

"*I don't know*. That's the whole point. I never had ferrets before. And now suddenly you start messing around with the book" — she waved imperiously, setting the bangles clinking again — "and now I have ferrets. There's ferrets in my office. There's ferrets in my house. In my car. There was a ferret on my *pillow* this morning." Her voice rose towards the end of the sentence, and she pressed a hand to her chest, apparently overcome by the very thought.

"This ferret?" Starlight asked, tickling the creature's tummy. "He's cute."

"Not that ferret. That one was in my handbag." She opened the bag to peer inside. "I'm going to have to disinfect it. Might even have to sell it, if it's going to have some sort of ferret whiff on it. And it's designer, you know."

"Right." I went back to the ledger. "What were the items you had to deliver, exactly? Maybe that'll help me work it out."

Half of Hollowbeck seemed to run on a barter system, but Norma had taken that to a whole other level. A lot of her deals had involved getting people to plant charms or deliver various unpleasantnesses to others, in order to fulfill her side of *other* deals. It was clever, in a horrible sort of way, keeping her at arm's length from everything. But the deals weren't simple, or easily paid. People were tied into them until Norma said otherwise, and until they were released, she could demand further payment, for as long as she fancied. Even her death hadn't released anyone, as the grimoire next to me bound the deals. Whoever had the book had the deals, and if any were broken, the thing had its own ways of enforcing payment. Apparently via ferret, in this case.

"Rabbits," Janice said.

"Rabbits?"

"Yes, I had to deliver rabbits. Four of them. I had to leave them at the corner of the organic greenhouses just out of town."

"Real rabbits?" I asked, mystified.

"Of course not real rabbits. They were … I don't know. Felt or something." Janice wiped a hand on her immaculate trousers, as if remembering a distasteful feel to them.

"What happened after?" I asked.

She wrinkled her nose. "There was a plague of actual rabbits in the greenhouses. Destroyed everything and put them out of business."

I wondered who that deal had been for. There were plenty of little farms around. No doubt someone hadn't wanted the competition.

"Wouldn't you have rabbits, if this was about your deal backfiring?" Starlight asked Janice.

"How would I know? I'm not the one with the damn ledger." She scowled at us. "Do either of you even know how any of this works? Because I'm starting to have my doubts."

"Rude," Starlight muttered, but it was a fair comment.

"Found it," I said, tapping the ledger. It felt like a small victory, at least, although all it consisted of was Janice's name, followed by a string of little runes, none of which looked like either ferrets or rabbits. I really needed to find out what Norma's code had been, but unless we found a key somewhere, it was looking more impossible all the time.

"So what do I do?" Janice asked, stepping forward and peering down at the ledger. "How do we reverse this?"

I moved the grimoire in front of her, the heavy leather of the cover slick and unnaturally warm under my fingers. It always felt like that, vaguely alive. Jacqueline put a paw on my hand, chittering at me, which could've meant anything.

"Ugh, you're not going to make me bleed on it again, are you?" Janice asked. "I didn't appreciate that with Norma."

"No, I should just be able to sign it off," I said, with as much confidence as I could. "Put your hand on it." She did, and I placed my hand over hers, then looked at Jacqueline. She twitched her nose at me, which I was starting to think was the rat equivalent of a shrug.

"Janice Thornbury, I hereby release you from your deal," I said, and we all looked at the book expectantly. I felt there should've been a puff of smoke, or a little electric shock, or pretty much *anything* to show it had worked. At least the ferret should've disappeared. But nothing happened.

Janice narrowed her eyes at me. "You really don't know what you're doing, do you?"

"It's a learning curve," I replied. "I thought I'd actually managed to release most people last week. No one's been bringing in tomatoes or anything, anyway."

"Well, I don't know how anyone else is getting on," she replied. "But I have ferrets. So evidently this may have worked on vegetables, but not on mammals."

I sighed. While I'd hoped that I might be able to simply take ownership of the book, make a couple of mystical passes with my hands, and declare all deals off, I should've known that'd be way too easy. It *had* seemed to work for a few people, but I think all that had actually happened was that when it came to the little deals that consisted of people bringing Norma homemade bread or fresh strawberries, or cleaning the shop windows, there were no consequences from them stopping. Maybe there had never even been a deal in the first place. I wouldn't have put it past Norma to have just *told* people they were bound by the book to keep her pantry stocked, and the threat would've been enough to keep them compliant.

"Right," I said. "I'll keep looking into it. Let me get back to you."

"*Ferrets,*" Janice snapped, then stormed out, the bells at the door tinkling wildly in her wake.

Starlight and I looked at each other. "That went well, then," I said.

"I think she's right. It might take a bit more investigating to figure out how to get people out of major deals."

I sighed. "We *really* need to get this sorted."

The ferrets weren't the only strange happening related to my trying to break the book's hold on the town. A man who had struck a deal that enabled him to set up a natural, carbonated spring in his garden, which he'd been bottling and selling to all the local shops and restaurants, currently had a geyser in his backyard that went off at regular intervals with an explosive force that had caught his visiting mother-in-law unawares and hefted her two fields over. She'd landed in a pile of rotting hay and had been unhurt, but it wasn't ideal (although he'd been grinning widely when he told us). He was now marketing the geyser to the local kids as a water ride, so there was that. But it didn't change the fact his entire property was awash in fizzy water and all the cows were burping.

So, no, releasing the town from Norma's deals wasn't

progressing well. Neither Starlight nor I knew enough about how the book worked, or the nature of the deals, or about being a witch, or about magic in general to be very effective. The only person other than Norma who might have done had been banished from town, due to the fact that she had killed Norma and had had a good shot at killing both Starlight and myself as well.

So I wouldn't have been inclined to ask her for help even if she had still been around.

I rubbed my forehead. "How're we going to fix this?"

Starlight played with the ferret's paw, ignoring its bared teeth. "We'll just have to go case by case. We'll figure it out."

"*When?* I feel like we've been poking about this bloody book *forever.*" I scowled at it.

"It's not been that long. And, I mean, people are bound to the book, but it's yours now. Just don't ask them to do anything."

"Sure," I said, "but it's still not *nice,* is it, them being bound like that? And what if someone else gets hold of the book? They'd have control of half the town."

Starlight wrinkled her nose. "You did claim the book," she said. "So *technically* no one can just take it."

"*Technically* isn't that reassuring."

She sighed. "They'd have to break your claim, so it's pretty safe."

"*Pretty safe* still isn't reassuring. How do they break a claim?"

"I'm not entirely sure," she said, not sounding that convincing. "Just keep it super-safe."

I wanted to say *great, I hadn't thought of that,* but I managed to bite it back. At least Starlight was trying to help, unlike my disaster of a brother, who barely bothered to come to the shop at all half the time. And he was the reason I'd been dragged into this whole mess in the first place.

I put a sticky note next to Janice's entry and wrote *ferrets* with a couple of question marks on it. "How did she end up with ferrets when she planted rabbits?" I asked.

"Don't apply logic to magic," Starlight said. "It never works. But maybe it's because people like rabbits more, which is very unfair. Ferrets are lovely." She cuddled the ferret a little closer, and it hissed at her, which didn't seem that lovely to me.

TWO

Stormy waters & fishy thin

STARLIGHT WANDERED into the back to make a cup of tea, and I decided that a morning of ferrets and irate estate agents had to have earned me a coffee. I took myself across the road to Bewitching Brews.

The little wrought metal tables and chairs under its green awning already all taken. There were a couple of women sharing a glass pot of tea, full of floating flowers and leaves that reflected the vines above, and an elderly man at the next table was trying to keep his cat sticking her paw in his cappuccino, without a great deal of success. A man and a woman in matching tweed jackets were playing some sort of speed chess, shouting abuse at each other and laughing helplessly, and the fourth table held just a black-clad woman with a pinched mouth who looked so displeased, I wondered if she was the mother-in-law from the farm.

I headed through the door, into the warmly lit and heavily scented interior. The bar stools at the counter were free, so I took one, watching James frown down at a cup as he poured a silky cap of milk into it. He set the cup on the counter and I peered at it.

"Is it a shamrock?" I asked.

He sighed. "It's meant to be a fern. You know, just the basic pattern."

"Oh. Well, it's better than last week's," I offered, although, to be honest, that was just because last week's efforts had been nothing more than Rorschach blotches.

"So encouraging." He put the cup onto a tray with a little plate holding a brownie. "Edith was really good at it."

"Yeah, but she was also slinging charms into people's mugs whenever she fancied," I pointed out, then watched him take the tray out to the grumpy-looking woman outside. She stared at the mug, then back at him, unimpressed even by his wide grin. She must be inhuman. I hadn't seen anyone of any gender who could resist that grin.

James came back in and set my own personal mug up on the machine — it had a picture of a grumpy cat on it, and the text read simply, *No*. "Are you sure you don't want a latte?" he asked. "I could do with the practice."

I made a face. "Too much milk."

"You're not helping me." He pointed to a clutter of mugs in the sink. "I've had about six cups already this morning."

"Just get one of those stencils," I said. "You know, where you shake the cinnamon on top and it makes a pattern."

He stopped what he was doing and stared at me. "That's cheating. *And* it's only good for cappuccinos. Imagine if I served Ruby a latte with cinnamon on top?"

"Fair point. And at least your designs aren't obscene anymore."

12

He wrinkled his nose. "You should've seen the one I did for Theodore last night."

"Theodore drinks *coffee?*"

"No, he just likes the whole ritual of it." Theodore was the entirety of the town's well-attired and endlessly courteous police force. Theodore was also a vampire, so, yes, not exactly inclined to drink coffee. That the town police force consisted of one supernatural being who couldn't come out in the daylight was less bewildering when one took into account the fact that the mayor was a ghost who liked to introduce herself as the Ghostess with the Mostess. Starlight's comment about not applying logic to magic could be extended to not applying logic to Hollowbeck, I felt.

And somehow, in the last month, this had come to seem perfectly normal. Before that, I'd been just like any other person, separated from my husband, ensconced in a run-down apartment, and trying to restart my life, having thrown in my boring but reliable job as the same time as I had my predictable and crushing marriage. Then my brother had marched into my life and completely ruined it, as he always did.

Thinking of him, I said to James, "Have you seen Ruiner?"

"I think I saw him go past earlier," he replied, pushing my coffee toward me. I sniffed it appreciatively. What James lacked in artistic skill, he made up for in really good coffee skills, which included roasting the beans in the room next door.

"Where was he going?"

James waved vaguely. "I don't know. I've never paid much attention to where cats go."

It was a fair point. I slid off the stool, planning to head

back to the shop, and stopped as I noticed a poster in the window. "What's this for?"

"It must've gone up last night," he said. "No idea but it looks like there's a carnival coming."

I poked my head through the door so that I could examine it the right way round. They'd leaned heavily into the vintage look, laughing clowns and sword swallowers and acrobats all rendered in heavy dark lines and reds and yellows, and lots of text shouting about "*The Great, the Incredible, the Unmissable MASTERS OF MAYHEM!!*"

"Like the name," I said.

"I know," he agreed. "I don't think I've been to a proper circus since I was a kid."

I looked at the poster again it. Among all the frantic forms, there was a lion, a couple of elephants, and some indeterminate forms that could've been donkeys or could've been really badly drawn horses. "Are they allowed to use animals still?"

"No idea around here. Acrobats and stuff will still be cool, right?"

"It actually would," I said, checking the date. It was coming that Saturday. Something about it gave me a shivering thrill, tapping into some childhood longing for magic and adventure. Not that I hadn't found enough of both here already, mind, but at least I could be a spectator at the carnival, rather than in the middle of it, which seemed like an improvement.

AS I CROSSED the road back to the Cosy Cauldron, I could already see the poster in the door. I frowned. It hadn't been there when I left, and when I looked down the street I spotted splashes of red and yellow on the lampposts with their heavy cargo of flower-stuffed hanging baskets, on the notice board outside the little grocery store, plastering the wood paneling outside Mystic Munchies, bordering the windows of both the touristy clothes shop and the one that was courting every esoteric wannabe with its corsets and capes, and even stuck to the bags of dog food piled outside the pet shop. It was as if that first one, pinned to James's door, had been the initial wisp of pollen, and all the rest had blown into town on the next gust of wind.

There actually was a friendly little breeze running about the place too, but the posters seemed impervious to it, not a corner threatening to curl. I dug my almost non-existent fingernails under the edge of the one on our door, but I couldn't even manage to tear the paper.

"Huh," I said, and had a sip of coffee.

"*Masters of Mayhem,*" someone said. "Is that preemptive? So if the lions start hunting the trapeze artists and the elephants stampede through the crowd, they can just say, *hey, it's totally in the name?*"

I looked at my brother. He was examining the poster with his ears twitching slightly in the breeze, his thick grey fur painted with soft warm undertones in the autumn sun. He made a very pretty cat, although it wasn't the ideal situation. Trying to fix that for him (as I always had to fix *everything*) was what had landed us in Hollowbeck in the first place.

"You would think that," I said.

"It's pretty good business sense, really."

"And thinking *that* goes a long way to explaining why you're a cat. Where've you been?"

"Here and there." He looked up at me, his eyes a familiar and deeply human blue. "Found a way to make me human yet?"

15

"Decided to tell me who turned you into a cat yet?"

"How should I know? Someone who took a baseless dislike to me, I imagine."

"I doubt there was anything baseless about it," I said, and waved at Jacqueline, who had appeared inside the display window, peering out at us suspiciously. She tended to stay close to the grimoire. As a familiar, she was its guardian, and while she'd gifted it to me (something I wasn't all that grateful for), she seemed to have well-founded reservations about my ability to look after it.

"Ugh," Ruiner said. "That bloody rat of yours. She keeps trying to bite me."

"I highly doubt that. Or she must have good reason for it. She's a very civilised rat."

"That's an oxymoron."

"Like a nice brother?"

He growled, and I grinned.

"Why're you swanning about on coffee dates, anyway?" he demanded. "You need to un-cat me."

"So tell me who did it, so that I have something to go on."

"*I don't know.*"

"Of course you know," I said. "You just won't tell me because you're embarrassed. What did you do to her?"

"Why would it be a her?"

"It has to be a her. It's always a her when you get someone really upset. And they must've been *spectacularly* upset to turn you into an animal."

He looked down at himself, then at Jacqueline. "At least I'm a decent animal."

She hissed at him through the glass, and he hissed back. I flicked his ear, and he hissed at me instead. "She started it!"

"You were rude to her," I replied. "Don't be rude to the nice rat."

He huffed. "You have changed, Morgan."

"And whose fault's that?" I asked him. "Who dragged me into all this?"

He shrugged, looking down the road. We could talk pretty freely in Hollowbeck, as half the population had an animal familiar. Like Jacqueline, they had their own ways of communicating, and seeing someone chatting to a non-human was commonplace. But I'd yet to meet any familiars who talked back, and given that we still didn't know what or who was behind Ruiner's transformation (I was still sure he'd been rude to the wrong witch), we tried to pretend he was just a regular-ish cat when anyone else was around. There was no one nearby, though, and I said, "Where've you been, really?"

"Trying to find some leads, since you won't."

I ignored the dig. "And?"

"And not much," he said with a sigh. "I heard Grace was back in town, though."

"Grace? As in something you're very short on?"

"Oh, hilarious. Grace the witch." He shuffled his paws uneasily, then added, "The one who was going to set up in opposition to Norma, so Norma got me to put some charms on her shop as part of my deal."

Oh, yes. Of course my brother had made a deal with Norma, and was still bound to the book. He really should be nicer to me, since it was *my* book and therefore my deal now. "The one whose shop you set on fire?"

"*I* didn't do that. It was Norma's charms. I just put them there."

"Ew, yes. Sneaking in, doing your seduction thingy."

"That wasn't *exactly* part of it. Anyway, apparently she's back."

I thought about it. "And she didn't curse you?"

"Not as far as I know."

"Then we should talk to her. Or we should talk to her either way, really."

"*Why?* I'm not exactly going to be her favourite person."

"She was a good enough witch to set up in opposition to Norma," I pointed out. "She might know something about breaking the curse."

"*No.* Definitely not."

"Why not? What harm can it do?"

"Morgan, I might not have burned down her shop, but I did set the charms," he said. "Plus, you know. We had a thing. She's probably a bit upset I broke that off, too."

"You really are a terrible person."

"Yeah, well. Maybe. But you see? Not only will she not be interested in getting me back to human form, she'll probably set a dog on me or something."

I shook my head. "You don't help yourself, you know."

He huffed. "We have other options."

"Such as? Norma's dead, Edith's banished, and the only other decent witch I know is Petunia, and all she deals with is weather." Which, admittedly, she did well. Hollowbeck was having the sort of autumn that seemed to belong on a postcard of New England, not to actual England. It was all trees lit up in flaming reds and oranges under luminous blue skies, rather than relentlessly grey days of mud and drizzle.

He nodded at the poster. "That."

"You want to join the circus as a talking cat?"

"*Morgan.* Read the damn fine print."

I rolled my eyes at him, mostly because I knew it annoyed him no end that cats couldn't roll theirs, and read aloud, "*The Talented Trapezing Trio! The Cavorting*

Clowns! The Bearded Babe! Jared of the Jungle, the King of Cats!
That one?"

"No, divot. *Legendary Lionel.*"

I ran down the list of attractions, then said, "Legendary Lionel the Wizard? What, they didn't make him
change his name to Wonderful Wallace?"

"You're missing the point."

"Which is?"

"*Wizard,* Morgan. Wizard!"

I scratched my jaw. "A carnival wizard?"

"It's got to be worth a try."

I looked at my brother, his eyes wide and guileless, and
sighed. Maybe it was. Probably it wasn't, but this was the
problem with Ruiner. It was really hard to say no to him,
even for me, and once he was set on something, he was
stuck, whether it made good sense or not. "Sure," I said.
"Can't hurt, right?"

"*Yes.* We're off to see the wizard!"

"*No.*"

He huffed cat laughter all the way inside.

RUINER and I went out for a drink that night, which
probably says something about my social life. Not only was
I going out for a drink with a cat, I was going out for a
drink with a cat who was my brother. Or maybe it should
be, not only was I going out for a drink with my brother,
but my brother, who was a cat. I don't know. Both options
seemed equally pathetic the more I thought about it.
Although, at least I had a rat with me as well, right?

Hollowbeck hardly seemed big enough to support a
cocktail bar as well as the three pubs scattered about the
place (a country one with low ceilings and open fires, a

gastropub for the fine diners, and a seriously old-fashioned boozer that had apparently never heard of smoking bans), but Tanya's place was always busy. It nestled among the shops on the main street, a narrow, deep building with a roof terrace crowning it, and Ruiner and I headed straight upstairs. We didn't need to stop and order drinks. No one did — we got what we were given here, and somehow it was always exactly what was needed.

Ruiner sprawled on the deep cushions of the pallet seating, and I settled next to him, grabbing one of the blankets that were laid out invitingly on the end of each bench. It was chilly but not uncomfortable out here, and I caught a whiff of rosemary from the herbs that were twined in among the potted roses. Mellow music drifted from speakers hidden in the trellises, and I waved at a woman at one of the other tables. She'd come in the other day for a dream catcher and something to stop fairy circles.

"You're settling in," Ruiner said to me.

"What choice do I have?"

He made a noncommittal sound. "No more notes?"

"Thanks. I'd almost managed not to think about them for five minutes." When we'd first got here, they'd kept turning up, warning me to stay away from Hollowbeck and what didn't concern me. There hadn't been one since I'd acquired the grimoire, but I kept waiting for another to arrive. Another threat, or one carrying consequences. Because I certainly hadn't listened. I was sunk up to my eyeballs in Hollowbeck, with my cat-shaped brother, my rat familiar, and the magic book I was so terrified of losing that at night I kept it hidden in the walls of the guesthouse we were currently calling home, where the frogs could keep an eye on it.

I didn't know why I was being warned away, if it was due to the book, or the shop, or because of Ruiner somehow. Most likely it was the latter — everything that went wrong in my life seemed to be to do with Ruiner. Ruiner or my ex-husband. Men, possibly, I think, is how that could be summed up.

"Maybe they've given up," I said now.

Ruiner didn't bother responding to that, which was fair enough. Nothing ever worked out that nicely.

Tanya appeared with a bowl of fishy-smelling soup for Ruiner, a little plate holding a couple of balls made of nuts and seeds for Jacqueline, and a pale purple cocktail that was smoking extravagantly for me. I gave her a questioning look.

"Stormy Waters," she said, grinning. Her canines were just slightly too long.

"Isn't Stormy Waters orange juice and rum?" Ruiner asked.

"Not here, it's not," she said to him. "Drink your bouillabaisse."

"I don't drink bouillabaisse," he said. "I'm a cat."

"When it suits you," I muttered, and handed Tanya a pot of salve. She took the top off and sniffed deeply, giving a little growl of pleasure. It seemed that all the cocktails wreaked havoc on her hands, and being a werewolf with bald paws was embarrassing. I tried not to think about werewolves too much, just as I tried not to think about Theodore and his gloopy red cocktails.

"It's cat-friendly bouillabaisse," she told Ruiner, then frowned in distaste. "Oh, there's that damn carnival again." She grabbed a couple of flyers which had blown underneath one of the tables and got wedged in the corner.

"Those things are everywhere. What did they do? A drone drop or something?" I asked her.

She gave me an amused look. "Drones don't get very

far in Hollowbeck," she said, and nodded at the crows lining the walls.

I stared at them. "They take out drones?"

"You should know by now that Hollowbeck guards itself." Her smile faded as she looked down at the flyers in her hands. "Not well enough though. I can't believe they're back."

"Back?"

"They keep coming around." She crumpled the flyers up, scowling. "Must be five years or so this time. Too soon, anyway."

"Is it that bad? Surely it's just a carnival."

"Can't you feel it?"

I looked around dubiously. "It's very warm for autumn," I offered.

Tanya gave a little snort of laughter and patted me on the arm, her skin surprisingly hot. "Never mind," she said. "You'll see."

She headed away, and Ruiner and I looked at each other. He shrugged and shoved his nose in his bowl. "I might like bouillabaisse," he said. I didn't reply, a ribbon of unease uncurling in my stomach. I had the sudden feeling that calling on Legendary Lionel might not be one of our better ideas.

THREE

That time of the month

THEODORE JOINED us not long after it got dark, threading his way through the tables with a pint jug of red liquid clutched to his chest. He'd evidently been at the fake tan again, his skin a luminous shade of orange that made his deep eyes and sweep of glossy hair startlingly dark in comparison. He slurped at his straw as he sat down next to me.

"Are you well, Morgan?"

"Not bad," I said. "Small problem with some ferrets."

"Ah. The deals?"

"The deals."

"I'm sure you'll work it out," he said, looking as if he were going to pat me on the shoulder, then thinking better of it. "You're very capable."

Ruiner snorted, splattering the table with bouillabaisse, and I scowled at him.

"I am," I said, and Jacqueline gave a little titter that I didn't appreciate very much

Theodore examined them both without letting go of his straw, then eventually came up for air — or a pause, as

23

I suppose vampires don't really need air — and said, "You're assembling quite the menagerie."

"Two," I protested.

"I'm not a menagerie," Ruiner said, soup dripping from his whiskers.

"And ferrets," Theodore pointed out.

I sighed and took another sip of my Stormy Waters, which tasted somehow of sunsets over distant seas when the fog's coming up and there's ice on the horizon. It made me shiver, but in a good way.

"What do you know about this carnival?" I asked Theodore, then immediately wished I hadn't.

His dark eyebrows drew down as he frowned, a little of the red liquid smearing the corner of his mouth. "I will be glad when it's gone."

"Tanya seems to feel the same."

"Everyone does."

"It's really that bad?"

He didn't answer, stirring his drink with his straw. The red liquid seemed to be steaming slightly in the cold air, and my stomach rolled over.

"If it's that bad, why don't you just stop them from coming? Ban them or whatever."

"It's not that simple."

"I don't understand why not. You're the police. Just say there's nowhere for them to pitch their big top or something."

Theodore sighed, which somehow served to make his cheekbones more dramatic than ever. Not even the orange skin could detract from them much. "Some deals are older than police. Older than towns, even. The carnival has always come. The carnival will always come and it will bring with it mayhem."

I had a feeling he wasn't talking about just the name,

and my stomach twisted again, but it was nothing to do with Theodore's drink.

The evening was subdued after that, and I went home feeling jumpy and unsettled, as if the night was charged with electricity. Ruiner got into a hissing match with one of the neighbourhood cats that turned into a spat, and I had to stomp around waving my arms and yelling to break it up. Then my brother was in such a huff he took a swipe at Jacqueline, she bit his tail, and when I pulled them apart, they both tried to bite me. In the end, I shut them both out of our attic room and slept on the bed alone. Or tried to — their combined yelling and scratching at the door finally forced me to let them in at some ridiculous hour of the morning. They both looked put out and dishevelled and we slept as far apart from one another as the bed would allow, none of us talking to the other.

I couldn't tell what was my own nervousness and what was some slowly gathering threat on the horizon, but I didn't like any of it. I checked on the grimoire five times in the night, and dreamed of it being wrenched away from me by faceless men in loincloths.

I'm not sure what the loincloths were about.

THE NEXT MORNING when I went downstairs, the kitchen was cold and there was no food left out, which was unusual. Our landlady never failed to leave fish or chicken in the fridge for Ruiner, and there was normally a loaf of bread or some muesli for me. I poked around warily, but there was something about Petunia's kitchen that made me reluctant to dig too deeply into her cupboards. It wasn't just the presence of many mysterious jars that could've held anything from ancient curses to fossilised chocolate oranges. It was simply the fact that we were guests in her home, and so far she had yet to charge me rent. Luckily, since I didn't have any money to pay it with. I had no desire to upset that balance.

I went in search of Petunia, the anxiety of the night before still gnawing at me. She wasn't in the living room or the dining room, and I was wondering if I was going to have to explore the house's extensive first floor to try and find her bedroom when I pushed the door to the lounge open. A conservatory had been added to the front of it at some point, and Petunia had apparently taken this as an invitation to turn it into a jungle of houseplants, and a perfect habitat for her extensive collection of frogs.

Today she was evidently going for the full, authentic jungle experience, as a fire was roaring in the grate and Petunia herself was sprawled in a large armchair with a towel underneath her, wearing bike shorts and a singlet. "I've made it much too hot," she told me as I walked in. She was dripping with sweat, and there were paddling pools full of frogs scattered on the floor.

"Um … is everything okay?" I asked her. I didn't know what constituted out of the ordinary behaviour in Hollow-beck, but this seemed out of character, if nothing else.

Petunia managed to give me a fleeting smile and shook her head. "Can't stand that carnival," she said. "I'm not moving till it's gone. I'll be in here with the frogs if you need me."

I opened my mouth to question it, spotted the half-empty bottle of whisky on the side table, and instead just said, "Let me know if you need anything."

She waved me off, leaning her head back against the chair, and I collected my two-animal menagerie and headed into town. At the corner, two men were screaming at each other over a fence, both of them armed with hedge clippers and taking swipes at the bush that divided them. Further on, a young woman was beating her mailbox with a shovel for no reason I could see, and an older woman a few houses down was pulling bits off a lawnmower, flinging them into the road while an elderly man clutched his head and wailed. I scurried past with my head down, trying not to be noticed.

Outside Bewitching Brews, two bicycles had run into each other, and a man and a woman were grappling on the ground. The woman was trying to haul the man's bag away from him while he screeched about assault and hit her around the shoulders with a battered loaf of bread. As I approached, James hurried out of the coffeeshop with a bucket of water and threw it over the pair, sending them rolling away from each other, gasping like stranded fish.

"Will you *stop* it?" he shouted, and they promptly started yelling back. I stood on the side of the road watching, then looked at Ruiner, who'd been following a couple of paces behind me.

"Do you think this is the mayhem Theodore was talking about?" I asked him.

"No idea," he replied shortly. "I can't believe you shut me outside with that rat."

"I can't believe you tried to bite me," I replied. On my shoulder, Jacqueline cuddled a little bit closer to my neck, which I took to be an apology. At least someone had the good grace.

James was shaking his bucket at the couple, and I grabbed his arm, pulling him into the coffeeshop. "What the hell's going on?" I asked.

"No idea," he replied. "It's been like this all morning." He plucked at his T-shirt. There was a distinctly coffee coloured stain running from the shoulder down to the belly, making the cloth stick quite nicely to his chest.

"Did someone throw a coffee at you?"

"Yes," he said with feeling. "They were offended by my latte art."

I made an encouraging noise, and he scowled at me.

"It wasn't *that* bad. Not rude or anything." He headed around the counter. "The usual?"

"Yeah, and give me a muffin as well. Petunia's hiding from the carnival, so there was no breakfast this morning."

He nodded and set the coffee machine going, then popped a large blueberry muffin on a plate and slid it across to me. "Loads of people are acting really weird."

"Theodore was last night, too," I said. "You don't think much would upset a vampire."

"Yeah. Do you feel okay?" he asked me.

"I think so. Hungry, mostly," I added, and tore a bit off the muffin.

"I'm fine too," Ruiner said. "If anyone's asking. Can I have a coffee?"

"No," I said to him. "Cat, remember?"

"I got some cat milk in if you want a bowl," James said, and Ruiner hissed. "Well, excuse me for bloody breathing."

"Behave," I said to them. "And give me another muffin and a coffee to go. I think it's going to be one of those days."

I LEFT BEFORE two other customers could come to blows over the last triple chocolate muffin, stashing my own in my bag until I could give it to Starlight. She was scratchy and jumpy, and came as close to being rude as I'd ever seen her be when I suggested we spend the day doing another search for the key to Norma's codes. She all but shouted at me that if there had been a key, didn't I think she'd have found it? Did I really think that she was that useless? Then she vanished out the back, and I could hear her crashing around in the kitchen.

Ruiner and I looked at each other. "Full moon?" he suggested.

That was entirely possible in Hollowbeck. Not the full moon, obviously. The full moon came at the same time as it did everywhere else. But the fact that people would go a little bit bonkers at the full moon seemed very on brand.

I shrugged, and drank my coffee until Starlight re-emerged, looking a little calmer.

"Is it a moon thing?" Ruiner asked her.

She drew herself up. "I hope you're not suggesting—"

"Oh, for — *No*," Ruiner snapped. "Not *your* time of the month, woman. *Full moon*."

She scowled at him. "They're sometimes called the same thing."

"They're not."

"You're a cat. How would you know?"

"I'm a *person*," he snapped.

"A *male person*," she retorted, in tones which suggested that meant he knew even less than a cat.

I pinched my forehead. "Do we have an almanac or something that will tell us if it's full moon?"

She sighed and looked at me. "You really need to pay more attention if you're going to be a witch. It's still almost a week away."

"Not Saturday night?" I asked, suddenly sure of the answer.

"Yes. Why?"

"That's the carnival night," I said. Because of course it'd be full moon. I couldn't have said why that made perfect sense and was entirely horrifying all at once.

Starlight clapped her hands together, bad mood banished. "The carnival! Of course! That's just what we need."

"That doesn't seem to be the general opinion around here," I said. "People seem to think it's going to be a problem."

"But carnivals are wonderful," she replied. "There'll be magic! That's so exciting!"

Ruiner and I looked at each other, and I said, "You do realise that we run a magic shop?"

She waved impatiently. "That's different. This'll be *proper* magic, not charms."

I wasn't sure if that was something we should be looking forward to at all. Not the way things were going.

THE MORNING BROUGHT MORE FERRETS.

Janice walked into the shop carting a massive cardboard box alive with scratching movement and dumped it in the middle of the floor. She glared at us, jabbed her finger at me, and said, "And there's more where they came from," and marched out again.

Starlight and I looked at each other.

"We're going to need to sort out the ferret situation," I said.

"How, though?"

I didn't want to mention looking for the grimoire key again, so I just shrugged. "Maybe we find somewhere that re-homes ferrets? A rescue or something?"

"Oh! They'd make good familiars," she said, then looked at her hand, which had a couple of Band-Aids wrapped around one finger. "Perhaps."

Despite her injuries, Starlight didn't seem too keen on

the idea of finding a ferret rescue somewhere. Instead, she made up a sign that read, *Ferrets Free To A Good Home!!!* with an exuberance of hearts and stars painted around it, and stuck it in the window. Then we corralled the creatures on the bathroom upstairs and listened to them scratching around the door.

"What do they eat?" I asked Starlight.

"I don't know. I tried lentils on Howard last night, but he wasn't keen."

"Howard?"

"My ferret." *Obviously*, her tone added.

"Right. I think we need a book." Hollowbeck's curious atmospherics meant no mobile phone signal, and its curious nature in general meant that the only internet was at the library, and it was sporadic at best.

"That's you off to the library, then," Ruiner said to me. "Off to hang with Benny Bestie."

"He's not my bestie," I said. "But he does actually have books, and we need one, unless you know how to raise ferrets."

He huffed. "I have no interest in ferrets. They're worse than rats."

Jacqueline hissed at him again, and he bared his teeth back at her.

"Honestly, is the whole town like this?" I asked. Starlight shrugged, and I wondered if it was even safe to go to the library. I couldn't imagine Ben, the town librarian, hissing at anyone or getting into an argument, but the assistant librarian was a little alarming. She looked like she could bite.

But I wasn't getting anywhere by sitting here listening to Jacqueline and Ruiner squabble, so I padded downstairs and headed for the door, opening it onto a cool day that was threatening rain at its crisp edges.

I'd barely stepped onto the pavement when I caught the whiff on the air.

It set my skin crawling, raised the hair on the back of my neck. A raw, feral scent, full of heat and excitement, whispering of long shadows and dark nights, and bright lights that painted the sky in wild colours. It smelled of half-tamed beasts and rough-hewn spells, of mystery and intrigue and a vague undercurrent of barely contained violence.

It made my heart stop in the chest, and it made me want to *run*. As if I was the sort of person who ever ran, but I still wanted to. I wanted to sprint toward that smell. I wanted to discover where it came from. I wanted to embrace the wildness and magic, to dance to tinny music, to be barefoot in the grass, and to twist and twirl across fragrant sawdust, to eat candy floss and toffee apples with a sticky mouth and gritty fingers, to smell strange creatures on the night and hear popcorn burst like gunshots in the distance.

I twisted on the doorstep, turning toward the scent without really being aware I was doing it, only half-aware that, across the road, Ruby and Jurgen were stepping out onto the pavement in front of Mystic Munchies. James was outside as well, a milk frothing jug in one hand and a tea towel in the other. All of us turned toward the lure that was more than simply scent, like weathervanes sensing a storm coming in.

At my feet, Ruiner said, "What the hell is *that?*"

Behind him, Jacqueline dug her claws into my jeans and scrambled up to my shoulder as Starlight pushed past me, barefoot on the pavement, already hurrying down the road. I came back to myself enough to run a couple of steps after her and grab her arm.

"Where're you going?" I asked.

"I want to see what it is," she said, trying to pull away from me. I tightened my grip. She was slight, but there was a wiry strength to her.

"Hang about," I said. "This isn't right."

Even as I spoke, half a dozen bikes tore out of town, kids hunched low over the handlebars, riding so hard that for a moment I wondered if they'd just robbed the bank, their eyes bright and their hair pulled back by the wind. A woman with a walker swung out of one of the dress shops and stood on the pavement, shading her eyes as she peered into the distance.

"They're here then," she said, and her voice was flat and hard.

"Who's here?" I called to her.

"That damned carnival," she said. "Can't you feel it?"

"Is that what that is?" I asked. "But it feels…" I trailed off. *Good* wasn't the word. *Exciting* was closer, but that wasn't it either. *Intoxicating*, perhaps.

She made an impatient gesture. "Oh, it feels nice enough now. But the rush always comes before the crash, doesn't it? Like bloody skydiving." She stumped back into the dress shop, flipping the sign to closed behind her.

Starlight and I looked at each other.

"It does feel a bit weird," I said. "Not safe somehow."

I could see her wanting to disagree with me, but she stopped pulling at my arm. We stood there, with that fierce wild wind washing over us and carrying the scent of magic and the promise of mystery towards us, and the cold nervousness of the night before started crawling about in my belly. This wasn't right. *None* of this was right.

FOUR

A Legendary (Lionel) hope

THE FLYERS HAD CHANGED. We spotted them that afternoon when we ran out to rescue our display of occult-themed postcards (mostly poorly printed Photoshops of fairies on toadstools and copies of tarot cards), which was making a break for freedom, driven by an urgent wind that hadn't settled since the carnival arrived. The poster plastered to the door had been joined by half a dozen others that had slid under the mat, and they all said the same thing.

Rehearsal night tonight!! Free entry! All welcome!

I frowned at the one on the door, trying to convince myself a new poster had been layered over the original, but I couldn't see any overlapping edges. When had they done it? We hadn't been wrestling ferrets for *that* long.

"Why would you have a free rehearsal night in a town this size?" I asked Starlight. "Surely they're doing themselves out of any sort of money. Who's going to come back and pay for a second night?"

She shrugged. "Maybe it's *really* good."

"That's a big risk to take."

Ruiner was pawing one of the flyers, and he looked up at me as Starlight went back into the shop. "This is perfect for us. We should go tonight and see if we can corner this Legendary Larry."

"Legendary Lionel," I said. "Should probably at least get his name right if you want him to help us."

"Whatever. But we're going, aren't we?"

I chewed my bottom lip. The wind was still unsettling me, the hunger of it, the way it had pulled everyone into the streets. Even now, anyone outside looked in the direction the wind was blowing, toward where the carnival must be, tugging at them even if they were walking in the opposite direction. The kids hadn't returned, either. Not this way, at least. I'd been looking for them, and their absence made me uneasy, as if the carnival might have devoured them. Not that it could have, of course, because that was ridiculous, and it wasn't like anyone would just let a bunch of kids vanish. Theodore definitely wouldn't. Although Theodore couldn't come out in the day, so who knew what could happen?

"Morgs?" Ruiner said. "We're going, right?"

"I suppose," I said, and hoped it was the right decision. Hoped neither of us would be devoured.

STARLIGHT, Ruiner, Jacqueline, and I stood on the pavement outside the shop, Starlight with Howard tucked into a soft cloth bag, his head poking out of the top, looking at us curiously. It wasn't dark yet, but dusk was heavy around us, running long fingers over the land and leaving streaks of blush in the clouds. I'd decided that the best way to approach a potentially creepy carnival was en masse, and before long, James jogged across the road to join us, and Ben came ambling down the pavement with his hands in the pockets of a dark green, quilted jacket that fairly screamed *town librarian*.

We all looked at each other a little awkwardly, and Ruiner said, "Come on, then. Everyone join hands and skip off into the sunset. Or are you waiting for a chaperone?"

"Shut up," I said to him, my cheeks heating up.

"Then let's *go.*" He turned and trotted down the street, his ears back against the wind.

"What happened to him not talking?" Ben asked.

"It was too good to last," I said. "Besides, you all know he's my brother. We need to find someone who doesn't know and hang around them."

"I can hear you!" Ruiner shouted.

We headed out of town, the pavements vanishing with the last of the shops and leaving us walking on the narrow road, pinned between drystone walls and the rich green of the fields beyond. There was a bite in the air, colder weather on the way, and the last of the sun painted the walls in deep shadows and soft greys. I could see a few people ahead of us, and a couple of cars passed, all heading in the same direction.

"So what do you think rehearsal night is all about?" Ben asked.

"What's a rehearsal?" Ruiner asked. "What do you *think* a rehearsal is, Word Boy?"

Ben raised his eyebrows. "It's a very small town and they're offering a free viewing. It's going to have to be a *really* good sell if people are going to come back and actually pay for it."

"Maybe they'll only show half the act," Starlight said.

"Like, they'll drop the curtain right in the middle of the knife-throwing, or just as the elephants are charging, so we have to come back tomorrow to see what happens."

"Just as the elephants are *charging?*" Ben said, his forehead furrowed. "Charging what?"

"Not entry fees," I said, mostly to myself, and Ruiner huffed cat laughter.

"Might be limited entry," James suggested. "Maybe they only let in a handful of people, then you go out and tell everyone else how amazing it was for the next night."

"Or they just magic the lot of us," Ruiner said. "You know, make us forget everything, then we'll just keep coming back and paying again every night because we won't remember anything about it. They could keep it up for months."

He marched on, unconcerned, while we all looked at him. After a little while, James said, "Do you think they could do that?"

Everyone looked at me and I spread my hands. "I have no idea."

"Well, you're the resident witch," James said, then winced. "I didn't mean it to sound like that. I meant it in a good way."

"What, like Glinda?" I asked, and Starlight gave a little snort of laughter.

"Just don't drop a house on anyone," Ben suggested. "Probably wouldn't go down too well."

THE CARNIVAL WAS SET up on a field not far beyond town, and considering it had only come in that afternoon, it had sprouted like a fairy city. Brightly painted caravans and striped canvas tents were pitched all around the edges, and a Ferris wheel rose in the centre, already shining with light and groaning its way through its first turns. I could see kids swinging in the seats, and I shivered slightly. Mobile rides always gave me the creeps. I mean, who knew how well maintained they were? Somewhere, something roared, and Starlight grabbed my arm.

"Was that a lion?" she asked.

I wrinkled my nose. "Circuses aren't meant to have proper animals these days."

"True, but this is a Hollowbeck circus," Ben pointed out. "It could have anything."

I really wish he hadn't said that. Now I was thinking of dancing bears and snake charmers and probably Cerberus dogs and chimeras besides.

We reached a wooden gate standing open onto the field beyond, and a big man with tattoos curling out of the neck of his jacket examined us, smiled, and said, "Welcome. The show is free. Everything else, you have to pay for."

"Yeah, I bet it's all marked up a hundred and fifty percent as well," Ruiner said in a low voice, and the man looked around, puzzled.

"I assure you it's not," he said. "It's just normal prices."

"Normal *carnival* prices."

I nudged Ruiner with my foot and returned the man's smile. "Thanks," I said. "It looks great."

"It's better than that," he said, his grin widening. "It's *magical.*" He waved us through with a flourish, then held up one finger in almost theatrical warning, glancing at me with a considering expression then turning his attention to Starlight. "None of your magic inside the grounds, though, little witch. The carnival doesn't allow outside magic."

Starlight looked him up and down. "*Little witch,*" she said, and sniffed. "I should turn you into a toad."

"Not inside the gate, you can't," the man said, and

grinned even more broadly. I took Starlight's arm and pulled her along with me before she could try it anyway. I had no idea how much magic she had, but I'd seen the results of some of her experiments. The last thing we needed was a carnival worker with webbed feet to deal with.

We trailed our way into the fairground. Given the way the town had been acting, I'd expected a horror show. Never mind the dubious welfare of circus animals, I'd been imagining awful, old-school attractions like weird creatures suspended in formaldehyde, and conjoined twins paraded about like they were monstrosities, and people with fake fingers stuck to their ears or something weird like that. Or maybe everything taken to a Hollowbeck level, shooting games with actual bullets or stalls where you could throw knives at your enemies, or dunk them in tanks of piranhas.

Instead, there was a grandmotherly-looking woman knitting furiously in a stall while a man shouted, "Beat Esther's knitting speed and win ten pounds!" Further down, two kids were frantically competing to eat as many chocolate cookies as they could with their hands clasped behind their backs, their faces smeared with crumbs and melted chocolate. A large sign above that stall proclaimed, *Beat the speed-eating record! There are no losers!* I thought that was probably fair enough, considering that if you got to stuff yourself with chocolate cookies, I didn't see how anyone could be a loser, no matter what the record was.

Further on were duck races with actual real ducks, all swimming around happily and wearing little vests with numbers pasted on them. As far as I could tell, the competition seemed to consist of throwing some birdseed into one end of a long tank, and the ducks would paddle toward it frantically, and may the fastest duck win. There was also competitive garland weaving and cake decorating, giant trampolines with competitions for the highest jump, and even a massive ball pit which a handful of kids were thrashing wildly across as we watched.

I looked around, unable to quite find the words.

"*Wholesome*," Ben said, a wondering note in his voice. "This is *wholesome*."

He was right. Even the food stands were simply *better*. Someone was making fresh pasta at one, and at another green juices were being blended up, and while there was popcorn, it was popcorn with half a dozen different fancy toppings. Even the candy floss promised to be made from pure organic sugar and no artificial colours. Everything about the place was simply *nice*.

"This is weird," Ruiner said.

"*So* weird," I agreed. "Why was everyone so worried?"

He lifted his chin towards the big top. "Let's see what it's like when we get in there."

I followed his gaze. All the fairy lights and fresh flowers and softly dancing garlands of leaves that decorated the funfair made it feel as if it had grown from the ground, full of blossom and life, but the old, stained canvas of the tent stood apart, heavy and dark and watchful. It crouched above us like a poorly camouflaged beast, sending a shiver through my stomach.

That felt much more familiar.

WE WANDERED around the carnival for a bit longer. I got pizza from a man who was doing the actual thing of throwing the dough in the air and spinning it around, and I watched with fascination as he eventually flung it down on a peel, scattered tomato sauce and a bunch of toppings on top, and shoved it into a wood-fired oven that was roaring behind him.

Starlight was tucking into a crêpe topped with ice cream, syrup, nuts, and so many different fruits I could barely see the crêpe at all, while Ben was eating a hot dog laden with almost as many toppings. And by the time I had my pizza in my hand, James had come back to join us, clutching a large cone of caramelised peanuts in one hand and chewing on a giant chicken leg he had grasped in the other.

"Did that come from a dinosaur?" I asked him.

"Turkey leg," he said. "I've only ever seen them on TV before."

"You've only seen turkeys on TV before?" Starlight said. "Where've you been living?"

"No, I mean, obviously I've seen legs on an actual turkey," he replied around a mouthful of meat. "I mean buying them like this, in a fun fair. I thought that only happened in America."

We all made agreeing noises, and Ruiner, who was sitting on the shoulder Jacqueline hadn't commandeered, hooked a piece of ham off my pizza and said, "Tell me this isn't weird."

"Of course it's weird," I said. "It's a funfair in Hollowbeck."

"We need to find Legendary Larry."

"Legendary Lionel," I said, and looked at the others. "Hey, I think we've got about half an hour before the show. Why don't we split up and have a wander around?"

"Should we split up?" Starlight asked. "Seems a bit dangerous."

"I'm sure it's fine," I said, not looking at the big top. "I'll meet you in a bit." I headed off before anyone could offer to come with me, munching on my pizza. It wasn't so much that it was a secret we were trying to change Ruiner back, just that I knew they'd all want to come and help, or interrogate Legendary Lionel, or have half a dozen probably well-founded suggestions why employing a carnival worker to lift an unknown curse was a bad idea. It was easier just to go and work it out ourselves.

"Have you seen any signs or anything?" I asked Ruiner.

"It's got to be around somewhere," he said. "Try the next row back from all the food stalls."

I did, stepping into an alley that was a little more like the fun fairs I remembered. There was a darts game, where a curvy young woman clapped cheerily as three men competed to pop a row of balloons with very little success, and just alongside that an enormous man in a very small leopard skin bodysuit offered to wrestle anyone who fancied taking him on. He feinted at me a couple of times, grinning broadly, and I waved him off, laughing. At the next tent a man sat in front of a chess board with a boy of about eight opposite him. The boy moved his king, and they both frowned at the board. A semicircle of adults watched, completely absorbed, and the sign said, *Chessboard Charles, Childhood Champ!* One woman's ice cream was dripping over her fingers and she licked at it automatically.

Further on was something called a tent of therapeutic butterflies, and beyond that, another with steam drifting from the seams announced itself as a sauna. A caravan painted in shades of purple and silver offered palm and tarot readings with the Fantastic Fiona, and then, finally, we spotted an old-fashioned gypsy caravan, listing a little to one side, with *Legendary Lionel* in slightly shabby paintwork on the side.

"That's it!" Ruiner jumped from my shoulder and ran to the steps.

"Slow down and let me do the talking," I said. "At least until we know what's going on."

He huffed irritably but stood back as I headed for the door.

"Excuse me!" someone called from behind me before I could knock.

I turned, startled, to see a curvy woman swathed in a swirling dress that matched the shades of the clairvoyant's caravan. The skirts swept the ground, but the cleavage would've given even Isabella pause. "Hi?"

"If you're looking for fortune-telling, you should come to me," she said, fluttering her hands at herself. "The Fantastic Fiona. I have a woman's touch, you see."

"Oh, it's not for fortune-telling," I said. "Thanks anyway."

"Are you sure?" She pressed one hand to her brow, closing her eyes dramatically. Her eyeshadow was purple, too. "I see … great distress in your future."

"Me, too," I said. "Probably involving a cat. Or ferrets."

She opened her eyes a smidge and sneaked a peek at me, frowning. "I mean, it'll be very distressing for you if you insist on getting your fortune from cut-rate *wizards.*"

"*Fiona!*" someone bellowed from behind us, and I spun around to see a broad-shouldered man leaning out of Legendary Lionel's caravan. "Stop poaching my bloody clients!"

She dropped her hand and glared at him. "I'm not poaching! *I'm* the fortune-teller here!"

"You heard her! She doesn't want her fortune read. If she needs someone to witter on about how tragic her love life is, I'll send her over later!"

"Ouch," Ruiner said. "They got you, Morgs."

"Shut up," I hissed at him.

"How about tarot?" Fiona asked me. "I will tell you how to find your one true love with a single reading!"

"*Utter bollocks!*" Lionel roared.

"No thanks," I said to Fiona. "One marriage is enough."

"But then it was not true love! Enter and I shall—"

"*Fiona!* Let the damn clients do what they want!"

"*Back off, Lionel!* You come in here with your crystal ball like you've any idea how to tell fortunes—"

"*I don't tell fortunes!* The ball's for my spells! How many times—"

"Likely bloody story," Fiona snapped, straightening her sleeves. Her bosom was heaving so dramatically I feared for the integrity of her dress.

"I don't want my fortune read," I said. "I just want to speak to a wizard." *Because I don't think I'm in Kansas anymore,* my head added helpfully, and I had to cough into my hand to stop a sudden bubble of laughter. *This* was how we were going to help my brother? A squabbling old man with flowers in his beard?

Ruiner looked at me with his ears back, and I had an idea he was thinking the same thing.

"See?" Lionel said to Fiona.

"Your loss," she muttered, and gathered up her skirts, sweeping back to her caravan with her head high.

Lionel turned to me, said, "Sorry about that," then cleared his throat, and in an entirely different voice boomed, "Greetings! I am the Legendary Lionel! Enter, enter, my dear. Tell me how I may be of service."

Ruiner and I exchanged dubious looks, but when the wizard stepped back, I edged past him into the caravan. A little wood stove rumbled at one end of the cramped space, with an armchair and side table to one side of it and a long bunk with beaded cushions dotting it on the other. Side lamps cast everything in a mellow glow, while the fire made it uncomfortably warm. A crystal ball sat on the side table, full of slow-moving, misty colours and giving me back my reflection in distorted angles, and I thought of that feral wind rushing through the town.

Lionel pulled the door closed with a final *clunk*, and my mouth went dry.

FIVE

The show begins

LEGENDARY LIONEL SANK into the armchair and waved me toward the bunk. "Come, come," he said. "Let us talk of what ails you."

I took a breath, steadying myself against that unexpected wave of fright. This was nothing more than a sideshow act. And even if it wasn't, what harm could it do? It wasn't as if some random carnival worker was going to have nefarious designs on my brother. Probably it'd all come to nothing, but at least we'd have tried, and I could go back to nagging my brother to tell me who'd actually made him cat-shaped.

"Nothing really ails me," I said, perching on the bunk. It was comfortable enough, but I had an idea it was likely also his bed, which made it feel a bit weird.

"So why do you seek out the Legendary Lionel? Is it insomnia? Heartbreak?"

"No and no."

"Curious." He tapped his chin and eyed Jacqueline. "An infestation of rats?"

Jacqueline hissed, and I scratched her back gently. "The rat's fine."

He looked at Ruiner. "Is the cat a problem then?"

"Definitely," I said, and Ruiner narrowed his eyes at me.

"I see." The wizard examined Ruiner, who jumped up next to me and sat down, tucking his tail neatly over his toes and returning Lionel's gaze with great interest. After a moment, the wizard looked back at me, green eyes sparkling.

"Your cat is not just a cat."

"Not exactly," I admitted, impressed in spite of myself.

Lionel grinned broadly. "Aha! It is an enchanted cat."

"Yes. And I'd like to get him un-enchanted."

"So you would like to be returned to your true cat-ness?" Lionel asked Ruiner.

"*No,*" Ruiner and I said together, and Lionel blinked.

"A talking cat! You're *terribly* enchanted, aren't you?"

"I'm a *human,*" Ruiner snapped.

"Oh, right." Lionel looked less impressed by that than he had been by the possibility of a talking cat. "That is indeed a conundrum."

"It's a bloody catastrophe."

"A *cat-astrophe,*" Lionel said, and grinned again. I couldn't help snorting with laughter, and Ruiner glared at me. The wizard rearranged his features into something more serious and said, "What brought about this catastrophe, then?"

"I have no idea," Ruiner said.

"He upset someone, as usual," I said over the top of him.

Lionel gave me an interested look. "Who? It must have been quite a powerful magic worker."

"He won't tell me," I said.

"Ah. A little shame, perhaps."

"He has no shame," I said and Ruiner hissed. I stuck my tongue out at him. "You know it's true."

Lionel nodded thoughtfully. "I'm sensing the cat is not your beloved."

"*No*," Ruiner and I yelped.

"He's my brother," I added. "He was a nightmare as a human, and he might even be worse as a cat."

"*I am not. And was not.*"

"*Hmm.*" Lionel tapped his fingers together under his beard, then sighed slightly. He took his wizard's hat off and set it carefully next to his chair, then scratched his beard and his head at the same time, burying his hands in the hair like he was going to tickle his brain into working. Then he pulled both beard and hair straight off. Ruiner and I both squawked in fright, even as he revealed a clean-shaven head and a neat white goatee. "Sorry," he said, dropping the fake hair and itching his chin furiously. "Bloody things are hot as hell. And you're not actually here for the performance." His voice had swung back from deep and booming theatre tones to cheery with a touch of Liverpool.

"Um, no," I said. "But we do need help."

"Are you even a *wizard?*" Ruiner demanded.

"'Course I am." He stretched, looking younger without the beard and hair. He had three piercings in his left ear and a cartoon dog tattooed over his right. "This is going to cost, though."

"Fine," Ruiner said at the same time as I said, "How much?"

My brother bared his teeth at me, and I glared back. "How much?" I repeated to Lionel.

"It'll cost what it costs," the wizard said. "We can work out a payment plan. It all depends how much you want it."

"I want it," Ruiner said. "I get *hairballs*. Hairballs!"

Lionel leaned forward, hands hanging between his knees, and regarded Ruiner almost eye to eye. "So tell me, my furry friend, who did this to you?"

Ruiner huffed. "Does it matter? It was done. I just want it undone."

Lionel glanced at me, and I shrugged. "Yeah, he won't tell me either."

"You don't remember?" Lionel suggested to Ruiner.

"I don't *know*."

They stared at each other, then Lionel looked at me. "I think you should probably leave."

"Sorry?"

"Your brother might talk to me when he won't talk to you."

"He bloody should talk to me, the crap he's put me through."

"I *am* here," Ruiner said.

I scowled at him. "So, you'll talk to your new buddy here, then?"

"Like a doctor, isn't it? Confidentiality and all that."

"More like a vet," I said, getting up. "Do *not* make any deals we can't afford."

"You're not the one stuck as a cat," he replied.

A moment later I was outside, listening to Lionel locking the door behind me. At least if he got Ruiner changed back, my brother would be responsible for paying his own debts. In theory, anyway. I sighed and headed for the big top, wondering if the next time I saw my brother he might be human again.

As it happened, the next time I saw my brother, he was

sitting on top of a dead body. Which was not an improvement in anyone's situation.

~

I WANDERED BACK DOWN through the fairground, where I discovered Starlight wrestling with Howard, who had spotted the ducks and was either terrified or hungry, I wasn't sure which. Theodore and Isabella had arrived, neither of them looking too happy to be there. Our ghostly mayor was resplendent in her eternal outfit of long dark skirt and dangerously low-cut blouse.

"Hello, dear," she said to me. "I hope you haven't sold your soul to anyone."

"Not to my knowledge," I said, thinking uneasily of Lionel and *it'll cost what it costs*. "Is that something I should be worried about?"

"You should be worried about *everything*," she said, scowling around the crowd, which had thickened while I'd been away. A man who'd evidently been sampling the organic cider fairly heavily stumbled through the edge of her skirt, and she tutted. I'd never seen Isabella tut.

"It doesn't seem that bad," I said. "The way everyone's carrying on, I thought it was going to be some sort of horror show."

Theodore was clutching a deep red and disturbingly *gloopy*-looking popsicle, and he frowned at me, his lips pink. "It might not *look* too bad. But can't you feel it?"

I looked around and shrugged. I honestly couldn't. There had been that fleeting unease in the caravan, which had dissipated somewhat when Lionel had revealed himself to be less Gandalf, more Gary from down the road, and sure, the big top was kind of creepy still, but here, in the midst of the stalls, everything felt kind of *nice*.

Holiday-ish, like we'd stepped out of everyday life for a moment into an oasis of homemade pasta and knitting competitions. My dread from early felt pretty unfounded. Jacqueline chittered in my ear, but I couldn't tell if she was chastising me or agreeing. Rat communication isn't an exact science.

"You will learn," Theodore said, in a way that was irritatingly paternal, especially when he only looked my age at most. He was currently, despite the dripping popsicle and luminous skin, looking exceedingly dashing in a well-tailored grey suit and a pale lilac shirt. At some point recently someone had apparently persuaded him to update his look with trainers, and rather than clashing with his more formal clothing, they somehow made him look both cool and pleasingly eccentric. I had an idea it was due to the cheekbones. A *lot* could be blamed on those cheekbones. He licked his popsicle with rather too much enthusiasm, and I looked away.

"I think the show's starting," Ben said, his hands tucked into the pockets of his jacket. "Should we go?"

"Into the den of the beast," Isabella said darkly.

Starlight joined us, her squirming bag clutched to her chest and her cheeks pink. "I think Howard needs more socialising."

"Or dinner?" James suggested, grinning at her, and she scowled.

"He had dinner! I made him roast vegetables."

"Are ferrets vegetarian?" I asked her.

"I don't know," she admitted. "But I didn't have anything else."

"Come," Theodore said. "I want to get good seats to witness the hellish capers of this carnival of carnage." He walked off, his back straight, Isabella drifting after him, and we looked at each other.

"Does he know he actually made it sound really cool?" James asked.

"You would think that," Starlight said. "This is why I left you."

"*I* left *you* because of the whole eye of newt and toe of frog in the Sunday dinner thing," he said, amiably enough, and I led the way toward the big top. I wanted good seats too, but less for the show and more so that I could see my brother when he arrived, whatever form he might be in.

THE ENTRANCE WAS WIDE open to the night, the canvas pinned back, and bright lights in the ring cast vast shadows against the walls. The scent of sawdust and sweat fought with the smell of popcorn and the sweet, fine aroma of candy floss, and I had a sudden shudder of anticipation, a memory of that wild excitement that had whipped through town on the wind earlier. The ring was set up against the opposite wall to the entrance, and seating rose in a semi-circle to face it. There were half a dozen rows of folding chairs on the ground, then the rest stepped upward like gym bleachers, climbing to meet the walls. The seating was only half-full, so apparently not everyone had succumbed to the carnival's siren song.

We clambered into the second row of raised seating to the left of the entrance, perching on the hard surface like a row of crows. Clowns were already tumbling across the ring, raising cheers from the audience as they shot brightly coloured water pistols across the sawdust and into the crowd, piling on top of each other and scrambling up ladders attached to the tent's hefty support poles, swinging from the trapezes, leaping and tumbling with an incredible degree of athleticism.

"I don't like it," Theodore mumbled around his popsicle.

Isabella sighed. "Neither do I, my dear. But we must bear witness, if nothing else."

Theodore growled slightly and crunched on a bit of ice, and I wondered if I should be sitting right next to a nervous vampire.

A moment later the lights went down and a hush fell across the crowd as the clowns cartwheeled out of the ring. Music rose up, reverberating in the suddenly hushed air, and I could almost feel it shaking the canvas around us. The beam of a spotlight spun through the space before lighting on a trapeze artist poised on the edge of an impossibly small platform, sleek and sequinned. Empty-handed, they launched themselves into the air, diving into a free fall that jerked a gasp from the crowd, plunging toward the sawdust that seemed both fatally distant and *far* too close. At what seemed to be the last possible instant another body flashed out of the darkness beyond the spotlight. They locked hands and swung back into the shadows, vanishing into nothing. An *oooh* went up from the crowd, and a smatter of awed applause.

Someone else plummeted out of the dark, legs hooked through the trapeze, let go, somersaulted three times and was caught by another person who snatched them out of the air effortlessly then swung off again, vanishing from sight. It was mesmerising, and I forgot about edgy vampires and missing brothers and plagues of ferrets, and simply watched, unable to look away for an instant.

Suddenly darkness fell entirely, and I felt Theodore stiffen next to me as a nervous ripple passed through the crowd. The music swelled to a crescendo, then cut off as a spotlight bore down on the on the middle of the ring. A tall, well-built woman stood dead centre in the light, her head bowed slightly and her face obscured in the deep shadow cast by her top hat. She had one foot in front of the other, toes out slightly, and she was wearing immaculately tailored black trousers and a matching waistcoat buttoned over a blindingly white, puffy-sleeved shirt. She didn't move until enough time had passed that people were starting to shift a little uncomfortably, then she abruptly swept her hat off and dropped into a low bow in the same movement.

She straightened up, both arms out to her sides and a heavy mane of glossy brown hair cascading over her shoulders, her smile broad and her eyes glittering in the light. "Greetings, Hollowbeck," she called out, her voice booming across the tent, even though I couldn't see speakers anywhere. "Are you *ready?*"

A little wave of applause went up, and her grin widened.

"Are you *excited?*"

The applause was a little stronger this time, and someone whooped.

"Are you, as the kids say, *pumped?*"

Laughter this time, and more clapping. Theodore looked at me. "Do the kids say that?"

"I have no idea what the kids say," I replied, still clapping.

"*The Masters of Mayhem return!*" the ringwoman roared, flinging her hat into the air and spinning in place, arms still wide. "We bring the *wild!* We bring the *impossible! We bring the **magic!***" The hat landed neatly back on her head and she grinned ferociously as lights flashed across the crowd, blinding us momentarily. My hands were hurting from clapping, and I was grinning almost as widely as the ringwoman, and I couldn't seem to stop doing either.

Theodore frowned and muttered, "Cheap theatrics."

"I am Aubrey, your Mistress of Mayhem. And now, my friends, my guests, my people — *the show begins!*" She spun, pointing to the side of the ring, still hidden in darkness. "The magnificent, the wonderful, the *inimitable* Jared of the Jungle and his *ferocious* beast!"

"*Oooh*," I said, along with the rest of the tent except Theodore and Isabella, and the vampire reached out as if to clasp my hands and stop them clapping, then evidently thought better of it.

The light snapped off Aubrey and another blazed down at the side of the ring, where I assumed some hairy man in animal skins should be running out with a lion or an elephant or (given that we were in Hollowbeck) a griffin. Instead, it took a moment for me to understand what I was seeing. I was still clapping automatically, my hands not caught up to my brain, and somewhere I heard Starlight gasp. My hands stilled, and the entire tent fell silent.

I had a wild thought that this was all part of the act, but what sort of act would start with Legendary Lionel sprawled on the ground, staring sightlessly up at the canvas, while my cat-shaped brother sat on his chest, blinking at the light with his ears back?

Then someone shouted, "Is he *dead?*" and someone else gave an uncertain little scream, as if they were trying it on for size.

"*Lights off!*" Aubrey shouted, and suddenly she was sprinting into the circle of light. "Gods be damned, *lights off!*"

Theodore dropped his popsicle and vaulted the seat in front, running for the aisle, and more screams went up. People started to scramble for the exit, but before more than a handful could reach the aisle, the entire place was plunged into shadowy darkness, lit only by the light creeping through the entrance, and lying in a yellow wedge from somewhere backstage of the ring, outlining scurrying forms. The screams multiplied, but I didn't pause to wonder what to do next. I bolted after Theodore. That was my brother down there, sitting on the chest of a dead man. The dead man who had promised he could turn him back into a human, whatever the cost.

SIX

Carnival rules

THEODORE GOT to the ring a lot faster and more gracefully than I did. I was still dodging fleeing carnival-goers and scrambling over fallen chairs, yelping apologies, by the time he'd reached Lionel. When I finally arrived, he was crouched over the prone form, one arm extended to keep Aubrey at bay and the other pointing an imperious finger at Ruiner.

"Stay where you are," he said to my brother as I finally made it through the chairs and sprinted toward them, my trainers slipping in the sawdust.

I dropped to my knees next to him. "*Theodore*. That's my brother."

He gave me a look that said quite clearly he was aware of this fact. "Your brother who's in the middle of yet another crime scene," he pointed out. "Hollowbeck had never been known for its murders until your arrival."

"That's not our fault," I protested. "You know Norma was nothing to do with us!"

"And this?" Theodore asked.

"Theo, dear," Isabella said from over my shoulder, and I barely swallowed a yelp. "He is a *cat*."

"Exactly!" I said, and Ruiner blinked at us.

"Murders?" he said, in a bewildered tone which suggested he was still catching up.

Theodore pointed at Legendary Lionel. "Until proven otherwise."

Ruiner looked at Lionel's face and made a little noise of distaste, then I saw his pupils widen. He looked down between his paws. There was a second where he didn't move, then he yowled, almost levitating off the body, and landed on the sawdust already scrabbling for purchase. He shot across the ring with his tail up and his back arched, yowling all the way.

"*Ruiner!*" Theodore and I both shouted, and he gave me a disapproving look.

"You need to control your brother," he said.

"*Control* him? He's a *cat*. Besides, what's he supposed to have done? *Hairballed* him to death?"

"Morgan," Isabella started, her voice soothing, and Aubrey talked over her.

"That's not just a cat. It was talking. That's an enchanted creature. Who knows what powers it possesses?"

"Mostly the power to make really terrible smells," I said, and she gave me a startled look. "He's my brother," I explained, since Theodore and I had already let the … well, *brother* out of the bag on that one.

She narrowed her eyes at me. "Then you're probably a part of it as well."

"A part of what? There's nothing to be a part of. Ruiner didn't do anything."

She pointed at the body on the floor. "I think Lionel would disagree with you." Her voice caught on the last word, then she pressed her hand to her chest, swallowing hard. When she continued, her tone was strong again. "We come here out of the goodness of our hearts to entertain you, and *this* is how you repay us."

"I—" I started, not at all sure how to defend myself and Ruiner from that. Isabella gave a snort that was so ungenteel I had to check it was actually her making it.

"*Out of the goodness of your hearts*, Aubrey? Really? That's never been a defining characteristic of the Masters of Mayhem."

Aubrey lifted her chin. "Isabella. Good to see you changed outfits for the occasion."

"You must be working hard, dear. You're looking positively haggard."

"Not dead, though."

Isabella huffed, folding her arms, and Theodore gave a long-suffering sigh. "Can I trouble you all to move out of my crime scene, please?"

"Well, I'm hardly going to contaminate it," Isabella pointed out.

"And it's my crime scene, anyway," Aubrey said.

Theodore frowned at her. "This is a Hollowbeck crime scene."

She shook her head. "It's taken place within carnival grounds. You know the rules."

Theodore grimaced, then stood up, brushing off his long-fingered hands. I looked from him to Aubrey. "What does that mean?" I asked, getting up as well. "What rules?"

Theodore hesitated, and before he could reply, there was a commotion at the entrance of the tent. Most people had already made it out, but I could see a knot forming, and a bit of a scuffle kicking off. We all turned to watch, and Aubrey clicked her tongue, waving to a tall, lean man clutching a leash that was attached to an actual *lion*.

"Jared, put Coltrane back in his quarters, can't you?

Last thing we need is someone panicking about him, as well." She turned her attention to the large man in the leotard I'd seen outside, and a skinny woman with knives slung from harnesses that hung across her body. "Franz, Mavis — make sure the tent's clear." She looked back at us. "Of *everyone*."

Franz hulked toward us, while Mavis went for an alarmingly relaxed stalk, her hands resting on the handles of a couple of extra-large knives that were strapped to her thighs like a gunslinger's holsters.

"Aubrey," Theodore started, and she rounded on him, one index finger raised. The light seemed to tighten on her, casting the rest of us in deeper shadow.

"These are the *rules*, Theodore Ianculescu. Do you challenge the rules of the carnival? *Do you?*"

He sighed, his jaw working, then looked at me. "I'm sorry, Morgan. I can't do anything."

"What do you mean?" My chest was too tight, and I couldn't seem to draw breath properly, as if the sawdust had got in somewhere. "Ruiner didn't *do* anything!"

"It means," Aubrey said, "anything that happens within carnival grounds is subject to our laws. We determine who is responsible and how they will pay. This is not Hollowbeck business."

I looked at her, the floor unsteady under my feet. *She* wasn't unsteady. There was not just a solidity to her, but a sense of deep-rootedness, as if she stood closer to the earth than seemed reasonable. *Implacable*, that was the word. "My brother wouldn't have hurt Lionel," I managed. "We went to him for help."

"Helping can be the most dangerous thing of all," Aubrey said. "It may have been exactly what killed him. If that's the case, you and your brother will be held responsible."

"No," Theodore said immediately. "Morgan leaves with us."

They stared at each other, and I could almost feel the heavy weight of history between them. I wondered how old Aubrey was, how long she'd been tirelessly driving the carnival ahead of her, treading and re-treading the roads and lanes and byways that riddled the country, while the appetite for carnivals grew smaller and smaller, and the audience faded, grew scarce and sceptical, and the magic in the world faded. I tasted something melancholy and lost under the heavy weight of painted-on makeup and sequinned suits, a slow fading that was worse than a collapse.

A triumphant shout went up from behind one of the sets of bleachers, and a short, rotund man with a huge beard and a leather waistcoat came striding toward us. He had Ruiner tightly by the scruff of his neck in one hand. My brother's eyes were pulled back into slits, and even from here I could see his laboured breathing.

"Stop it!" I shouted. "You're strangling him!"

"He bit me," the short man said, raising his free hand so that we could see the bloodied marks decorating his forearm.

"Wouldn't you bite if someone was trying to throttle you?" I demanded.

"Let him go," Theodore said to Aubrey.

She shook her head. "You may retain the sister for now, but this is in our hands. We will determine what happens next."

"At least let me assist," Theodore started, and she cut him off.

"You're no longer welcome in the carnival. Leave." She didn't raise her voice, didn't make any sort of arcane passes in the air, but I felt the change anyway. It was as if the tent were growing smaller around us, the canvas pressing close, threatening to crush us in its folds like some strangely formed python.

"Theodore," I started, and he took my arm, his fingers chill even through the cloth of my jacket.

"No," he said simply. "We have no choice."

"But—" I could barely breathe under the weight of the suddenly hostile tent, but that was my *brother.*

"*Morgan.* We have to go."

Theodore pulled me away, propelling me toward the exit, and I shouted, "Ruiner! Ruiner, it'll be okay! We'll fix this!"

My brother couldn't manage more than a strangled gasp.

"*Ruiner!*"

Theodore pushed me back up the aisle, which was lined with the carnival crew, their faces flat and hostile as they watched us pass. There were women in silken dresses and men in natty suits, and vice versa, wearing bowler hats and headdresses, while others were scantily clad and holding swords or juggling balls or knives. They didn't move to intercept us, but Theodore didn't let go of my arm until we were outside, the air cold and sharp on my cheeks. I was startled to find I was close to tears. I looked around to see Isabella hustling out of the tent behind us, her skirts gathered up in both hands.

"Uncivilized *hound,*" she spat.

"I know," Theodore said. He kept close to me, as if worried I'd turn and sprint back into the tent. To be fair, if the carnival crew weren't now filling the doorway, I might've tried.

"We can't just leave Ruiner," I said.

"We have to," he replied, letting Isabella lead the way toward the gate, still muttering. The crowd had already thinned to almost nothing, the sideshows shuttered and the music silenced.

"Why?" I demanded. "You know he didn't kill Lionel. He's a *cat*."

"He's more than a cat."

"Okay, sure, but you know he's not capable of *killing* someone."

"Do I?" Theodore asked, and he sounded oddly tired. "I know very little of you and Ruiner when it comes down to it, Morgan. I only really know you have been chosen as the new town witch after you found the previous one dead."

"You know Enid did that," I said.

"I *believe* Enid did that," he replied. "But how do I know that Ruiner wasn't behind it somehow? Enchantments work in many ways, and he is so very desperate to be human again."

I stopped just beyond the gate, the lane uncurling in either direction and full of people hurrying away from the scene. "You can't really think that."

"I don't know what to think," he said, watching me with dark eyes. "How did your brother end up with *another* dead body? You said you went to the wizard for help. Perhaps Ruiner's enchantment is what killed him."

"This is a setup," I said. "It *has* to be. Whoever killed Lionel set Ruiner up. It's the only thing that makes sense."

He spread his hands. "There's nothing I can do. The carnival has its own rules."

I very nearly stamped my foot, like a child no one's listening to. "You can't just give up. Even if you don't like Ruiner, we're part of your town now. I thought you protected *everyone* in Hollowbeck."

Theodore sighed deeply. "Not when they're so bent on self-destruction."

"He's not," I said. "He just wants to not be a cat anymore."

"At what cost, Morgan? Have you asked yourself that? And who pays?"

We stared at each other, mired in the deep autumn night, full of fright and loss and the drowning year, while the last of the carnival lights went off, and someone pushed the gate closed, the click of the latch ringing somewhere cold and distant on the very edge of my hearing. The smell of popcorn and candy floss faded to nothing and the carnival turned itself inward, locking Ruiner away in its depths. I was alone out here in the night without my annoying, horrible nightmare of a brother, who nevertheless was my only connection to the world as I knew it, and therefore precious.

"I'll pay what I need to," I said, and Theodore made an unhappy noise, as if he were unsurprised but deeply disappointed nevertheless.

STARLIGHT, James, and Ben were waiting on the edge of the narrow road, all of them looking a little anxious and uncomfortable. I had a momentary surge of annoyance, thinking that they *should* be feeling a little uncomfortable, considering they'd just abandoned us in the tent and hadn't tried to help Ruiner at all, but it was short-lived. Ruiner wasn't the sort of person who inspired anyone to go out of their way to help him, and given all the large and unnecessarily fit people lurking in the carnival, I wouldn't have been putting up much resistance to leaving either, if he hadn't been my awful little brother. I was going to have some serious explaining to do to our mum if I couldn't get him back. It was bad enough that I might still have to explain the whole cat situation at some point, but if he was a cat *and* I lost him … well, I wouldn't be getting any of her commemorative royalty plates in the will, put it that way.

Starlight threw her arms around me as soon as we arrived, hugging me tight. "This is awful," she said. "Poor Ruiner. Poor *you*."

I couldn't help shooting Theodore a resentful look. "It wouldn't be poor Ruiner if we'd been able to take him out of there. He's obviously innocent, and who knows what they're going to do to him."

"They won't do anything until he's proven guilty," Theodore said.

"But how long is that going to take?" I asked. "I don't imagine they've got a High Court judge waiting in a caravan just in case."

Theodore sighed slightly. "No. But he's not going to be summarily executed, if that's what you mean."

Starlight gasped, hugging me tighter, and I stared at Theodore, unable to find words. Ben winced, looking around the lane as if wishing he were anywhere but here.

"A bit harsh," James said.

Isabella tutted. That was twice in one night. "I know you're put out, Theo, dear. But that was unnecessary."

Theodore looked from one of us to the other, then clasped his hands in front of him and bowed his head to me. "I do apologise. The carnival does tend to ruffle me somewhat."

"*Ruffle?*" I managed. "*Put out?*"

Starlight petted my hair, making soothing noises, and I pulled away from her, scowling at Theodore. He offered me his arm. "Allow me to escort you back to Petunia's."

"I don't want you to escort me back to Petunia's. I want you to stay here and get my brother back."

Theodore gestured vaguely at the cluster of tents and caravans beyond the gates, full of dark and furtive movement. "Our welcome was revoked. I cannot go back in unless invited. Nor can you."

"You're the *police*. You can go where you want. It's *your town*."

We all stared at him, waiting, and he examined us, then looked at Isabella. She spread her hands in front of her and gave a delicate shrug. He sighed and turned back to us regular mortals. "None of you have encountered a carnival before, have you?" he asked.

No one replied straight away, and finally Ben said, "I've read a bit about them?" He sounded like he hoped he wasn't going to get tested on it.

"It's just a funfair," I said. "So they've booted us out. We just sneak back in, get Ruiner, and get out. It can't be that hard."

Theodore looked at Ben expectantly, and Ben sighed. "When he says they have their own laws, they really do. It's like a different country."

I pointed over the gate. "*That* is not a different country."

"Yeah, it is. Just like Hollowbeck is its own place."

I rubbed my face with both hands. "It's just a *town*. And that's just a bloody funfair."

"You know it's not."

And I did, really. Ben and I had even tried to find Hollowbeck on the ordnance survey maps once, but as far as they were concerned, it didn't exist. Technically we were in the Lake District somewhere, but the whole area was depicted as a confused muddle of contour lines, all mushed together until it was impossible to tell if they indicated a mountain or a valley, peaks or ravines. So, yes, I knew it wasn't just a town, and by extension the carnival couldn't be just a funfair. But I still turned around and marched back toward the gate, my hands in fists at my sides. James caught my shoulder and I shrugged him off, then Theodore had hold of me, both hands firm on my upper arms.

"You cannot go back, Morgan," he said, sounding almost regretful. "The carnival is protected."

"They have charms," Ben added. "Guarding spells and so on. Once it's closed, it's closed. You wouldn't get over the gate."

I almost fancied I could see the charms, shivering the night air, but that might've been the fact that my eyes were stinging. "But my brother," I said, and my voice almost broke on the last word. Ruiner was annoying. He was *beyond* annoying — he was unbearable at times. He'd got himself turned into a cat and promptly upended my life, dragging me out here and expecting me to fix it. And as if that wasn't enough, he'd now got me tangled up with *two* dead bodies, not to mention witches and ghosts and vampire police.

But for all that, he was still my brother. I jerked away from Theodore, crossing my arms over my chest. "*Fine*. I'm not going to try and break through their charms or whatever—"

"You couldn't," Ben said. "They'd zap you back or something. It's quite interesting. They—"

"Ben," Isabella said, raising her eyebrows.

"What? Oh. Right. Sorry."

I ignored them, still glaring at Theodore. "You *have* to do something, though. You can't just leave him in there like a … like a *stray*."

Theodore nodded gravely, his dark eyes glittering in the moonlight washing across the fields. "I will do all I can. But you must let me handle it. If you try to sneak in there, you'll only be imprisoned yourself. Then they'll hold you guilty of trespassing, or aiding and abetting, or whatever else suits them, and neither of you will ever get out."

I looked back at the carnival, and I could feel the weight of its scrutiny looking back at me, whether it was hidden watchers or some sort of magical security or simply the old, heavy consciousness of the carnival itself. It sent a shiver up my spine, and thinking of Ruiner trapped in there was enough to make my pizza want to make a reappearance.

"Alright," I said aloud, and looked back at Theodore. "For now."

He inclined his head just slightly, smiling faintly, and I could see his canines dimpling his bottom lip. Somehow it was less scary than the lurking tents beyond the wall, which truly showed how badly my references were off.

SEVEN

Tea can't fix everything

WE WERE HALFWAY BACK to town, none of us talking, just following the last of the crowd as they straggled home, all of them huddling together against the dark, when I suddenly grabbed for my shoulder.

"Jackie? *Jacqueline!*" I did a frantic pat down of my jacket, but there was no familiar, ratty presence, and quite suddenly I was on the verge of tears again, clutching my head as if to hold myself in place as I stood in the middle of the road.

Starlight stared at me with both hands over her mouth, looking like she was about to start crying herself, and Ben and James glanced at each other uneasily.

I'd lost my familiar *and* my brother in a single evening. I had to be the worst witch in the history of the world, let alone Hollowbeck. I didn't move until Starlight put an arm around me and coaxed me on, talking soothingly. I didn't register a single word she was saying, but at least it meant I didn't have to talk.

The others peeled off slowly as we got back into town, but Theodore and Isabella flanked me silently all the way back to Petunia's. By the time we got there, the night had set shivers deep into my bones. It wasn't that it was so cold, but I could feel the loss of Ruiner and Jacqueline like frostbite somewhere in my gut. I stopped at the gate, the posts capped by stone frogs, and looked at Hollowbeck's authorities, who both seemed somewhat discomfited.

"Morgan, dear," Isabella started, and I shook my head.

"I'm going to bed. I can't even think about this right now."

"Perhaps one of Ben's teas," Theodore said.

I made a face.

"I'm not having someone dose me up on *calming teas* again, thanks. I'd rather get a whisky from Petunia." I still hadn't quite forgiven Ben for that. He'd evidently meant well, but you'd think someone that smart would've realised that giving someone unsolicited calming teas was going to have the exact opposite effect.

"As you wish," Isabella said. "Come and see me first thing tomorrow, and we can formulate a plan."

"Well, no," Theodore said. "I'll be sleeping."

She patted the air above his arm. "We won't do anything exciting without you." But she dropped me a wink as she turned away that made me suddenly hopeful that she might actually know what to do next. After all, if the carnival came back, however irregularly, she must have seen quite a few of them. Tens, even. Twenties? *Hundreds?* I had no idea how old Isabella was, but however many it had been, surely she must know *something* about them.

I scraped one of the double gates open and let myself into the rambling, overgrown garden. It was given over mostly to wilderness, but a wilderness in which a certain order still existed. Clusters of fruit trees, feral veggie patches, and swathes of long, wildflower-studded grass that provided homes to squirrels and dormice and frogs and hedgehogs and all manner of other wildlife. Probably ferrets, too. I wondered distractedly if I should find out if Petunia was willing to extend her frog passion to some ferrets. We were going to be overrun if Janice kept turning up with boxes of them.

Despite my bold claim about the whisky (and a sneaking thought that it was actually quite a good idea if I wanted to sleep), I sneaked in as quietly as I could. I couldn't cope with a cheery, up-and-at-'em Petunia right now, and I certainly couldn't cope with a Petunia who was sulking in the conservatory with her frogs.

I crept up to the first floor instead and checked the bathroom. It wasn't my time slot, and even though, after over a month here, I had yet to encounter any other guests, when I tried to use the bathroom outside of my allocated time it was quite often occupied by a variety of users who seemed to splash about a lot but never left any traces behind except some rose petals in the drain.

Tonight, though, it was thankfully empty, and I sat on the edge of the big claw-footed bath as it filled, emptying some softly scented salts out of one of Petunia's dark glass bottles and watching them drifting quietly in the currents.

How could I have lost Ruiner? How could I have let that happen? I shouldn't have left him alone with Lionel. I mean, who knew what had happened? Maybe whatever spell Lionel had been trying to use to break the curse had somehow rebounded and killed him — although that didn't explain how they had ended up in the ring, my brother perched on the wizard's dead body.

My stomach flopped over again, making it hard to breathe, and I pressed both hands to my forehead. And Jacqueline. What had happened to her? Had she fallen when I'd been fighting my way to my brother? Had someone *snatched* her? Or — oh no — *eaten* her? There had been an actual lion there, after all.

How could I be a witch without a familiar? Not that I'd set out to be a witch, but I definitely felt more witch-like with a familiar. And how was I going to figure out—

"*The book.*" I shot upright and slammed through the door, pounding up the creaking stairs two at a time, jumping the broken ones and diving into our attic bedroom. It was dark inside, the lamps unlit, and I fumbled wildly at the switch until I could flood the room with light. I fell to my knees so hard in the corner by the bed that I knew I'd be bruised the next day, but I barely felt it. What if this had all been some ploy to make sure the book was unguarded? To distract me, to get rid of Jacqueline …

I pulled the bedside table out of place, hooked my fingernails into the skirting board, and tugged it so hard two of my nails bent back painfully. I hissed, but renewed my attack, and a moment later the board fell away. Four pairs of bright eyes glittered out at me and I took a shaky breath.

"Hi, guys," I said, and carefully removed the frogs. I had no idea what purpose Petunia's amphibian army served, but somehow the fact that they were still there reassured me.

I reached into the cavity, stretching up until I could hook a soft bag off a beam just within my reach. It clumped down, bringing some dust and spiderwebs with it, and I hugged it to myself, my heart slowing slightly. I still had the grimoire. That was something. It *had* to be something.

The frogs and I looked at each other, then I remembered the bath and jumped up with a yelp, sprinting out of the room and taking the book with me. Capping the night by flooding the guesthouse would seem to fit the day, but was also needlessly insulting.

The bath hadn't yet overflowed, and I pulled the chair over next to it to set the grimoire on while I got in. It was hardly the best bath-time reading, considering the weight of it, but I also had a suspicion I wasn't going to do much damage if I did drop it. A book like that looked after itself. I was more worried about what it might do to my bath-water — or me, for that matter.

A couple of frogs sat on the side of the bath watching me, but I ignored them, leafing slowly through the book. I'd been it through it so many times by now, staring at the jumble of recipes and spells and curses and strange little doodles done in half a dozen hands, but it still seemed that every time I picked it up I discovered something new. Not that I knew what I was looking for. Something to exonerate the unjustly accused, perhaps. Or *How To Break Into a Carnival Without Being Eaten or Stabbed. How To Find Your Missing Familiar?*

But whatever it was, I didn't find it. I stayed in the bath until the water went cold, and I thought I might even be able to sleep, then padded back upstairs and curled myself into the bed. It was cold and startlingly empty without Jacqueline curled on the pillow next to me, and Ruiner sprawled opposite, complaining every time I rolled over and alternating between quiet little cat snores and his rough unpractised purr.

I couldn't stand the fact that I'd lost them, and I couldn't wait on Theodore. I was going to have to come up with a solution.

∼

I DIDN'T SLEEP MUCH, not that I'd really expected to. The next morning, Petunia was still ensconced in what was rapidly becoming a sauna, so I topped up the frogs' paddling pools and took her a cup of tea, then headed into town, the grimoire tucked securely into my backpack. Hollowbeck's picture-perfect autumn weather was deteriorating along with the mood of its weather-witch, and hard low clouds scudded across the sky, a sharp wind ripping leaves from trees and setting dogs barking and cats bouncing sideways across lawns. Even the crows looked ruffled, and two of them buzzed me as I headed up the path to the town hall. I waved them off irritably and scowled at the handwritten note taped to the door, fluttering precariously. *At library,* it said simply, and I turned with a sigh and headed in that direction. I don't know why I was surprised. I'm not sure how other towns worked, but Hollowbeck's mayor seemed to spend precisely none of her time in her offices.

The library door opened onto a warm, book-scented atrium, full of the muted sounds of pages turning and covers sliding across shelves, and I stopped at the top of the few steps that led down to the main floor, breathing in paper and ink and a thousand unread stories. Dee, the assistant librarian, was at the round desk in the centre of the atrium, wearing heavy boots under a yellow tartan dress so glaring it made my eyes water. She nodded at me, then went back to stamping books. I'm sure one of the things that kept me in Hollowbeck was that they still stamped books.

Isabella came rushing out of the stacks as if she'd heard me come in, running across the main room with her long skirts swirling around her. She came to a stop in front of me and fluttered her hands over my shoulders, not quite touching me. I could feel the chill of them drifting against my skin as she examined me carefully.

"You didn't sleep."

"I got a little."

"It's not surprising. This is a terrible thing to happen, Morgan. I'm so dreadfully sorry."

My throat tightened, and I swallowed. "Thanks. But there has to be a way we can fix it, right? You said we'd come up with a plan."

She nodded. "Yes, and Ben and I have been looking all morning." She beckoned me to follow her into the rambling shelves, heading for Hollowbeck's extensive occult section.

"What've you found?"

"*Hmm.* It's not a simple task. Carnivals are old creatures."

"*Creatures?*" I stopped, staring at her. "Is that a figure of speech?"

She see-sawed her hand in the air.

"It's bunch of tents and popcorn stands!" Although, it hadn't felt exactly like that. It had felt like *more,* and the way it catered to everyone, all the organic this and home-grown that, every modern taste accommodated, seemed off. It had the feel of a carnivorous plant dangling the sweetest nectar over its maw.

Isabella nodded, as if she knew what I was thinking. "A carnival is not alive, exactly, but nor is it entirely inanimate. It recreates itself constantly, changes." She thought about it. "*Adapts.*"

I shuddered. "And, what — it *eats* people? Is that what happened to Lionel?"

"Oh, no. I've never heard of *that.*" She looked thoughtful, though, and I wondered what sort of adaptations the carnival might still have hidden in its canvas pockets. "But you're just in time. I was about to ask Dee to help me." She pointed at the shelves. "We need *that* one, and *that* one."

I stood on my tiptoes obediently and pulled down *A Treatise on the Complicated Matters of Magical Entertainment* by Enrico Alessandro Matiz, PhD, then *A Short Argument Regarding the Laws & Regulations of Travelling Fayres* by *An Interested Party*. That one was so big I had to use both hands to lift it down, so I hoped we didn't have to look at any long arguments.

"Can't you just float them down or something?" I asked her.

She frowned. "I'm not a *poltergeist*, Morgan." She swept off, head high, and I hurried after her, clutching the books to my chest and thinking that a) someone else evidently wrote her notes; and b) insulting a ghost had never been on my life bingo card.

Ben was leaning over the table in the library's staffroom, a pile of half-repaired books pushed to the side (the top one, rather than being some arcane tome, was titled *101 Best Biscuit Recipes*, and looked a lot as if someone had been bludgeoning the dough into submission with it), and a dozen more books scattered around him, sprouting bits of notepaper from the pages.

"Did you find—" he started, then stopped as he saw me. "Oh, Morgan. How're you doing?" His voice had gone from weary to that soft *oh dear* tone everyone had taken with me after I split up with Jason, even though I'd basically skipped out the door. Ruiner had been the only one who'd turned up with a bottle of bubbly and a half-price cake from the supermarket to celebrate rather than commiserate, a memory which startled me. He was so annoying, it was easy to forget that sometimes he got things right.

"Fine," I said, probably more shortly than was necessary. "Isabella says the carnival's *alive* somehow?"

"Sort of," he said, pushing his glasses onto his forehead. They'd left dimples on his nose, and without them his eyes were a warm, tired brown. "I only know what I've figured out from the books, though. Isabella knows more."

"No, no," she said, waving me to a chair. "You explain, Benji. Sometimes I forget what it is to not know about the magical world."

"Benjamin," Ben said absently, and went to the little kitchenette in the corner to put the kettle on. "Tea, Morgan?"

"Only if it's regular builders'."

He nodded amiably enough, but a shadow of irritation passed over his face. Well, it was his fault for feeding me *calming* teas, like I was some hysterical maiden. He leaned against the cabinets while he waited for the kettle to boil. "So, every time the carnival comes to town — to any town — there's a price to be paid."

"I'm guessing you don't mean the entrance fee."

"No." He hesitated, looking at Isabella, and she nodded encouragingly. "Someone is always … lost."

"Like they wander off in the night?" I asked hopefully.

"More like they fall from the Ferris wheel, or choke on a hot dog, or have a heart attack when the lion jumps a little bit too close to them."

I stared at him, then at Isabella. "That's *horrible*."

"It's the price," she said simply. "Everything has its cost."

"But why does anyone even go, then? Surely if everyone stayed away—"

"Could you resist it?" she asked. "Really?"

I opened my mouth to say of course I could, if I knew it

was going to *murder* me, then remembered that wild, twisting wind and its relentless invitation. "Alright, it'd be hard," I admitted. "But it's pretty good incentive to at least try."

"People don't necessarily know," Ben said. "The carnival doesn't come that often. There's no set schedule, and the deaths are always an accident, so I think it kind of gets overlooked, deliberately or not. I had to really dig through the archives to find the pattern."

"Plus it always happens to someone else," Isabella said softly. "It's what we always believe, isn't it?"

I looked at her, wondering how rude it was to ask a ghost how she died. Pretty rude, I imagined, and the poltergeist comment was already one strike against me, so I said, "Why don't you stop it coming?"

Isabella shook her head. "The carnival is part of the fabric of the world. A natural force, as it were. One can't stop it. It arrives and it goes, and the crew ebb and flow with it. There is always an Aubrey, there is always a Lionel, there is always a strongman, there are always acrobats, there are always clowns. The carnival is eternal."

I shivered. "You mean they're vampires like Theodore?"

"No, the people are simply people, for the most part. Of all kinds, of course, but they're not the ones driving the carnival. It has its own energy, and it always persists."

Ben put a mug of tea and an unopened packet of bourbon creams in front of me, and I just stared at them, then finally said, "I don't mean to be harsh, but maybe that's what happened with Lionel? The carnival ate him?"

"It doesn't *eat* people," Isabella said.

"Well, did whatever it did. Took its payment."

Ben made a thoughtful sound. "If that was the case, Ruiner would be in the clear."

Isabella wrinkled her delicate nose very slightly, then

shook her head, setting her dark curls shivering. "A nice idea, but I rather think not. After all, Lionel was *of* the carnival. If anything, the carnival will demand a replacement, or further payment. A balance has to be maintained."

"Oh, that's just bloody brilliant," I said. "So not only is Ruiner going to be executed by the damn carnival for killing someone he absolutely *could not* have killed, it's going to go after someone else as well?"

"It doesn't *go after* anyone any more than it eats anyone," Isabella said. "It's not a beast, hunting down its prey. Someone is merely lost to it."

"No, they're not," I snapped. "They're *killed* by it. The carnival comes to town and it *kills* someone."

"That's pretty much the gist of it," Ben said, and Isabella frowned.

"It's not really how we talk about it," she said.

"You should," I replied, standing up.

"Where're you going?" Ben asked.

"To work. I need to try and figure out what to do about this, and if all you can tell me is *it's how things work*, it's not getting me anywhere."

"There's nothing you can do, Morgan," Isabella said. "This evening we'll talk to Theodore and come up with a plan."

"Last night it was we'd come up with a plan this morning, now it's tonight? I don't think you intend to come up with a plan at all. I think you'd leave Ruiner there rather than upset your precious balance." My voice was rising, and I swallowed hard.

Isabella looked at me with her jaw set in uncharacteristically hard lines. "You do *not* understand what you're dealing with. You need to listen to those who do."

"I *need* to get my brother and my familiar back."

"If you get in the middle of this, you could make it worse for both of them."

"I can't make it worse than doing nothing," I snapped, then headed for the door.

"Morgan," Ben called, and I held a hand up to silence him, not turning back.

"If you offer me another bloody tea, so help me, I will *throw* it at your damn books!" I stomped out, my face hot, apologising silently in my head to the books. Of course I wouldn't do that, but there were some things tea couldn't fix, as astonishing as that was.

Coffee might, though.

EIGHT

A touch of Grace

I INTENDED to have a coffee then go to the Cosy Cauldron, I really did, but there appeared to be a brawl starting just outside the doors of Bewitching Brews between the Upstanding Ladies and a coven of crocheters in floppy hats. James stood in the middle with a jug of water in each hand, his messy hair even more disheveled than usual, so I didn't think coffee would be forthcoming just yet. Besides, given my current mood, if I ended up involved in the fracas, I just might slap someone, and with my luck I'd be cursed to be a crocheter for the rest of my life. Or an Upstanding Lady, and both of those possibilities filled me with horror.

So I headed straight to the shop instead, scratchy with sleeplessness and caffeine deprivation, and still furious at Isabella and Theodore and their unwillingness to help my brother. I mean, they didn't even know how annoying he was! They had no excuse for not helping him. If anyone should be not helping him, it was me, yet here I was, once again, cleaning up my brother's messes, and — I stopped myself, trying to take a deep, calming breath, as if all had to do was a bit of yoga and all my problems would go away. It didn't do anything, but it did slow me down enough that I had time to read the flyer on the shop door. It had changed again.

Opening Night Saturday! it proclaimed. *Come & make mayhem with us!* Legendary Lionel's name had vanished from the small print.

I scowled at the poster. Really? They were just carrying on like normal? Not even postponing the opening night? Someone had died, and they were holding my brother prisoner, and they were just *yes, come to our freaky circus!* I looked down the street in the direction of the carnival, as if expecting to see it looming over town like some sort of canvas Godzilla, but there was nothing except the layered grey sky. I wished I'd brought my car, but it rarely seemed worth it in Hollowbeck. Everything was walking distance. Besides, the whole curse incident not long after I'd arrived, when my car had taken on a life of its own and plunged off the road while I threw myself out the door into the woods had kind of taken a bit of the joy out of driving. Any time I got in it now, I was half-expecting it to take off in the direction of the nearest ditch.

Starlight's bike was leaning against the outside of the shop, fake flowers wound into the basket and the frame streaky with rust. It wasn't locked, no one seemed to bother about such things in Hollowbeck. I also knew from experience that only the front brakes worked, so it was steal-at-your-peril. I looked back down the road, as if the carnival might have crept into sight, then tightened the straps on my backpack and grabbed the bike. I wasn't going to ask to borrow it. She'd only tell me to listen to Isabella.

I swung onto the bike and pedalled off, the drop from the pavement to the road jarring my teeth and the frame creaking alarmingly. I half expected Starlight to come running after me, or for Isabella to do her freaky ghost thing of appearing out of nowhere, but no one tried to stop me. I headed straight for the carnival, the wind plucking at my clothes and freezing my hands, making my nose sniffly, while the fields unrolled beyond the drystone walls to either side, green and speckled with sheep.

I spotted the big top first, the canvas a grim, stained green against the sky, and then the rest slowly came into view. Everything looked a little shabby and rundown in the daylight, patches visible on the smaller tents and chipped paintwork marring the stalls. It looked about as magic as the ubiquitous, battered amusement rides in a seaside town, streaked with rust and salt and shattered expectations.

I leaned the bike against the wall next to the gate, then stood there staring into the field, one hand on the wooden rungs. I couldn't see anyone, but the scent of frying onions drifted from somewhere, and a shout rose up behind the stalls, accompanied by laughter.

I was lifting the hook of the gate's latch out of its eye when someone said, "We're closed."

I looked up to see an exceedingly short, exceedingly stout man standing just beyond the wall, his arms crossed over his chest and his beard bristling at me.

"Were you *hiding?*" I asked him, and he tipped his head at me.

"I was sitting behind the wall. Out of the wind, like."

"Oh." That made more sense. "I need to talk to Aubrey."

"We're closed," he repeated.

"I get that, but I really need to talk to her. It's about Lionel."

He examined me, then said, "You were with that murder cat last night."

"He's not a murder cat," I said, then looked at him more closely. "You were the one who tried to strangle him!"

He held his arms out to me, bare despite the wind. He had a tattoo around one huge bicep, all runes and sledge-hammers, and a large gold earring in one ear. "He bit me. *And* scratched me. Lucky it's not infected. I'd be after you for the doctor's bills."

"We have the NHS, and again, you tried to strangle him."

"He murdered Lionel."

"How on earth do you think a *cat's* going to murder anyone?"

"Well, he's mouthy enough. Gotta be a wizard in disguise, doesn't he?"

"He's just a *cat*," I said, then reconsidered as the man raised his eyebrows at me. They were almost as bushy as his beard, and he had a knitted green hat pulled down to meet them. "Okay, fine, he's not just a cat. And he's mouthy. But he's not a wizard. He's my little brother, and the only thing he's guilty of is being annoying."

The man shrugged. "Either way, can't let you in. Sorry. Aubrey's orders. We're on lockdown until she says otherwise."

"Can she come and talk to me, then?" I asked.

"She's pretty busy, like."

I gripped the top rung of the gate, feeling a sneaking pulse of what felt like electricity but was probably charms spilling over my knuckles. "I need to see my brother and make sure he's alright."

"You need to let go of our gate."

"You can't just keep my brother in there and not let anyone visit him. What about ... what about legal counsel?

He has a right to that if you really think he killed someone!"

"You a cat lawyer and all?" he asked.

"*No*. But I could find one." If anywhere had a cat lawyer, it'd be Hollowbeck.

He gave a snort of amusement. "Sure you could. But we don't allow prisoners to have any visitors, lawyers or not. It's the rules."

"What about the actual law?" I asked desperately. "It can't be legal, not even letting someone see a lawyer."

"It's the carnival, love. This is how we do things. Now off you trot." And he stared at me flatly, refusing to say anything else, even when I offered him half a dozen ferrets for five minutes with my brother. In retrospect, that probably wasn't a huge incentive, but I didn't exactly have any money to bribe him with. And one previously cursed car likely wouldn't have got me much further than the ferrets.

Finally, I grabbed Starlight's bike and wheeled it back down the road, muttering to myself under my breath, then stopped at a safe distance and shouted, "And your pizza was *awful!*"

"No it wasn't," he shouted back, and I huffed. He was right. It had been *amazing*, and thinking of it made my stomach rumble, reminding me I hadn't had breakfast. I hadn't even broken into the bourbon creams at the library, which showed just how upset I was.

I didn't get back on the bike right away, not least because I felt a little shaky and out of sorts, between not eating and not sleeping and arguing with someone who looked like he was cosplaying a dwarf warrior on a day off. I just kept walking until his gate was lost around a curve in the road, and another field appeared between where I stood and the carnival. There was a gate here too, and I dropped Starlight's bike next to it, clambering up a couple of rungs so I could see across the field and over the far wall into the carnival grounds.

This side was where the accommodation caravans were, by the looks of things, set at a decent distance from the big top and divided from it by a row of horse trailers and sturdy, unmarked trucks that would probably be used to cart the equipment. A couple of Clydesdales, three Shetland ponies, and half a dozen pretty, long-limbed horses (my knowledge of the varieties stopped with the very big and the very small, all the rest were just *horses)* were munching hay in a corner that had been roped off, and a bunch of goats cavorted around them, being studiously ignored by all sizes of equines. I watched two women in big jackets and baggy jeans wander past the enclosure, mugs in hand and shoulders hunched against the wind. There was no one else around, and I adjusted my bag, tightening the straps.

"I wouldn't," someone said, and I twisted urgently around, almost falling off the gate and thinking that I really had to get a lot better at noticing people sneaking up on me.

A woman was watching me from the centre of the road. She was straddling her own bike, a solid-looking town model with a low frame and white-walled tyres, one foot down for balance. I didn't recognise her, and I'm sure I would've noticed her if she was a Hollowbeck regular. She had long slim legs in skinny jeans, and was wearing boots and a Barbour jacket, looking like she was two spaniels short of a hunt meet. Her glossy brown hair was pulled into one of those careless ponytails that still somehow looked effortlessly polished, and I felt immediately even more sleep-deprived than I had a moment ago.

"I wasn't doing anything," I said.

"You were going to climb over. I saw you at the main

gate. Why d'you want to get in so much?" Her eyes were an odd colour, reflecting the grey of the clouds, but they were sharp.

"I need to talk to Aubrey. The ringwoman."

"Well, breaking in won't get you anywhere. They're charmed up to the eyeballs." She raised one hand and clicked her fingers, then pointed at the far wall that enclosed the carnival. A magpie bombed past her, heading across the field, and I watched it arrow over the wall. Or try to — it hit some unseen barrier with a squawk of alarm. The defence wasn't entirely solid, and the magpie froze mid-flight, its momentum carrying it forward a little, then it pinged back, rebounding like a finger pressed into a balloon. It was catapulted into the field just beyond the gate where I stood, and flopped helplessly into the grass.

I started to swing over the gate, some wordless sound of distress catching in the back of my throat.

"It's fine," the woman said. "Look, it's getting up."

It was, and I paused, frowning at her. "That was a horrible thing to do. It might not have been fine."

She waved dismissively. "But it was. And you see? You can't get through. All trying will do is tell Aubrey what you're up to. She's definitely not going to talk to you then."

"You know her?"

She shrugged, a liquid, graceful movement. "I know a little of how carnivals work."

We looked at each other for a moment, then I climbed back down and righted Starlight's bike. "I guess I'll have to think of something else."

"Maybe I can help you."

"Why would you do that?" I asked.

"The carnivals are dinosaurs," she said. "They should've gone extinct long ago. Did I hear you say they took your brother?"

"Yes."

She lifted her chin slightly, looking at the sky as if waiting for some clarity — or another bird to fling at the wall. "Your brother who's a cat?"

"Um. Why would he be a cat?"

She looked back at me finally, and her eyes were a deep, amused grey. "Not called Rainier, is he?"

I blinked at her. Technically he was, as our mum had a bit of a thing for European royalty, but I'd been calling him Ruiner for almost thirty years. "How'd you know?"

"Word gets around. Not too many new witches in town, or enchanted cats. And I kind of have a vested interest."

"Who are you?" I asked, although I had an idea I already knew.

"Grace," she said.

"Grace as in Grace who set up a shop in competition to Norma?"

"Yes. Also Grace as in your brother burnt my shop down."

"Right. He said he thought you were back."

"Just recently. Took myself for a little holiday while I licked my wounds, but all roads lead back to Hollowbeck, it seems." She sounded neither pleased nor upset, just accepting. I hoped that wasn't entirely true. I still intended to leave once my brother was de-catted.

I looked from her to the carnival grounds. "Why would you want to help Ruiner?"

She shrugged. "I want to see his face when I confront him. Maybe shave his belly or something. Neuter him?" She said the last bit consideringly, then grinned, revealing white but slightly crooked teeth, which were oddly endearing. "Joking."

"I get the sentiment." I kept watching her, trying to

read her expression. She just looked interested, and a little amused, as if someone were telling her a convoluted story and she was waiting for the punchline. She didn't *look* angry, or as if she were gloating over the idea of him being trapped. "You do want to confront him, then."

"Well, yes. I sank all my savings into that shop, and insurance does not cover Acts of Ruiner, I'll tell you now. I fully intend to at least chop his whiskers off, if nothing else."

"That'd be fair." And it'd be a tidy, hands-off revenge, getting Ruiner swallowed by the carnival. But she would've had to kill Lionel, and how would that have worked? The carnival didn't allow outside magic, and she didn't seem like she'd run in and bop him on the head herself. That didn't make it impossible, of course. She could've paid someone in the carnival to do it for her, or she could've dropped poison in his tea, or any number of other options. There was always a way. "Leaving him in there seems like it'd be good payback too, though."

"Not when I don't get to rub his nose in it." She tapped her fingers on the handlebars of the bike. "I got back about a week ago, and I've been trying to figure out what to do since. I almost came into the shop a couple of times, but I wasn't quite sure how to start the conversation. *Hey, your crappy brother ruined my life, can I give him a bit of a kicking?*"

"Again, I know the feeling."

"To tell the truth, I was at the carnival last night, and saw what happened. So this morning I thought I should talk to you, see if I could help, but then I spotted you heading out here so I followed." She shrugged. "Like I say, I don't love the carnival. And I want my shot at Rainier."

"Ruiner," I said.

"Huh." She considered it, smiling. "Yeah, you do know the feeling, don't you?"

"Most definitely." I couldn't trust her, obviously, but it was hard not to *like* her.

Her smile faded. "Don't try and sneak in. Even if you make it, they'll throw you in a cage as well."

"I can't just leave him in there," I said.

"We won't. But there are better ways to do it."

"Such as?"

She pointed back toward town. "Let's talk."

I hesitated, examining her, and she looked back at me, her face open and guileless, her stance relaxed. I could almost hear my brother screaming at me that this was a really bad idea, but he wasn't here. And no one else was stepping up to help me. No one else was even suggesting there was any way they *could* help. If she knew something about how the carnival worked, I couldn't afford not to listen to her. And that didn't mean I was trusting her. Not really.

Sometimes the only choice is a bad choice, but I suppose that makes it the best choice, too. I pushed Starlight's bike onto the road and fell into step with Grace, the birdsong rising and falling around us and the carnival festering like a sickness at our backs.

NINE

Smart witches

GRACE SEEMED suspicious of being overheard, and given the crouching presence of the big top lurking beyond the wall, I had very much the same feeling. So we walked our bikes silently side by side down the empty lane, like two lost members of the Famous Five in search of adventure.

Only once the carnival was well behind us did I say, "Why did you come back now?"

"I heard Norma had died, and that there was a new witch in town. Thought I should check you out." She gave me an appraising look, and I made a face.

"I don't think I'm a witch at all. But Jacqueline — Norma's familiar — seems to think so."

"Familiars are smart." She looked around, as if expecting to see Jacqueline trotting after us. "Where is she?"

I sighed. "I lost her last night, in all the Ruiner stuff."

"Ah. Now that *is* unfortunate." She sounded less surprised than regretful.

"Yeah. Another reason I have to get in there."

She nodded. "We'll figure it out."

I stole glances at her as we walked. She was taller than me, all lean and leggy, and had the sort of profile that should've been in a fashion magazine, her skin flawless. It was impossible to tell how old she might be, and I wondered if that was witch-related or natural. If it was witch-related, then I was starting to feel a bit more motivated to up my skills.

"So, given you're keen on neutering him, can I assume you didn't already have your revenge by turning my brother into a cat?" I asked.

She snorted. "I did not. Although, it's pretty impressive. I wish I'd thought of it. Not sure I could do it, mind, but it would've been bloody satisfying."

"I wouldn't be thanking you for it. D'you know how much trouble it's caused me?"

"Well, I'm sure," she replied. "But with Ruiner as your brother, I doubt it's the only trouble you've had to deal with."

I sighed. "No, not really. Haven't even had to post bail or bust him out of anywhere this time. Or break up any fights, and he's got fur now, so he can't be thrown out on the street naked when he gets someone's name wrong." I winced, suddenly remembering that he and Grace had had *a thing.* "I mean—"

"Oh, he never got my name wrong," she said. "I'd've set fire to some delicate areas if that happened."

"Right."

She gave me that crooked grin again. "Hollowbeck sounds positively relaxing for you in comparison."

"Eh. Not sure about that." I pushed my bike on in silence for a little longer, then added, "I don't suppose you know who could've cattified him, though?"

She shrugged. "There's plenty of witches with power in the world, and other magic workers as well. Hard to tell who'd have *enough* power for something like that, but plenty of possibilities. And I'm sure Ruiner could've upset any number of them."

"It is kind of his speciality."

She laughed, warm and easy, and we walked on in companionable silence for a bit, while I wondered how much I believed her and how much I just *wanted* to believe her. Wanted someone who knew what she was doing, and seemed like she might be willing to actually *do* something, even upset the balance a bit if that was what it took. I looked over my shoulder, as if the carnival might be creeping along the road after us on little popcorn feet, but it was empty, other than a handful of miffed-looking magpies.

"Alright," I said. "How do we get my annoying brother and my lovely rat back, then?"

She did the same check over her shoulder as I had, and I noticed tattoos running up the side of her neck, delicate, leafy things. "It's not going to be easy. It's a hungry beast."

"Isabella says it always takes someone. Like it's the price of it being here."

She nodded. "That's how it's always been. My gran used to make me wear charms when the carnival was near, so that it couldn't grab me. But just because something's always been that way doesn't mean it can't be changed."

I *did* like her. "You think we can change it?"

"Challenge it, if nothing else. But I'd like to see it sent away hungry."

"You hate it that much?"

She gave me a sideways look. "My best friend didn't have charms. We used to share mine, but one year my gran only gave me one. Jenny wouldn't take it, and…" She trailed off with a shrug. "And that was that."

I stared at her. "It took her?"

"Allergic reaction to a peanut."

"Oh, that's awful." I didn't say, *but it happens*, so I suppose she got it from my tone.

"She could eat her weight in Snickers bars, when we managed to get them in from outside."

"*Oh.*"

"Yeah. So I'm not fond of the carnival. I tried getting the town to boycott it last time it came, but no luck. Everyone seems to sort of wilfully forget what it does, or they're entirely fatalistic about it. If they just stopped supporting it—"

"That's what I said! If no one went, surely it'd stop coming."

She nodded. "Hollowbeck isn't quick to change. And I saw you with Theodore and Isabella. They're the very definition of unchanging. I wouldn't take too much advice from them."

I could understand what she meant, but that still seemed harsh. They'd been trying to help, after all. "Ben's been researching," I said. "Maybe he'll come up with something."

"Oh, *Ben.* Ben, Ben, the librarian man." She paused. "That doesn't work, does it?"

"No," I said. "There'd have to be multiples. Ben, Ben, the librarian men."

She gave me that crooked grin again, then said, "Either way, unless he's undergone a personality change since I left, he's as bad as they are. All he does is read old books. It's all *anyone* does around here, then they say, this is the way things have always been done, so therefore this is the way we shall continue to do them. Nobody *thinks*." She glanced at me. "But maybe you do."

"Hopefully," I replied, trying to not to be offended on Ben's behalf.

"Give yourself some credit," she said. "You're out here doing something, even if it's not very smart. Now, look — there hasn't been a show yet. Not properly."

I was at least slightly offended on my own behalf now, even if she was right about my daylight assault on the carnival hardly being well thought out. "I suppose there hasn't. They hadn't really started before the whole … before Lionel's body turned up."

"So no one owes them anything. They haven't put on a show, therefore they can't require payment."

"Okay," I said. "That makes sense. But how does that help Ruiner?"

"They can't demand him as payment."

"But they can still claim he's a murderer. Or take him in Lionel's place, apparently. Or both."

"Now *that* is going to be a bit trickier," she admitted. "But the next show's not till Friday. That's enough time to come up with something that gets Ruiner and Jacqueline out, and makes sure the carnival doesn't take anyone else."

She said it with such conviction that, offended or not, I couldn't help but believe her. "Do you have a plan?"

"No," she said cheerfully. "But two smart witches are basically a force of nature. We'll figure it out. Have you got Norma's spell book?"

The question ran into the rest of the sentence so casually I almost didn't notice it. I was too busy deciding if being called a smart witch cancelled out being told I hadn't been *acting* smart. But as the words sunk in I could almost feel Jacqueline's teeth in my ear, a sharp cold warning. "Why?"

"We're going to need some serious magic to take on the carnival. That book's our best source."

She wasn't wrong about the grimoire having serious magic. I could feel the innate power of the thing every time I picked it up. All those years and decades and, who knew, *centuries* of spells sunk deep into its skin. Just like the carnival, it had a life of its own, deep and silent and persistent, and it was *hungry*. The wrong person couldn't be allowed to get hold of it, not just because of the way the town's deals were enmeshed with it, but for the simple fact of the power it held — and the power it wanted. I still doubted I was the right person, but I'd been nominated for now. I'd claimed it, for what that was worth, and so I had to look after it, especially with Jacqueline missing. I could feel it burning into my back through my bag, as if just being mentioned had awoken it.

"Morgan? Are you alright?" Grace asked.

"Yeah. Sure."

"Lost you there for a moment." She smiled at me and stopped walking. We'd reached a junction, where turning left would take us back toward town, and right ran further out into the sweep of the valley. She nodded in that direction. "My cabin's on the edge of the woods. I think we should regroup later and start brainstorming. Where are you staying?"

"I'm going to the Cosy Cauldron," I said. Somehow, having Grace at Petunia's seemed ill-advised, as if she might start flinging frogs around like she had the magpie. Or searching for my hiding places.

She nodded amiably. "That works. I'll see you this evening."

She swung onto her bike and pedalled off, her back straight and the bike's chrome gleaming in the sunlight. I watched her go, then clambered onto Starlight's bike rather more clumsily and headed in the opposite direction, feeling scratchy and too cold and too hot all at once, and aware that I hadn't brushed my hair that morning, or put any makeup on.

But at least I had some help now.

Or I hoped I did.

I LET myself back into the Cosy Cauldron to find Starlight relabelling crystal balls on one of the less cluttered shelves, three ferrets curled into a basket next to her, two more tumbling across the floor in a whirl of soft fur, and another perched on the counter, eating something with a guilty haste that made me think it had been pilfered.

"More?" I asked her.

"There you are," she said, and gave me an accusing look. "You took my bike."

"Sorry. I've brought it back. It's fine."

She shook her head. "It's not *that*. You went back to the carnival, didn't you?"

"Of course I did. I'm not sitting around hoping they're going to suddenly shout, just kidding! and give Ruiner and Jacqueline back like nothing happened."

"You shouldn't have gone on your own."

I stooped to scratch a ferret behind the ears as it tried to scale my jeans. "No one seems keen to help."

"You didn't bother to ask!" Now Starlight looked properly upset, and she clattered the basket of crystal balls back on to the shelf hard enough to set the ferrets hissing and me wincing. "I didn't even know you were in town until James told me he'd seen you riding off on my bike."

"I'm sorry. I don't want to drag you into it."

"Do you know how friends work, Morgan?"

I opened my mouth to say I hadn't realised we *were* friends, but for once my brain caught up to my mouth in time, and my cheeks flushed with heat. I hadn't thought about it. I'd been so caught up with the deals, and Ruiner, and being saddled with the grimoire and Jacqueline and the Cosy Cauldron, that I hadn't stopped to think of Starlight as anything other than the young woman who'd come with the shop, like she was nothing more than another box of tat I had to deal with.

"I really am sorry," I said. "I didn't think."

She sniffed, digging around the shelves enthusiastically. "*Evidently.*"

"Can I get you a muffin?" I suggested, not entirely altruistically, although I *did* feel bad. I also had a headache starting from lack of coffee, though. "Hot chocolate? I'll get extra whipped cream."

"I wouldn't. Everyone's still a bit wound up from the carnival, and James is *very* snappy."

I threw a longing look toward Bewitching Brews, but there was no point pining. I was going to have to put up with tea and some mysterious biscuits from the local store. Which was a very nice store full of homemade cakes and local honey and mysterious teas, but which didn't stock any food brands I'd ever heard of. Everything was in strange packaging, other than the local produce, which had labels such as, *These potatoes were dug by Stan!* or *This is Mabel's cheese!* I'd never worked out if Mabel was the cow whose milk was used, or the person who made the cheese.

"Tea?" I offered.

"Mint," Starlight said. "With honey."

"Daring," I said, and she grinned at me, her irritation with me passing as fast as the clouds outside.

"It's all these ferrets. I need the energy."

"How many do we have now?"

She grimaced. "There was a box outside this morning. I think we're up to seventeen, but I may have counted some twice. They're *fast.*"

And also loose all over the shop, but I wasn't about to

make a fuss. They couldn't make it any more messy, anyway.

❧

FORTIFIED with tea and some biscuits that I'd hoped were chocolate chip but appeared to be spice and currant, we tackled the next shelf together, digging out three birds' nests, a golf ball, and a graveyard of wasps among a collection of *Witch's Daily Thoughts* journals and pencils made from twigs.

"I don't think Isabella and Theodore are going to help," I said, sweeping the wasps into the bin. "And Ben's just so *reasonable* that I'm sure he'll do whatever Isabella says."

"They don't think Ruiner actually did it, do they?" Starlight asked. "He's got to be the least magical person I've ever encountered." She shot me a look. "Although I didn't think you were very magical, either."

"I still don't think I am. But it's irrelevant — the carnival doesn't allow outside magic, remember?"

"*Oooh.* I forgot. How can Ruiner have done it, then?" she asked, examining the pencils. "These aren't even real wood. Look — they're plastic! How tacky."

I made suitably disapproving sounds. "Well, he wouldn't have anyway, because it really sounded like Lionel was going to be able to help him. Ruiner definitely wouldn't have hurt anyone he thought might help him get back to human form."

"Maybe someone else didn't want Lionel to succeed," Starlight suggested. "They sabotaged it somehow."

"But who knew we were talking to him? I didn't even tell you!"

"Again, you need to work on this friendship thing."

I accepted that with a nod. "Fair. But really — who knew?"

She shook her head. "Maybe it's entirely unrelated."

I made a dubious noise, and we went back to sifting through the shelves, accompanied by a soundtrack of squabbling ferrets.

Finally, Starlight said. "We should all go out there."

"To the carnival?"

"Yes. If we *all* go — you and me and Isabella and Theodore and Ben and James and anyone else we can drag along — and explain everything, they'll *have* to give him back."

"Isabella seems to think we should just let the carnival do what it wants.," I said. "She said I'd make it worse if I interfered."

Starlight put the journals back on the newly clean shelf and frowned at me. "Well, I know Ruiner's annoying, but we can't just *leave* him. That's very unreasonable."

"My thoughts too. But what do we do?"

"Maybe we can look in Norma's book. See if there's anything on tackling carnivals."

I nodded, not answering for a moment, then said, "I met Grace."

"Grace? She's back?"

"Seems so. She wants to use the book to get into the carnival too."

Starlight didn't answer for a moment, then she said, "You spoke to her about this?" There was a hurt note in her voice, and I looked at the shelf, scrubbing at a mark vigorously.

"She stopped me trying to sneak into the carnival. And she seems ... well, she seems helpful. And *witchy*."

"I suppose she is." Starlight ran her cleaning cloth

through her fingers. "You didn't show her the book, though, did you?"

"No."

"And it's safe?"

"I've got it with me."

She nodded. "Then let's have a look at it. Maybe we can figure out if there's anything in there that'll help, without you showing it to Grace. I mean, I'm sure you're right and she's just being helpful, but …"

But. I could feel the weight of it, and now that I was back in the shop, it seemed madness that I'd even considered sharing the grimoire with a complete stranger. A *witchy* stranger. A witchy stranger who'd probably know exactly how to break someone else's claim to the book and stake their own. Particularly with the book's guardian familiar missing.

"Let's do it," I said. "I'm going to talk to Theodore again tonight, but if he's still not going to do anything I need a plan. What's to stop the carnival just leaving with Ruiner any moment?"

"They're saying opening night is Saturday," she pointed out.

"I'm not sure how much I trust that."

Starlight nodded. "No. I wouldn't either."

TEN

Half-destruction is an option

STARLIGHT FLIPPED the sign to *Closed* on the door, then locked it against the day, and we went out the back to set ourselves up on the big worktable that dominated the back room, filling the space between the kitchen's old-fashioned wood cabinets and ageing fridge, and the living area with its little-used sofas.

The building that held the Cosy Cauldron was still set up as Norma's home, bedrooms full of clutter untouched upstairs and the witch's clothing still hanging in the wardrobes, along with an astonishingly extensive shoe collection and far too many souvenir bottles of mysterious liquors. I could've moved in, I suppose, but the place carried her presence like a stain in the air, and I could never walk back here without seeing her arm hanging out of the cauldron, pale and lifeless. Petunia's frog-infested guesthouse was more welcoming and less full of ghosts.

The table's long, scrubbed wood top was cluttered by pots of tinctures with neat labels on them, and more empty pots waiting to be filled, as well as bunches of herbs and bags of crystals and curious vials in all sorts of tints.

Beyond it loomed the blackened stone of the hearth, currently occupied by a huge cauldron that was so new it still had shiny bits on it. The old one had been removed along with Norma's body, and both Starlight and I were adamant we didn't want it back in the shop. So we'd bought a new one, and Starlight was using it with a variable level of skill to create some of the potions and spells that we sold in the shop itself. The size seemed to be a bit of an overkill, but there had been a couple of small explosions which it had contained pretty well, and even the mixes that went as planned often seemed to foam and froth a lot, particularly when certain words were said, or rosemary was dropped into them. I didn't know what it was with rosemary, but it definitely got magical things ticking.

I set the grimoire on the table, and we leaned over it together. I could smell Starlight's tea-tree shampoo over the whiff of mint tea, and she ran one finger over the cover of the book gently, as if in greeting, before she opened it. She was almost as familiar with it as I was, since she used it for some of the potion recipes. Although she'd been painstakingly copying them into her own notebook, along with some tweaks she made along the way, so I suppose I was still the one who used it most. If *used* was the right word for *read it late at night with no idea what I was looking at.*

"What are we looking for, then?" I asked.

"How to get into a carnival uninvited. Or how to destroy one," she said absently, turning the pages slowly, and I stared at her. She finally looked up at me. "I mean, we wouldn't destroy it completely, of course. Just as much as we needed to."

"As much as we needed to?"

"Sure. Like half, maybe."

"You think we should half destroy the carnival?"

"It would show it we were serious."

"Right," I said, then because I didn't want to upset Starlight any more by saying *are we even capable of that*, never mind all the other objections I had to blowing up a carnival, I added, "Would half a spell even work?"

"I don't know," she said. "We'd have to try it out."

I was starting to see why Jacqueline had given the book to me rather than Starlight. "I don't think that should be our first choice. We don't know what half we'll end up destroying, and it seems unlikely to end well." I pulled the grimoire toward me, as if the book might sense what she was looking for and deliver it. The last thing we needed was a devastated carnival to explain to Isabella.

I still couldn't quite get used to the feel of the book, no matter how often I handled it. The faint greasiness of the vellum under my fingertips, and the heavy scents rising from it, one moment redolent of cold sea foam, the next hot cinders, then rich spice, sweet and tart all at once, or a coppery, too-familiar tang that coated the back of the throat. The book was never cold, either. There was always a faint warmth to it, as if it had, at some stage, absorbed a much younger sun and was still reflecting it back.

The book was crammed with writing in half a dozen different hands, with spells for cleaning blackheads, ridding your home of sprites, ensuring a good egg supply, and cursing your neighbour with earwigs. There were also recipes, although none that I fancied trying. One for sticky toffee pudding required a certain mushroom that Starlight said was really inadvisable, while one for apple slice had an exclamation mark next to it which could've meant it was really good, really bad, or could be used to poison your enemies. There was no way to be sure. Interspersed with it all were passages that read like diary entries, and little snippets of lore that were less spells and simply knowledge preserved by long-dead witches, passed down over and over, going from quill and ink to fountain pen to ballpoint all in the space of one page in places.

But for all that accumulated knowledge, nothing seemed to relate to carnivals. Nothing about breaking into them, nothing about destroying them (luckily, as Starlight remained fairly set on the idea), not even anything about avoiding them. There was a spell for opening locks, which seemed it might be helpful when it came to breaking Ruiner out, but when we tried it on the back door, the whole frame melted and merged with the door itself, leaving us poking at a door-shaped outline in the wall and trying out various reversal spells, which didn't work in the slightest.

"That's annoying," Starlight said. "We'll have to go out the front."

"It's kind of a fire hazard," I said, jiggling the handle.

"We probably should've tried on something smaller first," she agreed. "But the spell could be handy."

I wasn't sure how, unless I wanted to ensure that Ruiner was locked in a cage forever. Which might be something I'd like to do at times, but it wasn't really what we needed right now. I put a Post-it note on the page anyway. I might want to use it in the future, once I had him back.

BY THE TIME the shadows were lengthening into mid-afternoon, we still weren't any further forward. Starlight had given up, opened the shop again, then gone to deliver some tinctures and charms to a housebound woman who was having trouble with gnomes (although Starlight confided in me that she thought it was likely mice, but the charms should work either way). I stayed in the back room, half-listening for the bell at the shop door while alternating between squinting at the footnotes in the grimoire, still in search of anti-carnival spells, and trying out different reversal spells on the back door. At some point, Ben knocked on it, and I had to lean out the kitchen window and tell him to go to the front instead.

"Did you know your door's got branches growing out of it?" he asked when he came in.

I pointed at it. "Moss on this side."

"I suppose it's atmospheric." He set two large books on the table and sat down opposite me.

I eyed the books. "What have you found?"

"One of them's a criminal history of carnivals," he said. "It cites a couple of cases where people did challenge the carnival's authority to hold people from their villages."

"Any luck?" I asked, and he made a slight face.

"One of the people who were taken spontaneously combusted before anything could be done, and the other they let out, but he'd aged about sixty years in a week and died of heart failure."

"Awesome," I said. "That's really helpful."

"Sorry."

I considered it. "How many lives do you think Ruiner has? Do cats really have nine?"

"No idea," Ben said, and tapped the other book. "This one is about the cost of the carnival."

"I don't really want to hear more about how people are *lost*, and everyone just accepts it."

"They don't always. I found one case where a village managed to make them leave without them taking a fee."

I blinked at him. "How?"

"It's tricky," he said. "The whole village had to be united against them, then circle the field and cast a joint spell which drove them out. Highly risky, apparently."

I sighed. "Well, that's not going to work. The carnival's

made everyone so edgy there's no way they'd all agree to *anything*. Plus, this is Ruiner. If he were a nicer person, people might be more inclined to help out, but he's *Ruiner*."

"And he's a cat," Ben said.

"Yeah, two counts against him."

We smiled at each other awkwardly, then Ben said, "It does suggest there are ways carnivals can be beaten, though."

"Do you think so?" I asked. I was aware my voice was wobbling just slightly.

Ben reached a hand out hesitantly and placed it on my arm, his fingers warm through my jumper. "I'm sure there's a way," he said. "We'll figure it out. I'm going to keep looking."

"Thank you," I said quietly, and we were both silent for a moment. Then I cleared my throat and moved my arm, leaning back in my chair to rub my eyes. "Do you think Isabella and Theodore will help?"

Ben looked at the books. "I don't think so. I mean, they'll ask, I'm sure, but if the carnival says no—"

"And they will."

"Probably, yes. Which I think they'll have to accept. There are a lot of stories in those books about people trying to escape from carnivals, or help others escape, and it just … it doesn't end well. In one case, a whole village vanished."

"What d'you mean, *vanished?*"

"I mean it was like the Marie Celeste. A young girl had joined the carnival, apparently, and her parents were adamant she'd never have done it of her own accord. The whole village were furious, so they marched on the carnival. They got her back — it was recorded in the town hall files — but when a couple who'd been away came back the next week, there was no one left. Cups of tea half-full, plates of food still on the tables. Even the pets were gone."

I stared at him, my mouth sticky. "They never found them?"

"Not a sign. The carnival was gone, and there's no mention that anyone dared follow it."

"But Ruiner didn't *join* it," I whispered. "Surely they can't just kidnap him. And what about Jacqueline?"

"I don't know," he said quietly. "But that's why Isabella and Theodore aren't going to rush to help. The whole town could be at stake if they do."

Neither of us spoke for a long time, my stomach roiling with sickness and threatening to reject Starlight's cauliflower salad. I'd never ask someone else to put themselves at risk for my brother or Jacqueline, let alone a whole village. That didn't bear thinking about. But I couldn't just give up on them, either.

"I'm going to keep looking," Ben said. "I'm sure there's something we can do. *Sure* of it."

I looked up at him finally. "Okay. Yes. Thank you." I cleared my throat and looked around the kitchen. "Do you want tea? I've got some spiced cookies that taste like cardboard, if you fancy them."

"Morgan. You're not going to do anything, are you?"

"No," I said, busying myself with the kettle. "What would I do against a bloody great carnivorous carnival?"

"I don't know — set a trap like you and Starlight did for Edith? Without telling anyone?"

I found two mugs and set them up with teabags. "I'd have no idea how to trap a carnival."

Ben looked unimpressed, but before he could argue anymore, someone appeared in the doorway to the hall, and we both looked up. Grace smiled at us, lounging into the room with an unconscious elegance that would've been really annoying if she hadn't been the only person who seemed to have any inclination to actually *do* anything about Ruiner. Other than Starlight, of course, and unless she was planning on raising an army of ferrets, I didn't have a lot of faith in what she could do.

But even so, I stepped forward and dropped a tea towel over the grimoire under the pretence of putting the biscuits on the table. "Grace. I wasn't expecting you until later."

"I got finished with a few things and thought I'd pop in a bit early," she said, smiling at Ben. "Hello, Ben."

He gave her a curious look. "I didn't realise you were back."

"Well, with Norma gone, I thought I may as well," she replied. "Might even start the shop up again." She winked at me. "There'll be enough business for two now Norma's not witching it up over her own personal empire."

I gave her a half smile. "Do you want a tea?"

"Sure." She sat down at the table, stretching her legs out under it and crossing her feet at the ankles. "What're you two up to, then?"

"Ben was showing me some research he's done into carnivals."

"Books! Of course." She grinned, taking the sting out of the words. "Useful?"

"Not exactly," I said, then when Ben frowned at me, I added hurriedly, "I mean, interesting. But not helpful for getting Ruiner out."

"It does give us a deeper understanding of the situation, though," he pointed out.

"Oh, very much."

"Well, can't say no to that," Grace said, taking a biscuit. "Were you staying?" she added to Ben.

He looked at me, eyebrows raised.

I grabbed both of his books and stacked them on top

of the tea towel-clad grimoire. "Thanks for these. Mind if I keep hold of them?"

"No." He looked at Grace, who smiled easily around her biscuit, then got up. "I guess I'll be off, then. I'll let you know if I find anything else."

"Perfect. Appreciate it." I gave him a thumbs up, and immediately wished I hadn't. "Um. Bye?"

"Yeah." He headed into the hall, and I waited to hear the bell jingle over the shop door as he left. I hadn't heard it go when Grace came in, but somehow that didn't surprise me.

Grace nibbled her biscuit, then looked back at me and said, "He's cute enough, in that bookish way. Not my type."

I thought that if she'd fallen for Ruiner's seduction routine, she should probably rethink her type, but aloud I just said, "He's a friend, is all."

She grinned, exposing those crooked teeth again. She had dimples too, damn her. "I'm sure he is. Did you bring the book?"

"No," I said, sliding Ben's books and the grimoire off the table in a stack and setting them on a chair before going to mash the tea. "I keep it locked up, so I thought we should talk things through before I go through the fuss to get it."

Grace grimaced. "We're not going to get very far without the book. If we're going to try and take on something as powerful as the carnival, we need something to back us up. A few charms and some willow sticks aren't going to cut it."

"Sure. But we don't need it to make a plan, do we?"

We looked at each other for a long moment before she shrugged and said, "Of course." Then she ran her tongue over her teeth and added, "Those biscuits are awful. You need to get some in from outside if you're going to be buying them."

"What is it with Hollowbeck biscuits?" I asked, sliding her tea across to her. But my voice sounded false to my own ears. I was more certain than ever that whatever help I was going to get from Grace was going to come at a cost.

But I already knew I'd pay whatever was needed, whether that was to the carnival or to the witch. I wouldn't sacrifice a whole village to save my brother and Jacqueline, but when it came to me?

That was a whole other question.

ELEVEN

My brother, my circus

I WENT into the shop to lock the door after Ben's departure, the grimoire and his books tucked under one arm as casually as I could manage. I stashed them under the counter, where a couple of sleepy ferrets chattered their teeth at me.

"Don't chew them," I whispered. "Or wee on them." The ferrets gave no indication one way or the other as to what their intentions were, but given the suspicious looks they threw at the tea towel, I doubted they'd touch the grimoire. It had that going for it, anyway.

I flipped the sign on the door to closed again and turned the lock, peering out into the late afternoon street. The Cosy Cauldron was open at erratic hours, which was, in theory, in order to serve some of the more nocturnal customers, but I suspected to was more to do with fitting around whenever Norma or (more usually) Starlight felt like opening. I had suggested that we print up a list of actual opening times and maybe even try to stick to them, but Starlight was very firmly against it.

"People will come in when we're open," she'd said, "and they'll come back if we're not." Which wasn't wrong, but it hardly seemed any way to run a business. I thought we might have to change our approach slightly if Grace did actually open her shop, but that was a problem for later.

I headed back into the kitchen and slid into the seat opposite Grace. She regarded me with some amusement and said, "Put those library books somewhere safe, have you?"

"Anywhere near the cauldron always feels a bit risky," I said. "Nobody wants a library fine. Besides, librarians are terrifying."

"I'm not sure I'd describe Ben as terrifying. Unless you mean his ability to quote entire passages of books no one's heard of."

"Not him," I said. "The other one." Dee, with her tartan skirts and heavy boots and multicoloured hair, who didn't come out in the sunlight. And who I'd once seen chewing on a chicken bone. Not chewing on it as in trying to strip the meat off. Chewing on it as in actually crunching it into tiny pieces and swallowing them. And, thinking about it, I'd only assumed it was a chicken bone. Imagining it wasn't opened the door to all sorts of even more horrifying possibilities that I didn't fancy thinking about right now. Anyhow, I was fairly certain she wasn't entirely human, but I still hadn't figured out how to ask about that sort of thing. The last thing I wanted to do was offend someone who could chow through bones in a single bite.

"Fair enough," Grace said. "She always gave me the creeps as well."

Which seemed a bit unfair. I mean, she didn't give me the *creeps*. I just had no intention of answering to her for a late fine or a missing book.

"So, what do we do about Ruiner?" I asked.

She looked at me levelly. "He's being held because they think he's the murderer. Or say they think that, anyway. He hasn't chosen to join the carnival, so they can't just *keep* him, and there's been no show, so they can't claim him as payment. So until they find him guilty, he can technically leave."

"With you so far, but how does that help? Since they're not going to *let* him leave. I imagine they're got him locked up somewhere."

"I'd imagine so too," she said. "So we have to find the actual murderer. That seems pretty obvious, doesn't it?"

"Does it?"

"Well, yes. It clears him, so they have to let him go. Then we've just got the payment to worry about, but we can deal with boycotting the show later."

"What about them needing someone to replace Lionel?"

"They still can't just *take* someone. Whoever it is has to choose to join."

I thought about it. "Alright, but we don't actually know it's murder. It might've been an accident, or some sort of side effect of Lionel trying to break the spell."

She made a little, impatient gesture. "*Might.* But this is your best shot at clearing him. And Lionel was a wizard, wasn't he? What's the likelihood he just tripped over a spell and killed himself?"

"No idea," I admitted. "But even if it is murder, how're we meant to find who did it? It'd probably be someone inside the carnival, and they're not allowing anyone in. I was kicked out the other night."

"Now that I have an answer for." She leaned forward, grinning at me. "You're not magic. Somehow you've ended up with Norma's shop, but you've got nothing magic about you. You're quite … *normal*." She made it sound both very not-normal and slightly distasteful.

"I know this," I said with feeling.

"So *you* join the carnival."

I blinked at her. "I'm sorry?"

"People do it all the time. Run away and join the circus, all that sort of thing."

"Yeah, I'm pretty sure they don't," I said. "I mean, maybe in books and stuff, but actual people don't. Not in this century, anyway."

She waved dismissively. "They do around here. And the fact that you don't have a magic whiff to you means they won't think you're involved with enchanted cats or likely to be a danger. They'll just let you in."

"And say what? I don't have any circus skills."

"Then tell them you want to learn. That you've always wanted to be, I don't know, an acrobat or something."

"Yeah, that's not going to work," I said. "The last time I did a somersault I was about nine."

She folded her arms over her chest. "Then say you want to see the world. Clean toilets or whatever." I grimaced, and she frowned at me. "Do you want to get your brother out or not?"

"Of course I do," I snapped. "Just … if I join up…" If I joined up, I was trapped. Stuck in the circus forever.

Grace looked puzzled for a moment, then her face cleared. "Oh, right. No — just don't sign anything."

"What?"

"Don't sign any contracts. Carnivals have laws, that's the whole problem. But it's also what saves us. Until you sign, you can still leave. But once you do that, you're bound to it forever."

"That's a really long contract."

"Carnivals have very long lives."

I scratched my chin, wondering if I could go and check this with Ben. But he'd just tell me not to do it, and probably get Isabella involved, and Theodore would be up soon, and then I'd never get within somersaulting distance of the carnival, let alone make it through the gates. I could go through Ben's books myself, of course, looking for guidance, but that'd take me all night and I'd probably still never have an answer.

"We can't find anything out from here," Grace said. "And the longer we leave it, the more time they have to do whatever sham trial suits them, and find Ruiner guilty, meaning they do get to keep him. And then they'll put on their show, and someone else will die, and off they'll go. But right now, we have a chance to stop all of it."

I looked at her. "We? Are you coming in too?"

"No. I'll be your contact on the outside. No point both of us being in there. Plus it looks more suspicious."

That made sense, but it also set shivers into my spine. The only person who knew I'd be going in there was the one person who had a reason to want to see Ruiner executed — okay, *one* of the people who had a reason to want to see him executed — and also someone who'd benefit from the new town witch vanishing. This was a really bad idea. I knew it with every twist in my gut, but also … she was right.

"Alright," I said. "But I was kicked out. Banned, or whatever. Plus Aubrey saw me last night, so she's going to recognise me."

"You can be invited back in. And she saw you in the dark, while she was more worried about dealing with a dead body," Grace replied. "And, sorry, you're cute, but you're not *that* memorable. The odds of her recognising you are pretty slim."

I made a small, doubtful noise, trying to decide

whether I was more complimented by being called cute or offended at being told I wasn't memorable. It was a close thing.

"We can dye your hair," Grace offered. "It'll help."

I wasn't sure if she meant help me blend in or help me be more memorable, but it hardly mattered. "There's really no other way?"

"I can't think of any. You saw the seal on the field. Even if we were to manage some sort of invisibility spell — which, by the way, is pretty much impossible — you're still not going to get through the seal. Plus you're doubly locked out if they banned you. And it's sure to have trip charms wired all through it, so you'd end up turned into a chicken or something if you tried."

"Cool." I drained my mug and went to the cupboard above the fridge. We'd discovered an extensive collection of single malt whiskies in Norma's office, and while it wasn't usually my thing, it was strong and I needed it. I grabbed two glasses and took them back to the table, slopping a generous measure into each.

Grace didn't say anything else, just took another biscuit and dipped it in her whisky, then nibbled on it with a quizzical expression on her face. I skipped the biscuit and went straight for the booze, trying to slow my panicky thoughts long enough to get a hold on them. Of course I wanted to help Ruiner. I *needed* to help Ruiner. But I couldn't help feeling I was being set up, that this was too tidy a solution for getting both of us out of the way. Then again, what connection would Grace have to the carnival? How *could* she set this up?

But if she really wanted revenge on Ruiner, and to take Norma's place as town witch rather more effectively that I had done, it'd be a good way to go about it. I thought of Starlight saying that the book was *technically* bound to me by the fact I'd claimed it. *Technically* wasn't close enough for witchy workings, and I wondered what being inside the enchanted bubble of the carnival would do to that claim.

"What're you going to do if I go in there?" I said aloud.

"Keep an eye on things this side. Be there to help pull you out once you have Ruiner and Jacqueline. Start stirring up some opposition to the carnival."

"How would we keep in touch? Smoke signals?"

She snorted and got up, going to the back door. She frowned at the moss (which had sprouted a few pretty, fluted mushrooms) and jiggled the handle, then looked at me with her eyebrows raised.

"It was meant to be a lock-breaking charm. I thought it might be helpful if Ruiner's in a cage."

"Probably don't do that," she said. "You'll melt it on him." She opened the kitchen window instead and leaned out, clicking her fingers.

A moment later, a wren landed on her hand with a flourish of soft brown feathers and tipped its head, looking up at her with small bright eyes. She smiled and stroked its chest with one finger.

"Do woodland creatures do all your chores, too?" I asked her, and she laughed.

"I've not cracked that one yet. I don't think I have the singing voice for it."

"Something to work toward, then," I said, and nodded at the bird. "I can't do that."

"You won't have to. I'll send them, and they'll come straight to you. You tell them what's happening, and I'll pass all the relevant information on to Theodore."

"The magpie couldn't get through the barrier."

"They don't have to get *through*. You just get close

enough to the wall to tell them the message. They'll bring it to me."

"You speak bird?"

She scrunched her face up. "I just understand them. It's a thing."

Of course it was. The more I thought about this, the more it seemed like a terrible idea, and the more it seemed like the only option. I slumped over the table, pressing the palms of my hands against my eyes until I saw stars.

"Alright," I said. "When do I start?"

"Immediately," she replied. "When else?"

WHICH WAS HOW, a few hours later, I found myself once more standing outside the gate to the carnival, the night creeping in across the fields and staining the sky. I checked over my shoulder, half-expecting to see Theodore sprinting down the road to intercept me, but it was empty. I was on my own, and while that was how I wanted it, I was also desperately wishing someone would come along and shake some sense into me. I looked at the wren, sitting on the wall watching me with glittering eyes.

"Here we go, then," I told it.

It tipped its head quizzically. I evidently did not have the bird speech thing, but as long as it was able to tell Grace was what happening, I supposed it didn't matter. I shifted my pack slightly, the heat of the grimoire making my back sticky even through my jacket. It might've been smarter to leave it hidden somewhere, but without Jacqueline to guard it, I didn't want it out of my sight. It was nestled into the clothes I'd collected from Petunia's when I went to change. I'd put on my best *running-away-to-join-the-circus* attire, which consisted of my oldest, baggiest jeans, a tank top I usually kept for my sporadic attempts at work-outs, and a scruffy army jacket that I'd bought at a charity shop in a sudden, misguided attempt at reclaiming a punk rock youth I'd never lived in the first place.

I took a deep breath, crossed my fingers that the cosplaying dwarf was off duty, walked to the gate and called, "Anyone there?"

A giant rose from behind the wall, making me take a step back. It was the muscleman from the night before, the one Aubrey had called Franz, only he'd swapped his leotard for a tie-dyed sarong that stopped just below his knees and a huge yellow fleece. The outfit was topped off with sandals and socks as well as a hat with earflaps, and we stared at each other in mutual bewilderment.

"Hi?" he said finally.

Definitely not the grumpy guardian from earlier, anyway. "Hi," I said. "Can I come in?"

"We're closed."

"Yep. But I want to join, not visit."

He examined me, frowning slightly. I looked back at him steadily. I could still smell dye and bleach, and from the corner of my eye I could glimpse the blues and greens running through my hair. Grace had sworn that the more striking it was, the less people would be looking at my face, but she'd also got to work with some heavy, Goth-y makeup that I wasn't sure I'd be able to recreate, and a nose piercing that was smarting insistently.

"I'm not sure we're hiring," Franz said.

"Oh, go on," I said. "I've been waiting ages for this. You're not easy to find, you know. I had to track you all over the country."

He looked toward the tents as if hoping for assistance. "What's your skill set?"

"I can cook. And clean. I've been horse riding once.

Well, donkey, but it's the same thing, right? And I'm good with heights, so I could climb things?"

"You can climb things?"

I let my shoulders slump. "Okay, look, I know that's a really pants skill set, but I really, *really* want to join a circus. *This* circus. I'll do anything. I don't even need to get paid."

"The boss'll like that, at least," he said, scratching his beard.

"Can you ask her? Please? Come *on*. This is my child-hood dream."

He snorted. "You should have had better dreams. I wanted to be an astronaut." But he turned and started toward the accommodation tents, his calves flexing alarm-ingly. "Stay there."

I did, rocking on my heels and trying to look both highly employable and eager to be a circus lackey, as well as unlikely to be any sort of spy. Music was drifting out of the carnival grounds, and good-natured shouting, and someone was making something that involved a lot of frying garlic. If it weren't for the big top looming above it all, it would've been enchanting in the deepening shadows, a world of magic and possibility run about with fairy lights and illusion. But it didn't have much appeal when I knew my brother and Jacqueline were trapped in there some-where, and I was doing my best to join them.

And I had no idea how or if any of us were getting back out.

TWELVE

Mind the alligator

I DIDN'T HAVE to wait long before Franz came back, Aubrey striding ahead of him. Rather than the elegant three-piece suit she'd been wearing the night before, she was clad in baggy combat trousers rolled at the ankles, and a t-shirt with a big flannel shirt unbuttoned over it, the sleeves rolled to her elbows. She had a set of heavy leather gloves clasped in one hand, and she pushed her other back through her hair as she examined me. I returned her gaze with as much confidence as I could, hoping Grace had been right about the previous night being chaotic enough that Aubrey wouldn't have paid much attention to me. That, or my *unmemorableness*.

"Yes?" Aubrey said, without giving any sign she recognised me.

"Hi," I replied. "I love your carnival, and I've been following it for ages, and I was really hoping for a chance to join."

She sighed. "Franz says you have zero training."

Franz gave me an apologetic shrug.

"I'm a really fast learner," I said.

"We're not circus school. You can do that on your own time."

"Okay, but I can clean toilets and serve candy floss and brush horses and … and make popcorn, or … I don't know, polish throwing knives, or—" I stopped as she raised her hand cut me off.

"Basically you have no skills, but you want a job." Her tone added *kids today* with a head shake.

"I'm not looking for payment. And I'll do any job you give me. Please. I really want this." My voice wobbled, and I let it. I *did* want this. I *needed* this.

"Will you clean the showers?" Franz asked. "And scrub the fish tanks?"

"Anything," I said, wondering how a travelling circus kept fish tanks going.

Aubrey sighed. "What we really need is another bloody wizard." She tipped her head at me. "Can you do any magic tricks?"

"Actually I can," I said, which wasn't entirely a lie. I used to put on magic shows for Ruiner's birthday when we were little. I just needed ready access to a trick shop, a bunch of gullible seven-year-olds, and preferably a YouTube tutorial.

"That's something."

"As long as you don't do tarot," Franz said. "Or palm reading. Fiona doesn't like competition."

"Don't know either of those," I said.

Audrey shook her head. "Shame, really. Fiona keeps sending the punters out in tears, so she could do with a bit of competition." She looked at me for a moment longer, then said, "Alright, you're in. Unpaid trial for the first month, and we'll see where you fit after that. Deal?"

I started to say *deal,* then had a momentary panic when I remembered Grace saying, *just don't sign anything.* What if this was the verbal equivalent? I tried to change to *okay* instead, so what came out was, "Deedy-ay!" Aubrey and Franz stared at me, and I grinned at them desperately, then added, "It's slang. Like, *indeed* and *okay* all at once."

"Great," Aubrey said. "Just what we need." But she clicked her fingers, and the air shivered as the charms dropped. "Come in."

I opened the gate and edged through, half expecting the grimoire to give me away somehow, to set off some unseen protective alarms that would start screeching warnings, or for the barrier to recognise me from the night before and come crashing back into life, sending me flying across the lane. Or, worse, for Aubrey to give a ghastly grin and order Franz to lock me up with Ruiner, dooming us both to be carnival sideshows, eternally touring fading, unhappy villages and leaving a trail of death in our wake.

But Aubrey just examined me from closer quarters, then said "Well, you look like you should be able to do some work anyway. Settle in tonight and you'll start first thing in the morning. Bunk her in with Willow," she added to Franz. "And make sure she meets Gus. He can get her started." She turned and walked off again, leaving Franz and I looking at each other warily.

"Come on, then," he said, and started toward the accommodation caravans, his stride long and easy. "I'll show you to Willow's."

"Who's Willow?" I asked, hurrying after him.

"She's nice," he said. "Everyone likes Willow."

"And Gus?"

"Head of maintenance. No one likes Gus."

"Oh. Good to know."

He led me past the semicircle of parked trucks and into an area lit softly by lights hanging from caravans and campers, holding back the night as it deepened around us.

A big tent with the sides rolled up was backed up to the trucks, and inside were rows of tables and benches and folding chairs, already filling up with people clutching beer bottles and mugs. They were of all ages, all sizes, every form and description possible, some in sequins and hats and feathers, others in overalls and boots with greasy gloves hanging from their pockets. A kitchen was set up along one side of the tent, and I could hear the sizzle of hot pans from here.

"That's where we eat," Franz said, rather unnecessarily. "Willow doesn't always come down, but you come on over and I'll buy you a beer."

"Thanks," I said.

"No worries," he replied. "It's hard being new." He held one hand out to me and I took it, and he enveloped it in his own, shaking firmly. "Franz."

My mind went suddenly blank. I couldn't use my own name. What if Aubrey had heard it? Or Ruiner had been asking for me? "Liz," I blurted, using my mum's name since it was the first thing that came to mind.

"Pleased to meet you, Liz," he said, and pointed at a slightly tired-looking caravan that had been granted some life by pink bunting hanging from the roof and potted shrubs wreathed in fairy lights by the door. "This is Willow's. See you soon?"

"Sure," I said. "Thanks." I watched him walk away, then turned to the door. It had been surprisingly easy to join the circus. I just had to hope I could get out without too much more trouble.

I knocked firmly, and inside someone shouted, "Who is it?"

"I'm new," I called back. "Aubrey sent me."

"Oh, sure. Come in. Just mind the alligator."

"The *what?*" I asked, just as a hissing shadow rushed

out from under the caravan, the light shining off its generous array of teeth. I shrieked and hauled the door open, diving for safety and expecting my leg to be taken off at the knee at any second.

"Marvin!" someone shouted. "*Bad reptile!*" A chicken leg sailed out of the caravan as I rolled onto my back, scrabbling away from the door as well as I could in the tight confines, and I spotted an actual, real alligator snapping the meat out of the air before slinking away again. He had a glittering purple collar on.

"Sorry," someone said, and I looked up to see a curvaceous woman with glossy dark hair and a luxuriant beard, both plaited with red ribbons, looking down at me. She offered me her hand and helped me to my feet. "I'm Willow."

"Liz," I said. "Why is there an alligator under your caravan?"

"A gift from an admirer," she said, turning and heading into the little living space. "Plus I think he likes my TV shows. Do you like *Friends*? I'm on season four, but I can catch you up if you want."

I followed her in, clutching my bag to me and with my heart still going too fast. "What's wrong with roses?"

"I don't know that show," she said. "Is it good?"

I shook my head mutely. If alligators were a sign of affection, I wasn't at all sure I was going to survive long enough to help Ruiner and Jacqueline. After all, what happened if someone *didn't* like you?

THE BEARDED LADY'S trailer was beautifully decorated, with small watercolours of villages and gardens fixed to the bulkheads, flowers in a vase on the little kitchen worktop, and a neat collection of throw pillows in the U-shaped seating area that were neither too gaudy nor too twee, nor too nondescript at the same time. Willow settled herself among them, hit play on the TV that was mounted among the paintings, and picked up a nail file.

"Are you more a Chandler or a Phoebe?" she asked me, buffing the ends of her nails carefully.

"Um — don't know," I said, standing in the little entrance area and unsure whether I should join her or not. She had her long legs stretched out on the seating, the toenails painted a deep red.

She looked up at me. "Haven't you done any quizzes?"

"Not recently."

"*Oooh.*" She clapped her hands lightly and swung her legs off the cushions, leaning over to open a drawer in the kitchen area. It was easy enough to do — the caravan wasn't roomy. Behind me was an open door that revealed a double bed with tiny built-in bedside tables to either side of it, and next to me was a closed door that probably held a toilet, judging from the mingled smell of chemicals and air freshener. Otherwise there was just the seating area and the kitchen, with a little under-counter fridge and a two-burner gas stove with a metallic red kettle set on top of it.

Willow brandished a handful of magazines at me. "You know *Friends* is really popular again, right? There are *so many* quizzes!" She patted the seat next to her. "Come on!"

"I think I'm meant to meet Gus?"

"Tomorrow," she said, waving dismissively. "No rush for that."

I had zero desire to do a *Friends* quiz — I hadn't even been that into the show when I'd been a kid — but if Willow was going to be my roommate, it seemed best to go along with it. Especially given the alligator. So I took my bag off and set it by my feet as I sat down next to her, dutifully specifying my coffee order, favourite dinosaur, and Christmas side dish.

Finally she added up the totals, nodded once as if it confirmed what she already knew, and said, "You're a Joey."

"I am?"

"Yes! That's wonderful."

"I'll take your word for it."

"Everyone underestimates him," she said, smoothing her beard. "He's much smarter than he seems."

"Right." I adjusted the bag. "Um — thanks for letting me stay with you."

"It's fine." She pointed to the room at the other end of the caravan. "That's my bed there. You can sleep on the sofa — it's actually pretty comfortable. You'll be assigned some permanent accommodation once they decide who you fit best with."

"Okay. I'll try not to get in the way too much."

She shrugged. "I'm used to it. Anyone new starts here. It's as if they think that just because I'm not throwing weights around or turning somersaults or blowing smoke rings or whatever, that I don't need my own caravan." She gave an elegant wave of the hand then grinned at me. "I don't really care. I'd rather share than have to scrub out rhinoceros enclosures."

"Rhinoceros?" I said. "There's rhinos here?"

"There were," she replied. "But they kept busting out and terrorising the villages. Then we had Komodo dragons. Or maybe they were monitor lizards. I don't know. Some sort of big toothy lizard anyway."

"Toothier than alligators?"

"Oh, there's only Marvin. And he's fine, really. Stops anyone sneaking in to steal my DVDs."

"Handy," I said, wondering how the Hollowbeck GP

would cope with alligator bites. Considering his affection for salves over antibiotics, it was probably best not to find out.

"You'll be fine," she said, and stood up to take a packet of crisps from a cupboard in the kitchen. "I think we're down to goats and horses now. The lizards bit a few too many people, and elephants are *so boring*." She waved the packet at me. "Hungry?"

"I might go over to the food tent thingy. Franz said he'd buy me a beer."

"Canteen," she said, grinning as she opened the crisps. She offered me the bag and I took a handful automatically. "And good plan. Franz wants to be friends with everyone, so he can show you around."

"You're not going over?"

She held up the crisps. "I need a break from people now and then." She gave me a curious look. "What's with the green hair?"

"It seemed like a good idea at the time," I replied, examining the ends.

"I suppose you were going for the mermaid look. We're out of mermaids at the moment. Might be an opening for you there if you're good with a fake tail."

"What happened to the other mermaids?" I asked.

She crunched on a crisp, her face suddenly drawn. "We haven't had any for a long time. The tanks are too small."

"Too small for tricks?"

"Too small for mermaids," she said, giving me that look as if I were being slow again.

"For people dressed as mermaids? What, do they bump into each other or something?"

"No, Liz. Too small for actual mermaids."

"*Actual* mermaids? You said fake tails!"

"I said *you* could use a fake tail. Have you never met a mermaid before?"

"*No.*" Because they don't exist, obviously. But then again, I'd never met a witch or an enchanted cat before, either, so … "Do they leave, then? Because of the tanks?"

"No one leaves," she said quietly, and then there was no sound but her eating steadily through the crisps, and scuffling under the floor from Marvin. All I could think of was Franz asking if I could clean fish tanks, and how small they must be after the endless vastness of the ocean, how desperately suffocating to circle and circle like an orca in a pond, and how dull with nothing to look at but the gawking faces of carnival-goers. How maybe, even if one *could* survive in the jostling water of moveable tanks, maybe one just *wouldn't*, because life's meant to be more than simply survival. It *has* to be more than just survival, otherwise what's the point?

I HEADED to the food tent not long after that, jumping the steps and jogging away from the caravan with my backpack strapped down tightly, looking over my shoulder in case Marvin was giving chase. I heard a guttural hiss from the shadows, but he didn't emerge.

Willow sent me off with the advice not to eat with Franz and his strongmen buddies. "Hideous," she said. "Eggs. Everything's just eggs. Or sometimes protein shakes. Or protein shakes *with* eggs."

But Franz had evidently already eaten, because when he waved to me from one of the tables on the edge of the tent, he had a large bottle of what looked like home-brew beer in front of him, and two glasses.

"Liz!" he called, and for a moment I thought he'd

mixed me up with someone else, then remembered my new name.

I waved back and went to join him, aware of the weight of gazes on me. The tent was still only half-full, a painfully skinny and uniformly blond trio munching through giant plates of salad at one table; the gate-guardian from earlier in deep conversation with a pleas-antly plump, curly-haired woman who I took a moment to recognize as the purple-clad Fiona from the night before; and a few other tables occupied with little knots of people, glasses or plates or both in front of them. There was an air of relaxed satisfaction about the place, an end-of-day contentment, and I slid into a seat opposite Franz.

He grinned at me. "Settled in?"

"You could've warned me about Marvin."

"Oh, he's fine. Barely ever bites anyone." He topped up the spare glass and slid it across to me. "Eugene's special."

"Eugene?"

He nodded at the man I'd met at the gate that morn-ing. "Dwarfs make the *best* beer."

I sniffed the glass and wrinkled my nose. "Isn't the correct term *little person?*"

He raised his eyebrows. "If you want him to have at you with a battle axe."

"Oh." He really was an actual, fairy tale dwarf, then. I should've known. I took a sip of the beer. Language conventions and hoppy whiff aside, it was actually excellent.

Franz pointed around the tent. "Those are the trapeze artists," he said, pointing at the pale trio with their salads. "Don't go calling them string flyers or something."

"Got it."

"Amelia, Alan, and Art."

"What?"

"Triplets." He shrugged. "Or we think so. They're never actually said. They all share one caravan, eat together, and dress the same, so either they're related or they've just spent so much time together they may as well be."

"Okay."

"And … that's Fiona's talking to Eugene there," he said, nodding at them. Fiona's off-duty garb consisted of slacks and a cardigan that would've looked at home in a Women's Institute meeting, but her curly hair was piled on her head and skewered with a glittery black skull-shaped clip.

"She's the one who doesn't want anyone else doing tarot?"

"Yeah, there was a whole thing when Lionel joined. He's … he *was* a wizard." Franz stopped, and took a deep breath. "He was a good sort."

"Was?" I said. "What happened?"

"This cat up and murdered him."

"A cat did?"

"An enchanted one." He scowled, and I was suddenly aware of the bulk of him, looming above the flimsy table. "Either a wizard in disguise himself, or working with a witch."

"How *awful*. What happened to the cat?"

"Oh, Aubrey locked him up quick-smart. He's not going anywhere."

I wanted to ask where, but that felt like it might be pushing the limits of first-day questions. So I just said, "Good to hear. Are you going to hand him over to the authorities?"

Franz snorted into his beer. "We're our own authorities. He'll answer to Aubrey soon enough."

"He hasn't yet?"

"No, but I think she's just deciding on a suitable punishment, to be honest. I mean, he's obviously guilty. The mouth on him, too. Horrible creature."

Of course Ruiner would be talking himself in deeper. *Of course* he would. "No one else could've done it? Like you said there was a *whole thing* about the tarot between Fiona and Lionel? Could that have got out of hand or something?"

He gave me a puzzled look. "Of course not. Fiona and Lionel might have disagreed, but the carnival's a family. Why would you think someone else did it?"

"Well, just, you're talking about a *cat.*"

"An *enchanted* cat. And rumour is, his sister's a *witch.*" He whispered the last word, leaning toward me and looking around as if afraid he might summon such a dread creature just by saying the word. "Fiona saw them go into his caravan. She said they looked like trouble."

I took a gulp of beer to hide my face, then said, "So what can I expect tomorrow?"

"Lots of cleaning," Franz said, straightening up. "That's how everyone starts, unless they've already got an established act."

"Definitely in my skill set," I said, brightly as I could. And it was. More so than being a witch, anyway.

THIRTEEN

Pigeons 0, Morgan 1

WHEN I GOT BACK to Willow's caravan, she offered to turn the TV off and drop the table down to convert it into a double bunk, but I waved her off, happy to just curl myself into the pillows on one side of the seating, cradling my bag between myself and wall, and doze off to the laugh track from *Friends*. Dwarf beer is *strong*, and I didn't even hear Willow when she went to bed.

But once the beer had worn off, I found myself restless with anxiety, my sleep reduced to patchy stints. I startled awake to the whinny of horses and the clatter of pans, to scuffling under the caravan and the roar of something unidentified that sent old, deep instincts into flight mode. Eventually, though, I fell asleep properly, only to be woken what felt like five minutes later by the TV going on and the kettle clanging onto the stove. I opened one eye and looked at Willow.

"Morning," she said cheerfully. Her hair was loose, tumbling almost to her waist, and she examined the ends. "Do you think I should dye my hair green?"

"No," I said, licking my lips. My mouth tasted *awful*,

and I'd only had two glasses of beer. "Your hair's beautiful."

"What about my beard?" She ran her fingers through it. "Would a green beard be good?"

"I think it's impressive enough as it is," I replied truthfully.

She nodded in satisfaction, petting the beard like it was a small animal. "Probably for the best," she said, finding a couple of mugs. "I'd have to bleach it first, and that does *terrible* things to your hair. The bathroom's free if you want it."

I took my bag with me into the tiny wet room, and stashed it in the cupboard while I showered and brushed my teeth, and tried to copy Grace's makeup from the day before. I emerged feeling better but looking like a refugee from a 2000s emo music video. It was going to have to do, though.

Willow had a tea waiting for me, laden with too much milk and sugar, and she said, "You can get breakfast at the canteen."

"That's alright," I said, wrapping both hands around the mug. "I should probably just start."

She nodded, leaned over to carefully remove an eyelash from my cheek, and said, "Give your face a chance to dry next time. You'll look less like a panda."

My cheeks flushed with heat, and I gulped my tea hurriedly. "Thanks. Can you tell me where to find Gus?"

"I'll take you in a moment. First, thought — what're you doing joining the carnival?"

The sharpness of her gaze startled me, after all the *Friends*-fixation and makeup and hair talk, and I blinked at her, then offered, "It's been my childhood dream?"

"Rubbish. It's a man, isn't it?" She tipped her head suddenly. "Or a woman?"

"Um …"

"Midlife crisis?" She picked up a couple of locks of my hair, examining it, and while I was still veering between horror that she'd think I was *midlife* (I was sure that didn't start until mid-forties, so I had almost a decade to go still) and horror that she'd figured out why I was really there, she added, "This is terrible. I'll give you some of my beard conditioner."

"Thanks?"

"What'd they do?"

"Who?"

"Your ex," she said, in tones that suggested I was being slow on the uptake.

"Jason? Oh. He was just…" I waved vaguely, trying to take in the fact that it wasn't what he'd *done*, but rather all the things he'd *never* done, like have a steady income or any sense of responsibility or ability to pick up his own socks.

"Ah." She nodded, as if she understood completely. "*Men*. Joining the carnival seems like a bit of an overreaction, though." Her voice softened as she spoke, and she glanced at her hands, running the fingers of one over the other's ring finger in an unconscious movement that made me think she did understand.

"It just seemed like a good chance to change things completely, you know?"

"Sure. But you should leave yourself the chance to change them back." She looked up at me again, then smiled. "But you're here now."

"I am," I said, cheerily as I could.

"And you best not be late. Gus *hates* people being late." She took a scarf from a hook on the wall and flung it dramatically around her shoulders. "Come on."

I took another gulp of tea, put the mug in the sink, and grabbed my backpack.

Willow gave me a curious look. "You can leave that here. It'll be quite safe."

"It's got my passport in it," I said.

"You're not going to need that."

"Well, no." I didn't move to take the bag off, and she rolled her eyes, then held a hand out.

"Give it here."

"Um …"

"Sweetie, how safe d'you think lugging it around all day's going to be? It'll get eaten by an alpaca, covered in Clydesdale poo, and drowned in the duck pond."

"All at once?" I said weakly.

"And that's if Gus doesn't sling it to the goats because he's sick of seeing you carting it around."

I hesitated, then reluctantly took the bag off and handed it over. She had a good point, and I supposed stashing it in some cubbyhole in the caravan was safe enough. It wasn't like anyone here knew about it, and no one from outside could come in and get it. I hoped.

Willow pulled the carpet back in the kitchen area, exposing a hatch secured by a couple of clasps. "This is where I keep my hair serums," she said. "The good ones, you know?"

"Okay."

"Also my DVDs," she added, unfastening the clips and lifting the hatch. "People think they can just — *bad reptile!*"

Marvin surged into the gap with a hiss, jaws snapping wildly and his purple collar glinting in the soft light of the caravan's lamps. Willow bopped him on the nose almost casually, then dropped a chicken leg to him. He snatched it up and crunched on it a couple of times, eyeing us balefully, and she pulled a different latch, sliding a container into view from under the caravan's floor like it was hidden drawer. It was packed with an assortment of neatly labelled bottles and a collection of DVDs, but there was enough room for her to squeeze my bag in as well. She slid the container back into place, latched it, and closed the hatch while Marvin hissed murderously at us.

"Happy?" she asked me.

"Actually, yes." Although I wasn't sure how I was getting my bag back without Willow's help, I didn't think anyone else was getting their hands on it either.

We left the caravan, Willow not bothering to lock it behind us, and I fell into step with her as we crossed the fairground. The day was damp and grey, a steady drizzle holding back the dawn, but the carnival was already alive with movement, the canteen full of people tucking into full Englishes and stacks of toast, and others ambling about with no haste but a general sense of purpose.

As casually as I could, I said, "I heard there was a bit of a thing the other day. On rehearsal night. Did someone get hurt?"

"Oh, it was awful," Willow said. "Poor Lionel!"

"Who was he, exactly?"

"A stage magician."

"Really? I saw his name on the flyers. Legendary Lionel, wasn't he?"

"Can't believe everything you read," she said with a grin. "Can't exactly pull the punters in with *Mediocre Mike*, can you?"

"Fair enough. So he wasn't a proper wizard, then?"

She snorted. "If you were a proper wizard, would you be working for a carnival?"

"I suppose." Of course he hadn't been a proper wizard. What had he been doing, saying he could help Ruiner, then? Was that why he ended up dead? He tried something that was way beyond his abilities and it all went wrong? "So what happened?"

"The theory is a cat killed him," she said, her tone noncommittal.

"You don't think so?"

She shrugged. "Seems like a stretch, but weirder things have happened in carnivals."

"That does seem pretty weird, though. Do you know where the cat is now?"

"Being held for judgement," she said. "You'll probably meet him. No one wants to be on litter box duties. He's bloody rude, apparently, as well as everything else."

Well, I'd be volunteering for it the first chance I got. This could be easier than I'd hoped.

The maintenance shed was actually a truck, the interior stacked with plastic tubs labelled in black markers with things like *Tie-downs* and *Eye-hooks* and *Splicing kit please return.* Great coils of rope and electrical cables and bungee cords and bundled nets hung from the ceiling, and tool kits were corralled in a corner with more labels that declared they were for *Electrical* or *Plumbing* or *Misc.,* as well as *Gus's!! Touch it & I'll cut your hands off!*

Gus himself was a tall, rangy man whose arms seemed disproportionately long compared to his short legs, and he looked me up and down critically, one hand on his hip and the other holding a cigarette with the tip tucked into his palm.

"Can you climb?" he asked me.

"Reasonably," I said.

"Good, because we've got some pigeons trying to nest in the big top. You can start with scaring them off."

"Okay."

He wedged his cigarette into his mouth, picked a clipboard up from a bench set up on the grass next to him, and ran a finger down a list. "After that, you can muck out the horses' enclosure and check the fencing. Can you handle that?"

"Absolutely," I said, with as much confidence as I could, trying not to think about how big Clydesdales were.

"Off you go, then." He pointed at the big top, and I hesitated.

"Do I get a harness or anything?"

"You'll be fine," he said, putting the clipboard back down. "Just don't let them get in your hair."

I hadn't actually been worried about pigeons getting in my hair before then, but I added that to the list of carnival-specific risks, alongside being crushed by oversized ponies and eaten by guard-alligators. At least rhinos and Komodo dragons were off the list of possibilities.

I trotted dutifully towards the big top, Willow waving me off enthusiastically and Gus frowning like he expected me to trip over my own feet any moment. At least it didn't look like I was going to get much supervision, which left plenty of room for finding my brother.

I'D HEADED off confidently enough, but it took me a bit to find my way into the big top, the canvas sides all pinned down and secured. Eventually I spotted a flap with a couple of ties holding it closed, and I undid them, half-expecting someone to yell at me, or for the whole thing to unravel like a collapsible dome tent. Instead, I slipped into a muted, low-ceilinged darkness, the scent of sawdust rising all around me. A string of mellow lights were suspended above me, old-fashioned bulbs illuminating a narrow corridor, one side of which was taken up with racks that held jackets, feathery things that might've been hats or might've been some inventive bodywear, gauzy wings and umbrellas and platform boots and bags of soft foam balls. A quartet of unicycles were stacked in the corner, along with some torches in a bin that reeked of kerosene, and there was a fearsome display of swords and knives stuck into a giant polystyrene block that someone had stuck the image of a certain universally disliked politician on, which for some reason was the most bizarre thing of all.

I grabbed an umbrella, since there was nothing labelled *pigeon-chaser* hanging about the place, then headed down the little hall until I found another set of loose canvas flaps, these ones not tied back. I pushed through them and found myself at the edge of the ring, lit in the same low light as the backstage area had been. I stood there for a moment, looking at the corner where we'd been just two nights ago, Theodore and I crouched over a dead body while Ruiner fled with his panicked screech. It still made no sense to me, not the death, or Ruiner's connection to it, or why he and Lionel had been in the big top at all.

A flutter of wings and some low cooing pulled my attention back to the task at hand. The sooner I got the pigeons out, the sooner I could try and track down my brother. I trotted up the aisle to the main door and tied it back, letting a gust of cool wind and grey light into the tent, then turned and headed back to the ring, peering up into the far reaches of the roof.

"Off you go," I called. "Much nicer out."

The pigeons either weren't listening or didn't believe me, as my only answer was a deposit that narrowly missed my upturned face.

"Rude," I muttered, and crossed to one of the heavy support poles, peering at it dubiously. It had … not *handles*, as that implied they were big enough to grab hold of with your *hands*, but notches in the old wood, leading up to an equally minuscule platform too far off the ground to be reasonable.

"Ruiner, you owe me *so much*," I shoved the umbrella up the back of my T-shirt and tucked the handle into my jeans, which was uncomfortable but manageable. Then I kicked out of my trainers, peeled my socks off, and started up before I could think about it too much. I kept my eyes on the pole, avoiding looking at the ground receding below me, or the precarious feel of the tiny notches beneath my hands and bare feet.

It felt like I climbed at least three tents' worth of pole before I finally reached the little platform and scrambled onto it. It was just big enough for me to have both feet wedged on, my belly pressed to the pole and both arms wrapped tightly around it. The wood creaked under my feet and I swore softly, trying to calm my breathing. A coo drew my attention and I looked up to see three pigeons perched on the support cables that ran to the other poles, watching me curiously.

"Shoo!" I said to them, and they cooed back, sounding suspiciously like they were laughing at me. "Go on, get out!" I let go of the pole gingerly with one arm and waved at them, which had precisely zero effect.

"Snacks," I suggested. "Peanuts? Do you like peanuts? I'll give you peanuts if you go outside." They stared at me, not giving me any indication of their position on peanuts. We looked at each other for a little bit longer, then I reached behind me and carefully disentangled the umbrella from my clothes. The pigeons shifted a bit more, and one of them dropped a mess on my shoulder.

"Oh, *ew.*" I huffed, then flailed at them with the umbrella. "Get out! Get out, before I put pigeon pie on the menu!"

My aim with the umbrella wasn't great, considering I

still had the pole in a death grip with one hand, but somehow I connected with the wire they were perched on. The pole shuddered with the echo of the impact and I shrieked, but the birds exploded into flight, tearing around just underneath the canvas and calling to each other in panic.

"That's right," I yelled at them. "Go on! Or I'll turn you into taxidermy doorstops!" There was no way to direct them out the door or give chase, so I just stayed where I was, flailing out with the umbrella every time one came close, yelling an increasingly deranged selection of threats while my whole body shook with the effort of holding on and the pigeons wheeled and cooed and decorated half the tent with their droppings.

I thought I was going to have to give up and climb down while my arms still worked when one of them either spotted the grey light from the door at last, or decided dealing with an unhinged human was too high a price to pay for a nice perch. It zoomed out the entrance and the other two followed, vanishing into the drizzle. I gave a yelp of triumph and dropped the umbrella, hugging the pole and pressing my cheek to it. My arms were shaking so badly that I wasn't at all sure I was going to make it down, and I wondered, not for the first time, how I'd ever thought this was a good idea.

But I'd conquered the pigeons. That had to be a good sign, right?

FOURTEEN

The carnival creeps on

I MADE it all the way to the bottom of the pole and collapsed into the sawdust with a whimper before someone started applauding. I looked up without moving from my prone position to find three ethereal figures watching me, the low light of the tent rendering them ghost-like, their hair drifting silver and their skin almost translucent. The trapeze artists. Ambien, Amtrak, and Ampersand, perhaps? My brain couldn't come up with anything better.

"Well done," one of them said. "That was highly entertaining. I was betting you were going to fall, to be honest."

"It was very hard to bet against the falling," the person on the left said, and the one on the right sighed and said, "I'd even figured out what points to allocate dependent on the style of the fall."

"Thanks so much," I managed. "I appreciate the confidence."

They all leaned over me, their features in shadow, and I sat up rapidly. There was too much of an alien autopsy vibe going on to stay where I was.

"She did get the pigeons out," one said.

"I did," I said, and stood up, still feeling a little wobbly. Now I was upright, they were less alarming. Their height was as uniform as their long thin noses and wide-set eyes, and I was taller than all of them, which was a novel experience around anyone over the age of twelve.

"They made a mess, though," one said, and drifted languidly to the pole.

"Less of a mess that if I'd left them in here," I pointed out, and watched them scale the pole effortlessly, almost running up it. None of them answered, the second one wandering off to scale a different pole and the third looking at me with pale eyes, a small frown line crinkling their forehead. "Yes?" I said.

"You look familiar."

"I saw you in the food tent — the canteen — last night. I'm Liz."

They tipped their head. I was still struggling to remember their names — one name had been distinctly feminine, but I couldn't have said which of them it belonged to. There was something oddly undefined about all three of them, making it hard to be sure of anything other than their paleness and homogeneity.

"It wasn't then," they said, but held a hand out. "Art."

"Hi," I said, and shook their hand. It was cool and strong, callouses hard under my grip.

"Amelia," they said, pointing at the creature who had run up the pole I'd just about fallen off. I could see them dimly, standing casually on the little platform and stretching. "Alan. Or Al, rather." They pointed to the other one. "Don't worry if you get us mixed up, though. Everyone calls us all *A*, because it's easier."

"You don't mind?"

They shrugged. "Saves us remembering anyone else's names if they won't remember ours." They grinned, displaying small sharp teeth, and looked up at a sudden rush of movement. I looked up too, in time to see Al sweeping through the air, one arm clutching a trapeze carelessly. Amelia dived to meet him, and the next moment they were sweeping back the other way, both holding the same trapeze with one hand, their bodies tracing identical arcs through the air that made me feel for a moment as if I had double vision.

I really wished I could just say *what **are** you*, but instead I said, "Amazing. You're all really talented."

"Yes," Art said, without any sort of boastfulness, simply a statement of fact. "It's a good job."

"I imagine. You know, if you like heights."

They examined me again, then said, "We do. We can see everything from up there." Then they were gone, swarming up the pole like a ghost, and a moment later all three of them swung past, swapping trapezes and somersaulting through the air, meeting and parting like physics was merely a suggestion.

I watched them for a bit, thinking about when they said, *"we can see everything"* and then went to close the main doors before the bloody pigeons came back. Questioning strange little flying creatures would have to wait. The horses were calling.

GUS handed me a broad shovel and pointed me across the fairground, toward the wall that cut us off from the next field, the one I'd been considering scaling the day before. I threaded my way through the semicircles of accommodation trailers that had the big top and the canteen as their centre point, trying to see if one had a big sign on it reading *Carnival Jail*, or *Murderers Kept Here*. None did, though. In fact, most of the caravans were plain and nondescript, no different from the dozens of old, genteelly rusting contraptions that proliferated on the roads every summer, usually towed by an equally mature Volvo estate with at least one dog hanging its head out the window. Only a handful of the more characterful ones — a fancy American-style motorhome, a campervan that looked like someone had built a wood cabin on top of an old Transit van chassis, and a few beautifully painted wooden caravans, had any signs on them, and they were all for various attractions.

One of those was Legendary Lionel's, which had evidently been moved back here for safekeeping, and I slowed as I passed it. But there were too many people around for me to risk peeking in the windows, and what would it get me anyway? He hadn't died in there, unless someone had carried his corpse through the crowded fairground to the big top, which seemed unlikely. He'd been pretty solid. He wouldn't have been easy to move.

So I kept going, passing a group of about six people who were attempting to build a human pyramid. They were shouting and swearing at each other, all of them trying to direct the others at once, and one woman stopped to bellow, "Did any of you even *go* to clown school?"

"Clown school?" An older man with huge muscles in his arms and a shock of white hair yelled back. "In my day—"

"You arm-wrestled Churchill? We *know!*"

They kept arguing, ignoring me as I passed, while I wondered what arm-wrestling Churchill had to do with clown school, and if he meant *Winston* Churchill, and how old that made him. But given the A-team and their trapezes, and Aubrey and her charms, I was willing to bet I might be in the minority here as far as being strictly human.

The makeshift fence that penned the horses in was simply a roll of plastic webbing that they could've walked through likely without noticing, but they were just standing there docilely, looking off over the wall as if dreaming of wider fields. I clambered over the fence and stood staring around the enclosure, eyeing the Clydesdales nervously. If one of those stood on me, it'd be as bad as a nip from Marvin.

On a more practical note, big horses create a *lot* of muck, and they weren't the only ones in here. The Shetlands and the medium-sized horses (they were very pretty and looked like they were the most likely to bite me, but that was as well as I could categorise them), were in here too, so there were piles of manure in a whole variety of sizes to deal with. Plus the goats seemed to come and go as they fancied. Two were head-butting each other next to a plastic water trough, three were fighting to stand on the highest point of the wall, and one was standing on the back of a Shetland pony, looking pleased with itself. There were also four alpacas looking superior in one corner, and I eyed them suspiciously. I had an idea they might spit. They *looked* like they would, going by the expressions. But, on the upside, I might get stomped on, kicked, or spat at, but I couldn't fall off anything and plummet to my death.

There was a wheelbarrow leaning against the wall just outside the fencing, so I started shovelling the manure into it, talking to the horses as I did so, mostly so they realised I was there and didn't kick me. Even the Shetlands looked like they could put some muscle into it. One kept following me and shoving its head into my side, so I alternated patting him and fending off the goats, who wanted to jump into the wheelbarrow.

I kept my eyes on the fairground as much as I could while I worked, looking for someone carrying cat-sized bowls or bags of litter, or sneaking around with a murderous demeanour. There was plenty of movement, people carting fresh-painted signs, or stacked plates, or bags of unpopped corn, or mysterious parts that probably belonged to sideshow games, all hurrying about in the persistent drizzle. Every now and then music popped up somewhere, ran for a bit, then went off again, or a loud-speaker crackled and died. There was a lot of shouting, but it was mostly short-lived, with no sense of urgency in any of it. And nothing suggested anyone was off to care for a cat.

The shovelling was easy and repetitive, but calming as well, and the soft rain beaded my hair and soaked my skin, cold and soothing. I listened to my breathing as I worked, and for the first time since I'd seen Ruiner in the big top, my heart seemed to slow a little. Simply *doing* was better than running around worrying about things, and this was *doing* in the right direction. I'd get on, and make myself useful, and wait until everyone stopped paying attention to me. Then I'd find my brother and Jacqueline and get them both out. The details would come when they came.

It wasn't much of a plan, but it was all I had. It was going to have to be enough.

BY THE TIME the field was clear of muck and I'd topped up the trough up with water, then petted the friendly Shetland on the head for a little longer and persuaded him not to try charging through the fence after me, I was starving. The day was too dull for me to have much idea what time it was, but it felt like I'd missed lunch. I was going to have to get a watch. Not carrying a phone all the time was still something I wasn't used to.

I trailed back to the maintenance shed with the shovel over my shoulder and found Gus examining the insides of a clockwork mechanism, his cigarette dangling from his lips and a pair of smudged glasses perched on his nose.

"Finished," I told him.

"I can smell that," he said, not looking up. "Bites?"

"None."

"Kicks?"

"None."

"Escapees?"

"None. Although the grey pony tried to follow me out."

"Yeah, that's Ferdinand. He likes women." He looked up finally. "Had lunch?"

"No."

"Well, you're probably too late."

"Great," I said with a sigh. "I don't have a watch."

"Get one." He looked at his clipboard. "But Mike and Cheryl can always do with some help. Head over to the canteen, scrub some dishes, and Cheryl'll feed you."

"Okay. When do I come back?"

"You can stay there through dinner," he said. "Come back tomorrow morning for some more jobs. We're pretty quiet — everything's already mostly set for opening night."

"When's that then?" I asked.

"TBC. Was going to be Saturday, but I think Aubrey's getting a bit restless. Might be sooner."

"Why?"

He shrugged. "How the hell do I know? I just make sure things turn on when they should and off when they should."

He went back to his clockwork thingy, and just like that

I was dismissed. I wandered off, sniffing my shirt as I went. I *was* pretty fragrant after the scramble around the big top and all the shovelling, but scrubbing dishes for the rest of the day was hardly going to improve things. I headed straight to the canteen, where about half the tables were once again occupied, people drinking tea and munching on sandwiches or slices of cake. No one was at any risk of going hungry while at Masters of Mayhem, anyway.

The kitchen consisted of a food truck parked next to the tent, which offered a griddle, a four-burner gas stove, an industrial double oven, and a couple of huge fridges. A free-standing sink and scullery area was set up along the tent wall next to it, along with a prep area, all in well-scrubbed stainless steel, and a row of more stainless-steel trolleys both separated it from the rest of the tent and created a service are. A burly man was leaning over a small woman in the food truck, pointing at an enormous pan from which drifted the scent of softly cooking onions.

"Do you call those caramelised?" he was asking as I approached, sounding more curious than irritated. "I've never seen caramelised onions that pale. What sort of caramel are you thinking? White chocolate?"

The woman gave him a bored look and said, "If they go any faster, they'll burn."

"If they go any slower, they'll go backwards and end up raw again."

"Have you been watching *Kitchen Nightmares* again?"

He spluttered, but he was grinning as well, and they both looked up as I stopped by the service area.

"Can I help?" the woman asked.

"I'm new," I said. "Gus said I should come and wash dishes, stack plates, that sort of thing."

"Excellent," the big man said, clapping his hands

together. There were burns on the back of both of them. "Mike, Cheryl, and you can start by clearing some tables. Think you can handle it?"

"I should be able to," I said. And this time, at least, I was telling the truth. Waitressing was one of many part-time jobs I'd had, both before I'd gone into bookkeeping and during it, when my wages hadn't been enough to cover both myself and Jason, and often to bail Ruiner out of his latest problems. For the first time since arriving in Hollowbeck, I was actually doing something I was familiar with.

I took the apron Mike threw me and put it on, less to protect my already filthy clothes and more to make sure I didn't shed bits of straw (or worse) on the tables, then headed out to start clearing empty plates and stacking glasses. It was as easy and mindless as mucking out the horses had been, but, even better, it let me do a lot of eavesdropping. Carnivals were no different from anywhere else, apparently. Nobody notices the people who clean up the debris of life.

The discussions ranged from the predictions of crowds at the next town, which was somewhere I'd never heard of but which sounded like it could be in Wales, given the excessive amount of syllables and consonants. Another table was arguing about the relative merits of Taylor Swift over Nicki Minaj, neither of which I had an opinion on, and at a third they were speculating on what the clowns' new act was likely to be. Apparently they had something spectacular planned for opening night.

All of it was interesting enough, but no one seemed to be talking about arrested cats or dead wizards, which seemed weird. Surely something like that happening in the middle of rehearsal should warrant at least a *little* discussion. But it seemed that life at the carnival went on regardless, as if Lionel had simply been swallowed up, vanished as if he'd never been there at all.

I cleared all the tables I could find, then set to washing dishes, the water gurgling into the sink from a big drum set on a stand behind it, and the hot water coming straight from a tank fitted with a gas heater that just about took the skin off my hands the first time I switched it on. As soon as that lot of dishes were done, I went back out to the tables and started the whole process over again, pausing only to munch on a salad-stuffed wrap Cheryl had handed me, dripping dressing and marinated mushrooms all down my top, which was actually an improvement on the muck already on it.

Things slowly got busier as I did my circuits of tables to sink to tables, and before long I found myself too busy for eavesdropping. The plates went back out at least as fast as I could get them in and clean them, piled with sandwiches or cake or salad or fish 'n chips or steak or duck crepes or aubergine curry or half a dozen other dishes that made me wonder how the little kitchen could possibly keep up. I didn't know if there were a disproportionate number of crew at the carnival or if they were just disproportionately hungry, but the pots and pans never stopped. Neither did Mike or Cheryl, both of them deceptively fast. Mike stomped and swore and bellowed at me, Cheryl, the carnival crew, his pans, his knives, and the kitchen gods in equal measure, and next to him Cheryl calmly chopped and seared and stirred and plated, barely breaking a sweat. I just tried to stay out of both of their ways, and not drop too much.

At some point I realised that it felt like I'd already been doing this forever, and would still be doing it in twenty years' time, or more, caught in the endless cycle of the carnival, and I waited for a wave of panic to pass over me.

It didn't, which should've scared me. Instead, I just went back for more plates, and the day bled on into evening, one step closer to opening night. One step closer to Ruiner and I being lost forever.

FIFTEEN

You're not lion

WHEN THINGS FINALLY EASED OFF, the tent still full of people but most of them moving onto after-dinner drinks, Cheryl presented me with a plate of shepherd's pie and shooed me off to eat it. I grabbed a beer from the big communal fridges next to the food truck, collapsed at the nearest table, and settled down gratefully to scoff both. My feet were sore, my back ached, and I'd added a cut from a broken glass and a burn from a hot pan to my skinned knuckles from the pole climbing.

I wanted to crawl back to Willow's caravan and fall asleep on the nearest flat surface that'd have me, even though I knew I should be searching for the murderer, or finding where my brother was being held, or looking for Jacqueline. That all felt oddly less urgent, though, as if such concerns belonged to the outside world, which was too far away to really matter right now. And I knew that lack of urgency should've worried me even more than the possibility of being sent after more pigeons, but I was too tired and too hungry to make myself care.

As I shovelled the shepherd's pie down (it was excellent,

flavourful and topped with perfectly creamy mash, with bright fresh peas on the side and lashings of gravy), I wondered if Theodore had discovered I was gone yet, or Isabella, and how I was meant to find the wren so I could get a message to Grace once I found something out. Was the bird going to hang about the walls waiting for me to do the fairy tale princess thing at it? Or would I have to figure out how to do a wren call?

Just like my concerns about murderers and missing brothers, though, I couldn't seem to get up the energy to worry that much. The carnival was its own place, an island in the world, so utterly cut off from what passed as everyday life that I could almost have believed that Hollowbeck didn't even exist outside its waters, let alone more concrete places like Manchester or Leeds. Could have believed there was nothing at all beyond the canvas tents and the wooden caravans, the scent of sawdust and good food and peanuts, all tied up with the lingering traces of popcorn and sweet friend dough and strange enchantments that might've been magic and might've been illusion, and it was impossible to tell which. It was hard to really worry that much about anything when everything felt as surreal and impossible as the softly falling rain.

I was staring at my empty plate with something like surprise, wondering when I'd finished it, when someone flopped onto the bench on the opposite side of the table. I looked up, startled, and found a tall, dishevelled man staring at me. Despite the rapidly cooling evening, he was only wearing a T-shirt, which was torn at the neck, and his messy hair hung to his shoulders. He yawned, looking from me to my plate, and licked his lips.

"Hi?" I said.

"Hi," he said, and I blinked. I was more tired than I'd

thought, because it seemed like his voice was coming from the wrong direction — just off to his right somewhere.

"Um ... can I help you?"

He reached out and put two fingers on my plate, pulling it toward him, then gave a sudden yelp and stopped, staring down at the ground next to him. "Your name's not Liz," he said.

"What?"

He looked from the floor to my plate and back down again, scowling, and ... was he *growling?* "I know who you are," he said, and I leaned around the table to see what he was looking at, because someone was *definitely* growling.

"Bloody *hell!*" I yelped, and pulled my knees up as if I thought the full-grown male lion looking back at me could be avoided as long as I protected my ankles. "Should he be in here?"

"He's very well trained," the man said, and I stared at him. He had a new growth of stubble, but if I imagined him with slicked back hair and a spotless white shirt, ruffles running all down the front ...

"You're the lion-tamer. George of the Jungle?"

"*Jared,*" he said, with a touch of exasperation, still staring intently at my plate. He obviously wasn't great with eye contact.

"Why d'you think my name's not Liz?" I asked, but I already knew. He'd been there, right beside Lionel and Ruiner. Right beside *me.*

"I saw you," he said, his voice low and gravelly. Kind of sexy, to be honest, especially with that wild hair, but I didn't have time to think about it, because the next thing he said was, "You're the cat's sister."

"That's ridiculous." I could hear the way my voice went up and down, turning the word into a question.

"It's not, though, is it?" He reached across the table

again, and I watched him pull the plate toward him, finally giving me a quick glance with deep brown eyes.

"Help yourself," I said.

"What?" he asked, then bent over the table and started licking the gravy off the plate.

I watched him for a moment, not quite sure what to think. I mean, he was obviously planning to threaten me or blackmail me or something, so was this some sort of carnival intimidation technique? It was definitely unsettling, seeing him cleaning the plate thoroughly with his tongue. "Um … I think there's still some left in the kitchen. Can I get you a plate?"

"Oh, for—" He hissed and jerked upright, gravy still on his chin, eyes darting to the lion. "No, I don't need a plate." He wiped his chin, then licked his hand, saying around it, "We need to talk."

"Okay?"

"Not here. Meet me by the knitting booth after the canteen closes up."

"Is this about my brother?" I asked, since there wasn't any getting around the fact he'd recognised me. "Is he okay? Do you know where he is?"

Jared looked away, toward the kitchen, where the smell of cooking bacon was drifting toward us. He wrinkled his nose. "Just meet me there." He got up, starting toward the food truck, and the lion barged into him, sending him staggering toward the open side of the tent. He gave an irritated growl and said, "*Walk on*, dammit."

I watched them leave, Jared still throwing longing looks at the kitchen as he went, and the lion so close to his side that he kept tripping over him. "Walk on," he kept saying. "*Walk on.*"

"Jared!" Mike bellowed after him. "Put that bloody lion away, can't you? What are you, joined at the sodding hip?"

"He's very well trained," Jared shouted back, but they vanished out into the dreary night.

I sat there for a moment longer, then took my plate to the sink, collecting a few more on my way.

"Poor Jared," Cheryl said to me, taking the plates and giving me a couple of homemade custard creams in exchange. "Coltrane didn't bother you, did he?"

"Coltrane?"

"The lion. Ever since the murder, Jared won't go anywhere without him. I think he's scared, poor boy."

I squinted at Cheryl around a mouthful of biscuit. "Coltrane?"

"No, Jared."

"Oh. Jared's scared of the murderer? But I thought it was the cat, and you caught him."

"I think Jared saw the whole thing," she whispered. "He was *right there*. Imagine!"

"Imagine," I echoed, and when she shooed me off, I left without argument, trailing back to Willow's and managing a shambling run up the steps, shouting at Marvin as he charged me, "*No!* Behave!"

He hissed wildly, but didn't get close enough to nip, and I stumbled into the warmth and canned laughter of the caravan, closing the night out behind me. I leaned against the door for a moment, trying to get my thoughts in order, and Willow called, "How was your first day?"

"Weird," I said, honestly.

"Sounds about right."

AS MUCH AS I wanted to simply melt into the sofa (once I'd showered, as Willow let me get exactly one step into the living space before she yelled at me to stop stinking up the place, mostly good-naturedly), I forced myself to stay awake, sitting up with my bag clutched to me and the grimoire nestled like a hard-edged and potentially venomous animal inside. I'd told Willow I needed my journal out of it, and she'd shrugged and told me to throw Marvin another chicken leg from the tub in the fridge to distract him. I'd ended up using two, and she'd muttered about making him fat, but he hadn't bitten my arm off, so I figured it was a fair trade.

Now I listened to the steady snores coming from the bedroom, and when I was as sure as I could be that they weren't about to stop, I got up, fetched another chicken leg from the fridge, and eased out the door with my bag on my back. I heard the charge of hard feet and sleek belly on the ground under the caravan, and hurled the chicken at Marvin before he could start hissing. The charge stopped and the crunching started, making me shiver. I shut the door gently and hurried down the line of caravans and campers, the night air cold on my cheeks. The rain had stopped, although the moon had a halo of cloud around it still, and the stars were hidden.

The canteen had shut a good hour ago, one string of multi-coloured lights still illuminated and turning it into a landmark among the dark shapes of the trucks and vans. The big top loomed above everything, a deep shadow cut out of the night, and I almost fancied I could feel it watching me as I skirted its edges and headed into the tangle of shuttered sideshows. In the dim moonlight the paintwork was all greys, and there was something both melancholy and sinister about the whole place, bereft of people and purpose, like it was just waiting to grind into vampiric life.

I was still trying to find the knitting booth, peering at the signs in the shadows, when the lion loomed out of the night on soft, silent paws, the dull moon reflected in his eyes. I froze, my heart going too fast, and said, "Jared?" It came out in a little squeak, which felt quite justified, considering the *wild animal* staring at me. Its mouth dropped open, revealing long white teeth, and I hissed, "*Jared!*"

"Shh!" he said, and I tried to look around for him while not looking away from the lion.

"Where are you?"

"Here — heel, you mutt." Jared emerged from behind the stall, still in his torn T-shirt. He was barefoot, his toes digging into the grass, and he sidled up to the lion, staring at me with a disconcerting intensity. Apparently the eye contact thing was only an issue when shepherd's pie was involved.

"Where's Ruiner?" I demanded. "Where's my brother?"

"I can show you," he said, "but you have to help me."

"Help you with what?"

He didn't answer straight away, still staring at me, then finally said, "You're a witch, right?"

I grimaced. "Not really."

"You're *not*?" He sounded honestly horrified. "How are you not? You have a cat for a brother!"

"That's not my fault! He got into that situation all on his own."

"But you're friends with that vampire police officer, and the ghost. You *have* to be a witch."

"I mean, only by accident."

The lion slumped to the ground, apparently exhausted, and Jared said, "He *said* you were a witch."

"Who?" I asked, although I was already sure I knew.

"Your brother. He said that you could help."

I sighed. "Ruiner may have been a little overly optimistic. It's a character trait."

"What do I do now?" Jared asked. "What do I do *noooooowww?*" The last word ended in a gravelly wail, and I stared at him. He just stared back at me and licked his lips. I looked from him to the lion, whose mouth was definitely open, eyes squeezed shut in anguish.

"Oh no," I said.

The lion looked up at me. "Pretty much," he said.

"HOW?"

"I have no idea," Jared-the-lion said. Jared-the-man, whom I supposed I would now have to call Coltrane, scratched behind one ear and stared into the night, head tipping slightly. "I was backstage, ready to run on, and it felt like someone shoved me in the back. I fell over — I *thought* I fell over — and when I tried to get up, I was like this." He shook a paw at me. "Then the lights went on for me to go into the ring, and there was poor old Lionel and a damn cat, just sitting there. When they grabbed your brother, I heard someone say he had to be a wizard, so I thought he might know how to help me out."

"Wow," I said, and looked around for somewhere to sit. I was tired for a start, but also this was just … I needed a seat. I slid to the wet ground, ignoring the old rain soaking through my jeans, and said, "And he said I could help?"

"He said he wasn't a wizard, but you were a witch, and that if I could get you into the carnival, you'd be able to fix me."

I put my elbows on my knees and buried my face in my hands. "*Fix* you? I don't even have a plan for how I'm going to get us out."

"I can help with that," Jared said, then growled. "Coltrane! Sit!"

I looked up to see Coltrane rolling on his back, arms and legs in the air. "No one's noticed this yet?"

"Not yet. But it won't be long. That's why I grabbed you as soon as I could."

We watched Coltrane roll onto all fours and sit back on his haunches, hands on the ground in front of him. "You can really help us get out?" I asked.

"If you get me back in my right body."

I had zero idea how I was going to do that, given the fact Ruiner had been a cat for well over a month and I hadn't been able to do so much as shrink his tail. But if he could get us out, I was willing to promise pretty much anything. "Take me to see Ruiner," I said aloud. "We can work this out."

"D'you think?" he said, sounding far too hopeful for me to say, *not really*.

Instead, I fished a smile from somewhere and said, "Sure. I know a smart witch."

Jared led me into the darkness, Coltrane ambling next to him and shaking the rain out of his hair. We walked purposefully, as if there was every reason for us to be wandering around in the middle of the night, and Jared took us straight to Legendary Lionel's caravan, which sat slightly apart from the rest of the accommodation. A few people had left flowers on the little steps at the back, as well as a flask-sized bottle of whisky that had been substantially sampled.

I stared at the display, and then turned to Jared. "They've locked Ruiner in a dead man's caravan?"

"Well, he's not using it," Jared pointed out, and jerked his chin toward the door. "Hurry up. No telling who's up at this hour."

I hurriedly grabbed for the door handle, but while it turned easily, there was a shiny new hasp attached to it, with a bolt slid across and a padlock to keep it closed. "It's locked."

"Of course it's locked," he said impatiently. "He's a *prisoner.* The key's hanging under the caravan. Left-hand corner."

I crouched down, and sure enough, there was a hook with a key dangling invitingly from it. I grabbed it and straightened up. "Secure."

"No one from the carnival's going to release him. It's just so no one can sneak in and break him out."

"Past the charms?"

"You did."

I acknowledged that with a grunt as I unlatched the padlock and opened the door. The instant I did, a fluffy black missile powered out past me. I bit back a yelp, and Coltrane whipped around with startling speed, throwing himself full-length and pouncing on Ruiner. He grabbed my brother in both hands and rolled onto his side, trapping him against his chest, lips pulled back in a snarl. Ruiner gave a matching snarl, throwing some startlingly descriptive curses into the mix as he twisted in Coltrane's hands, burying his teeth and claws in the man's forearms. Coltrane growled and tried to bite Ruiner's head.

"*No!*" Jared hissed. "No biting!"

Coltrane gave him a betrayed look, and licked Ruiner instead.

Ruiner spluttered. "Ugh, *gross.*"

"*Ruiner!*" I said. "Stop messing about."

He looked up at me, his claws still firmly embedded in Coltrane's bare arm and his pupils huge in the dark. "Morgan?"

"Hi," I said.

SIXTEEN

Two cats and a man

"ABOUT BLOODY TIME," my brother said, and strained to get away from Coltrane. "I've been here *forever*."

"It's been two days."

"Exactly! What took you so long?"

I sighed. "It's not been that easy. Now get back inside, can't you?"

He peered up at me, ears back. "Why? Aren't you here to break me out?"

I glanced at Jared, whose tail was ticking back and forth irritably. "That's in progress," I said. "Come on, move it. We need to talk."

"Can't we just make a run for it?"

"No," Jared said.

"Why not?" Ruiner demanded. "Look, my sister's here now, we just have to get over the wall—"

"You can't *just get over the wall*," the lion said. "Plus you need to sort me out before I help. Can we get out of sight? My body needs to put you down. He's going to keep grooming you otherwise, and I really can't watch that."

165

Coltrane was still licking Ruiner's head, my brother's ears flat with distaste.

"Yeah, he definitely needs to stop," Ruiner said. "I'm not enjoying this."

"You'll have to grab him," Jared said to me, and I sighed.

I approached Coltrane and reached for Ruiner, but Coltrane curled himself tighter around my brother, growling. "Is he going to bite me?" I asked Jared.

"He can't do that much damage with human teeth. Besides, I'm vegan."

I wasn't sure what relevance that had. "Vegan or not, I still don't fancy being bitten. Even with human teeth."

"That says something about your love life," Ruiner said, wriggling. "Just help, can't you? He won't stop *licking!*"

"He's just being friendly," I said, but crouched down and cautiously extricated my brother from Coltrane's grip. Coltrane growled the whole time, but didn't do anything more than nip me lightly when I picked Ruiner up, then lick my hand. "Ugh."

"Now you know how I feel," Ruiner said, twisting in my grip and straining toward my shoulder. "Let me go. This is weird."

"*This* is what you find weird?" I asked, lifting him into place.

"Coltrane, come," Jared said, jumping into the caravan somewhat clumsily. It shook under his weight, and Coltrane followed, moving on all fours and stopping just inside to sniff the air.

"We could just run for it now," Ruiner whispered to me.

"I don't think we can," I murmured back. "The charms on the field are pretty hefty. I don't know if we'll be able to get through them."

"You didn't *check?*"

"And get turned into a chicken?"

"A what?"

"Never mind. But I wasn't going to give us away by trying to get out before we were ready."

"Hurry up," Jared said in a low voice from inside. "Someone's going to see."

I clambered into the caravan before Ruiner could complain any more, pulling the door shut behind us. Inside it smelled of wood smoke and tomato soup, the cosy space deeply shadowed and the light from the windows doing little more than reveal them as slightly lighter shades of darkness. I stumbled forward, Ruiner and Jared both offering helpful but conflicting instructions, until I collided with the wood stove. I yelped as I barked my shin on what was probably a wood basket, then fumbled around until I found a chair and lowered myself into it, taking my backpack off and tucking it behind my knees. Breath immediately washed over my cheek, and I flailed out, connecting with Coltrane's broad chest and pushing him back.

"Bad lion!"

Jared sighed. "Sorry. He's very well trained, but things like sniffing and licking aren't anything I've ever tried to stop him doing."

"It's fine," I said, trying to hold Coltrane off as he leaned against my hands, evidently still intent on reaching Ruiner.

"It's not fine," Ruiner said. "He's going to eat me."

"He can't. He's a human," I pointed out.

"Vegan human," Jared added.

"Does he know that?" Ruiner demanded. "Besides, if he doesn't eat me, then he'll lick me again, and I'm not good with that either."

"Neither am I," Jared said. "I'm going to end up with hairballs."

"Can humans get hairballs?" I asked.

"Apparently I'm going to find out."

Ruiner and I both made sympathetic noises, and Ruiner said, "Why couldn't I have got *your* body? I wouldn't have minded being a lion. I'm still stuck as a bloody house cat, and there you are, a *lion*."

Jared wrinkled his snout, revealing those impressive teeth. "You're not so badly off. At least a cat can come and go as it wants. I've got to walk around doing a ventriloquist's act."

"It's very good," I said, and he growled.

"It's not. It's just that everyone knows lions can't talk, so I'm getting away with it."

"Anyway, I *can't* come and go as I want," Ruiner said. "I haven't been able to get out of here, have I? And when you finally turn up, you say we can't leave."

I didn't have to be able to see him to know the last bit was directed at me. "I've joined the bloody circus for you, Ruiner. And I don't want to end up trapped here with you, so we need to think this through to make sure we get it right. You know, like you never do."

There was a pause, and for some misguided reason I thought he might actually apologise for dragging me into yet another untenable situation, then he said, "What the hell did you do to your hair? Is it a midlife crisis?"

"*No*," I snapped. "It's a disguise."

"You're disguised as a midlife crisis?"

I tried to bop him on the head, and he fled to the back of the chair. Jared looked from me to him and said, "I can see why you're working so hard to rescue him."

"*Thank* you," I said, and Ruiner hissed. I ignored him and added, "So what happened? How did you end up swapping with Coltrane, Jared? And Lionel…" I trailed off. I didn't know how to say, *did one of you kill him?* I suppose only cops are much good at those questions.

"No idea," Ruiner said. "Lionel and me had a bit of a chat in here, then he said he needed access to more power."

"Power? Like electricity?"

"Yes, Morgan, he was a battery-powered wizard."

"Well, I don't know!"

"He wasn't even much of a wizard," Jared put in. "I mean, I'm not sure what the wizardly scale is, but he was more kids' party tricks than throwing down with Saruman, you know?"

I sighed. "So I heard."

Ruiner gave a squawk, and I twisted in the chair. I could dimly see Coltrane had hold of him again, and was either trying to gnaw his head off or clean his ears.

"Can you *please* call off your beast?" Ruiner demanded.

"That's my body," Jared said. "It's not a beast."

"It is when it's trying to eat me."

"Aw, he likes you," I said, grinning, and Ruiner spat at me. "Focus," I said to him. "What did Lionel mean about needing power, then?"

"He said reversing the curse was going to be difficult, and he needed a lot of power to do it. The big top's the centre of the carnival's magic, apparently." He growled, and I could hear him scuffling.

"That's true enough," Jared said. "The big top's *old*. It's the heart of the carnival, and it's how all the charms are sustained. If he could tap into it, I suppose that would've given him a lot of strength."

"Okay," I said. "But then what happened? I mean…" I swallowed, then managed to continue. "How was he killed? And how did this happen to you two?"

There was silence in the caravan, and with my eyes adjusted to the dark I could just see Jared and Ruiner looked at me blankly, and even Coltrane left off cleaning my brother to stare at me.

"I thought you might be able to help with that," Jared said. "You know, being the town witch."

"*Ruiner*," I growled.

"Well, you are."

I sighed. "You really have no idea what happened?"

"No," my brother said. "We went in there, and he did a bit of waving around and chanting and so on, and—"

"When?" I asked.

"Just as the show was starting. He said that was when the magic was at its strongest, because of the anticipation of the crowd feeding it. He seemed to think we could do the reversal and get out again before anyone saw us."

"And then?"

"And then I don't know. He was doing all the chanting and stuff, and I came over a bit funny. Next thing I know, old Theo's yelling at me and Lionel's a goner."

"Nice."

"Well, he was." Ruiner gave a final squirm and managed to free himself from Coltrane by the simple expedient of wrapping his paws around the man's wrist and biting him as hard as he could. Which probably wouldn't have gone well if Coltrane had had his original form, as he immediately stopped grooming Ruiner and tried to bite him back. But human teeth are no match for cat teeth, and my brother twisted out of reach, leaping back to my shoulder and spitting at Coltrane, who lunged at me.

"No!" Jared snapped, as I tried to fend his body off. "Down!"

Coltrane growled, but dropped onto his haunches, his

eyes locked on Ruiner. Ruiner hissed, and I bopped him on the nose.

"Oi! Bloody great thing was licking me."

"Well, you probably need a bath," I replied, and looked at Jared. "Did you see anything else?"

"No. I was backstage. Like I told you before — I just came over weird and the next thing I know I've got a tail."

"You don't know anyone who'd have a grudge against Lionel? Might have rigged his spell to backfire somehow?"

He shook his head. "There's always conflict here and there. We all live on top of each other, so it happens. But no one would *kill* someone else. The punishment's too high."

"What is it?" I asked, wondering if people were fed to Marvin.

"You get exiled," he said. "No carnival will work with you ever again. You become *normal*."

Ruiner and I were both silent, and finally I said, "That hardly seems like a huge punishment for murder."

Jared huffed. "Carnival time passes differently to outside time. All those years catch up. Ten, or twenty, or a hundred. It's a death sentence like any other."

Now that *was* creepy.

"Could it've been an accident?" I asked the two of them, and they gave matching feline growls of doubt. "Great," I said, and leaned my head back in the chair. "Cool."

We were all silent for a moment, then Jared said, "So what do we do now?"

I looked at him. "About?"

"About getting me back into my body. I'm not going to be able to hide this for long."

"I'm not really a witch," I said.

"Your brother said you had a spell book, though. Is there something in there that could help?"

I turned my head to scowl at Ruiner from close quarters, and he looked away. "I was trying to figure out a way out," he said. "I needed some leverage."

I looked back at Jared. "I don't know," I said. "And I don't fancy trying anything in here anyway, after what happened with Lionel. Why can't you just go to Audrey? Surely she'd understand."

He gave a little huff of amusement. "Understand what? That having a lion in the body of a man, and a man in the body of a lion would make for a *far* more interesting act than a tired old lion-taming show? We were being phased out anyway. No one likes seeing exotic animals being kept captive anymore. Coltrane's the last we've got left, and we don't even perform every show, only when it seems like the town'll accept it. But *this* ... this is new. She'll do everything she can to make sure we never swap back."

I stared at him. "She'd trap you like that?"

"Absolutely. And your cat here—"

"Not her cat," Ruiner said, at the same time as I said, "Not my cat."

"Whatever. You're not going anywhere either, even though she knows you mightn't have actually killed Lionel."

"Didn't," Ruiner interrupted. "I *didn't* kill him."

"Doesn't matter either way. She's going to declare you guilty, and keep you in a cage, and you'll have to wear little sequinned outfits and sing Eighties hits, or tell the punters what their cat's inner thoughts are."

"I'm not doing that," Ruiner said.

"You're not going to have a choice," Jared said. "Neither of us are, unless we can get out of here." He turned his heavy head toward me, the thin light seeping in the windows painting it in silver and grey, majestic and deeply sorrowful. "And you're not getting out either."

"I haven't signed anything," I said.

"Doesn't matter. One out, one in. Lionel's gone, you turn up."

I was suddenly struggling to catch my breath. "No."

"Yes. You were trapped the moment you walked in. But you help me, I'll help you. I can get you out, but you *have* to get me back into my body."

"But I don't know how," I whispered.

"Then figure it out," Jared said. "And quickly. This is your window. You have to get out before the carnival moves on. Once it leaves, the deal's done. You're signed on, and you're not getting back out."

Ruiner and I both said something unrepeatable, and Coltrane rested his chin on the arm of the chair, staring at Ruiner.

"He's trying to lick me again," he said.

"He can't even reach you from there," I said, my voice cracking on the edges. But at least arguing with Ruiner felt *normal*, as if we were still free and still had a chance, no matter how slim.

"He's thinking about it."

"He's being friendly. More than you deserve."

"Hey!"

"You *bit* him. He's bleeding."

"Please don't bite my body anymore," Jared said. "The last thing I need is toxoplasmosis."

"I'm not *infectious*."

Coltrane put a hand on my arm, half-raising off his haunches, and growled slightly.

"Down," I tried, and he growled again.

"Pat him on the head," Jared said. "He just wants some affection."

"I'm not doing that," I said, and Coltrane head-butted me, smelling of crushed grass and sweat. "Oh, for — fine." I patted his head gingerly, and he slumped back to the floor. "Look, has anyone seen a rat?"

"You've lost *Jacqueline?*" Ruiner asked.

"Yes. I hoped she'd stayed with you."

"No. We're not exactly besties."

"Jared?" I said, and he shook his head, mane shivering.

"I've not really been in the mood to look for rats."

I sighed. "If we can find her, she might be able to help me with a spell. But in the meantime, I can try to get a message out, get some help."

"No one can help from the outside," Jared said. "The carnival's closed unless you're invited in, and even if they somehow forced their way through, any charms they tried wouldn't work. Only carnival crew can use magic."

"You're just a ray of bloody sunshine, aren't you?" Ruiner asked, and I poked him in the side.

"Shut up. Alright, if they can't get in, what if you get us out, Jared?"

"Not until you change me back. You're crew now, your magic'll work in here. You fix me, I'll get you out, then tell Aubrey you magicked me into helping you escape. She should buy it. Witches are a sneaky lot."

I scowled. "Nice. Why don't you just leave with us, if you're so worried about her?"

He shrugged, a fluid, warm movement. "She still holds my contract. The consequences aren't worth trying to break it. And even if I did … well, I've been here a while. Don't know how old I'd be on the outside."

I shivered, a full body judder that made Ruiner stare at me.

"Best get thinking," he said.

"You could help," I pointed out. "You know more about magic than me."

"You're the witch. Plus this is all your fault."

"It's not."

"It is. You were the one that suggested I talk to Legendary bloody Lionel."

"He has a point," Jared said. "And then you lost your rat and sneaked in here with no idea what you're doing, so…"

I scowled at him. "Great. I've got two of you now."

"Three," Jared said, and we all looked at Coltrane, kneeling on the floor with his hands between his knees, looking from one of us to the other. He still had that intense, unnerving stare, and I could almost imagine his tail twitching behind him.

"Great," I said again, and we sat there in silence for a while, myself, two men in the bodies of cats and one cat in the body of a man.

Things were not looking up.

SEVENTEEN

Can you smell a rat?

"WE NEED A PLAN," I said, when it became clear the other two weren't going to come up with anything. "First we have to make sure no one figures out what's happened to you, Jared. You need to stay clear of everyone as much as possible. Cheryl already said you were acting off."

"Bit bloody hard not to," he said, then added, "What if you helped me? Be easier for you to work on the reversal then, too. I could request you as an assistant."

"Seems like a better plan than chasing pigeons."

"Come to my trailer in the morning and you can get Coltrane changed. It took me an hour to get those clothes on him yesterday. He can't work out if I'm still his trainer or another lion and kept trying to wrestle me."

I sighed. It felt very on brand for my love life that the first time I got to undress a man in ages, he had the mind of an animal, and not in the figurative sense. "Sure."

"What about me?" Ruiner asked. "What do I do?"

"You stay here and try not to be too rude to anyone," I said.

He flopped dramatically across the back of the chair,

head and front legs dangling next to me. "I hate it in here," he complained. "It stinks of old man."

"Lionel wasn't even that old. And if we let you out before we're ready to make a run for it, it's only going to end up with you locked up somewhere even more secure."

"I hate it when you're right. It's the *worst.*"

"You should be used to it," I said, and got up.

"Where're you going?" Ruiner demanded.

"Back to my own quarters," I said. "I can hardly stay, can I?"

"This is a really shoddy rescue."

"Coltrane, walk on," Jared said, getting up and padding to the door. Coltrane followed reluctantly, throwing backward glances at Ruiner, and I went to open the door for them.

"I'll find you in the morning," I said to Jared.

"You're not coming?"

"I need to talk to my brother for a moment."

"Alright." He yawned, displaying those alarmingly large teeth, then headed off, Coltrane shambling next to him. I watched them go, then pulled the door gently shut and looked at Ruiner in the shadows.

"Is that really our best plan?" he asked. "The Cowardly Lion and Tintin?"

"You realise those are two entirely different universes?"

"Whatever." His tail was twitching urgently. "We've got to get out of here quick as we can, Morgs. I'll be a cat forever otherwise."

"We'll both be carnival crew forever otherwise," I said. "You really don't know anything more about what happened?"

"No," he said with a sigh. "It's like I lost time or something. Blinked, and then everything changed. It's not like I was sitting on top of Lionel to start or anything. I was standing in this little circle he'd made in the sawdust, and he was outside it, and then *boom*. Dead man for a bed." He said it breezily, but his tail was going to dislocate itself if he whipped it any harder.

"You didn't see anyone? Not Jared, or Fiona, or—"

"Who?"

"The fortune teller. The one who shouted at us outside Lionel's caravan."

"No. The clowns were running about, and the flying bloody monkeys were doing their thing, and that ring-woman was ordering everyone around, but that was it."

I rubbed my forehead. "You didn't notice *anything?*"

"I was a bit busy getting ready to be human-shaped again. And why does it matter, anyway? You find a reversal spell, Lion-man gets us out, and we're all good."

"I don't know if I *can* do a reversal. And I absolutely can't do it without Jacqueline. I'm certain of that. So if we can find who the actual murderer is and tell Aubrey—"

"Nothing's going to change, because she's still going to keep us here."

"We don't know that."

"Lion-man seemed pretty sure."

I ran my hands back through my hair. "I can't do this, Ruiner. I'm not a witch."

"You are," he said, and I looked at him, startled. His voice was serious, and he stared at me in the dimness. "No one gets chosen by a familiar if they're not. And the way you fell into Hollowbeck so perfectly? You're more magical than I am, and I was *working* at it. Plus you're smart, and inventive, and persistent. You'll figure this out."

I swallowed, my throat clicking. "Who are you, and what've you done with my brother?"

"Why d'you think I always knew I could call you for help? You *get things done.*"

"I never had a choice," I pointed out.

"Doesn't change the fact."

I pressed my hands over my face. Ruiner being nice to me made the world feel like it was coming loose at the edges. "I still need help."

"So we'll get some. Does Theo know you're here, or Isabella?"

"No," I admitted. "They wouldn't have let me come."

"Starlight? *Benjamin?*"

"No."

"Who does?"

I scratched the back of my head. "I … had to look elsewhere."

"Who?" he asked, and when I didn't answer straight away, he said, "Who did you talk to, Morgan?"

"Grace," I said.

"*Grace?*"

"She offered to help. And she's a proper witch."

"Exactly! She's a proper witch who *hates me*. I take back what I said about you being smart."

"She helped me get in. No one else was going to do it."

"And now you're stuck here, and there's no one in the way of her becoming town witch."

I winced. "Okay, yes, there's that. But she was really nice. And we arranged a way to send messages."

"Oh? How's that working out for you?"

"It's only been a day," I muttered.

"Brilliant," he said. "Just brilliant. I'm going to spend the rest of my life as a cat-shaped Boy George impersonator."

∾

THE MORNING CAME in bright and clear. It wasn't quite cold enough for frost, but I could feel it sneaking around on the skirts of the dawn as the first of the sun outlined the trees with startling clarity. Either Petunia had shaken herself out of her carnival depression, or we were having one of the Lake District's rare perfect autumn days (as far as Hollowbeck could be said to be in the Lakes, or England, or the world as I knew it, for that matter).

I yawned my way through a giant mug of tea in the caravan, the grimoire safely back in its alligator-secured hidey-hole, then stumbled over to the canteen, where Cheryl took one look at me and handed over a giant mug of coffee and a bacon butty that I doubted I'd get my jaws around.

"Rough night?" she asked me sympathetically.

"Could say that."

"The first few weeks are always difficult. Come in here any time you need a bit of a pick-me-up, alright?" She put one hand on my arm as she spoke, brown fingers long and scarred with burns.

"Thanks," I said, and was startled by a wobble in my voice. I turned away and carted my breakfast to an empty table in the corner of the tent. I didn't fancy making small talk with anyone — or even less so than I usually did.

I was tackling the second half of my sandwich, feeling marginally less like I'd spent the night tussling with Marvin, when Coltrane picked his way into the tent with Jared strolling next to him. Coltrane was wearing the same torn T-shirt and jogging bottoms, a big Army coat unzipped over the top. He was still barefoot, and I crammed another bite into my mouth. I'd *intended* to go and help him, but breakfast had seemed more urgent.

Coltrane sniffed the air, head raised, and headed straight for the kitchen area. He leaned over the counter and patted a loaf of bread with one hand, setting Mike bellowing abuse. Cheryl shooed Mike away and handed Coltrane a large bowl of muesli and yoghurt, liberally decorated with fruit. He sniffed it and gave her a suspicious look.

"Bloody vegans," Mike said. Coltrane growled faintly, and they glared at each other.

Cheryl held what looked like an entire leg of mutton out to Jared, who recoiled in horror, then took it delicately in his mouth, snout wrinkling. "He shouldn't be eating in here, really," she said to Coltrane, who still had the bowl in both hands, staring at it doubtfully. I saw Jared trying to say something around the bone and jumped up.

"Jared!" I called. "You wanted to talk about a new act?"

He turned and trotted toward me, heavy shoulders rolling under his mane, and Coltrane trailed after him, eyes fixed intently on the mutton.

"You're *welcome!*" Mike shouted, and Cheryl put a hand on his arm, shaking her head.

Jared circled the table to sit between me and the canvas wall. He dropped the bone, gagging, and Coltrane fell to his knees, not looking away from it. "*No,*" Jared said, and Coltrane growled.

"Morning," I said.

Jared glared at me. "You were meant to come and get my body dressed."

"You don't think my sneaking into your trailer in the early hours of the morning might've raised some questions?"

"Less than my sitting on the floor drooling over a bone. I was going to get you to bring us some food rather than this."

I looked at Coltrane. He really was drooling. "Oh." I stood and picked up the bone and the bowl. "Come on."

I led the way out of the tent with them both trailing after me, Jared hissing, "Up! *Up*, you lazy beast!"

Coltrane grumbled, but he stayed upright, so I had some hope we might get out without drawing any attention. The bar for weird behaviour had to be pretty high in a carnival, anyway.

We almost made it, too, but Gus strode in as we reached the entrance, a heavy jacket zipped to his chin. He scowled at me. "Late on your first morning, newbie?"

"Second," I said. "And no watch."

"I told you to get one."

I pointed at Coltrane. "Jared wants me to help him with a new act."

Gus glared at Coltrane. "What, you're poaching my recruits now?"

"I've done some work with animals before," I said, pulling his attention back to me. "This seems a better use of my skills."

"Lions?" he asked sceptically.

"Well, no——"

"She's going to do the glamorous assistant thing," Jared said. "Damsel in peril, all that. Goes down well with the punters."

Gus looked momentarily puzzled, then said, "Put some bloody shoes on, mate. You sound sick as a dog already."

"It's grounding, being barefoot."

"Bloody vegans," Gus muttered. "Off their heads." He headed for the kitchen while I had a momentary confusion over whether he'd said off with *their* heads. I couldn't be sure.

"So I'm good to help Jared?" I called after him.

"Whatever," he said, waving one hand vaguely above his head and not looking back.

"What about the mucking out?" a rotund man at a nearby table asked. "Who's doing that?"

Gus paid them as little attention as he had me. "Do you pony prancers some good to look after your own horses."

"Hey!" a tall, well-muscled woman yelled back. "We *do* take care of them! All the time! But we're *artists*." A murmur of agreement went up around her, and I headed out of the tent before we could get dragged into some sort of carnival turf war.

Jared's surprisingly modern caravan was split into two, the back half given over to a small travelling pen for the lion, and the other half a cramped living area. We squeezed ourselves into it, and I dressed a fairly docile Coltrane in a fresh T-shirt and zipped his fleece to his chin while Jared gobbled down the muesli.

"You shouldn't be eating that," I said to him, letting Coltrane slide to the floor and start chewing on the bone. I found a hairbrush among an extensive collection of hair care products, and tackled Coltrane's tangled locks while he ate.

"I'm starving," Jared said, licking the bowl.

"You've got a cat stomach now. Take it from someone who knows, just because you're a human in there, you can't eat the same stuff."

"I'm not eating *meat*."

Coltrane growled, as if understanding his meal was at risk, and gripped the mutton bone in both hands. I sighed. We needed to figure this out before one or both of them got food poisoning.

~

TEN MINUTES later we were back out in the chill of the day, me pulling a borrowed woollen hat down over my ears. Coltrane should've been wearing it, but he pawed it off every time I put it on him. I'd had about as much luck with shoes, too, so I was getting second-hand frostbite watching him padding toward the big top, sandwiched between Jared and myself. I had a whip in one hand and a stool in the other, and a bag of dried apricots and one of dried meat stashed in my pockets. The apricots were to make it look good if we really had to pretend to be practising, and the dried meat was to keep Coltrane happy.

Our first mission was to find Jacqueline, and while she hadn't emerged when I'd been clambering around the big top yesterday, I was still holding out hope that she was hiding in the bleachers somewhere. I'd stopped back at Willow's and retrieved my bag, so with any luck she might sniff the grimoire out and come hunting for me herself. We had to be due a little luck, surely?

I pushed through the heavy canvas flaps into the backstage area, Jared slinking after me. Coltrane growled and huffed as he got tangled in the cloth, so I reached back and pulled him through, then crept into the dimness making little smooching sounds like I was calling a cat who wasn't my brother.

"Jackie?" I called. "Jacqueline! It's me."

There was no response, and I dug through the piles of costumes and props, hoping she might be snoozing away somewhere, but between the low light and clutter she could've been right beside me and I'd never have known. I looked at Jared.

"Can you smell her?"

"I'm not a bloodhound."

"No, but you must be able to smell *something*."

"Myself, mostly," he said with a sigh, but joined me in

pawing through the jumble of feather boas and juggling clubs and fur stoles and tiaras.

We'd worked our way through most of the racks and baskets when a swirl of cold air and Coltrane's growl let us know we weren't alone. I straightened up, pressing my hands into the small of my back, and eyed the trapeze artists as they drifted in, the sunlight turning their hair to spun silver and making their skin luminous.

"Hello," one said, smiling at me, and since they were the only one doing so, I thought they might be Art.

"Hi," I said, and tried to ignore Coltrane leaning toward them, sniffing hopefully.

"What're you doing?" one of the others asked. "This is our training time."

"We're just finishing up," I said.

"Finishing what up? Dismantling the whole place?" They looked around pointedly, nose wrinkled.

I looked at the debris strewn across the floor and had to admit they had a point. "I lost one of Coltrane's treats," I said. "Didn't want it stinking up the place."

"Ugh." One of them moved forward, passing us with an easy, fluid gait. "Well, just pick it up, can't you? And don't make any noise. We have a new routine to practise."

"Stay out," the second said, shaking a finger at us like a pantomime villain, then grinning as they prowled out into the ring.

The one I thought was Art lingered. "What're you looking for, really?" they asked.

I hesitated, then said, "You were in here when Lionel was discovered the other night, weren't you?"

"We'd just finished up."

"I don't suppose you saw anything, did you?"

"No, once we're performing, we have to be pretty

focused." They hesitated, glancing at the entrance to the big top.

"Nothing before or after?" I asked.

"I did see Lionel beforehand. He had his crystal ball and the cat, and they sort of sneaked off into the corner. I thought it was weird. He does a few fill-in bits, but it's more rabbits out of hats and things. No reason for him to have a crystal ball with him."

I nodded, trying to remember the caravan. I hadn't seen the crystal ball last night, but maybe it had been put away for safekeeping or something. "Nothing else?"

"No. I assumed he'd leave before Jared and Coltrane went on."

"Suppose he did, at that," Jared said, and Art frowned slightly.

"Are you alright, Jared? You don't sound quite like yourself."

"Got a cold," he said.

Art nodded. "I have to go. Rehearsal. Sorry I couldn't help."

"No, that's great," I said. "Can you tell me if you see a rat in there, though?"

"A *rat?*" he said, pressing one long-fingered hand to his chest. "Why would there be a rat?"

"I'm just asking."

He hesitated, then said, "Megs and Mace aren't doing their job if there's a rat."

"Who and *who?*"

"Aubrey's terriers. They're pest control," he said, and slipped away into the ring.

I turned to Jared, hands on my hips. "*Pest control?*"

"It doesn't mean they caught her," he said. "But we should probably move on to you working on the reversal spell, rather than waste any more time, don't you think?"

"No, I don't think. This makes it even more urgent we find her."

"We're not going to find a rat in a fairground," he said. "She's probably holed up in the popcorn stall, happy as anything."

"That doesn't help. I *need* her."

"Then you'd better figure something out," he said. "Time's going."

I pressed a hand to my chest, feeling bands of fright tightening down harder and harder, making it difficult to breathe. *Terriers.*

EIGHTEEN

Witches always burn

I SPENT the rest of the morning poking around the shuttered stalls with Jared and Coltrane, me waving the whip and stool at Jared-the-lion whenever someone walked past.

"Good kitty," I announced, as Franz headed for the gate with a smoothie shaker in hand.

He stopped, looking at me quizzically. "What're you doing out here?"

"Trapeze lot are using the big top," I said.

"And she really needs the practice," Jared added. I shook the whip at him again, and Coltrane growled.

Franz looked from one of us to the other, frowning, then said, "I'd quite like to do lion taming. My knees won't keep up with being a strongman for ever." He did a couple of half-squats, and I could hear the crunching from where I stood. I winced.

"Ouch."

"Exactly. I thought maybe I could work with the goats, you know? Just sort of walk around with them on my shoulders. But Aubrey said it wasn't enough of an act."

"What do the goats do now?" I asked.

"Just hang around looking cute," Franz said, taking a swig of his smoothie and grimacing. "I mean, it'd be better than that, right?"

"You'd have to talk to Aubrey if you want to swap," Jared said, and Franz sighed.

"Yes," he said. "And we all know how that goes." He raised his smoothie to me, then plodded off toward the gate, his shoulders sagging.

"What, he can't change what he does?" I asked.

"Not unless Aubrey says he can. And a strongman is one of the oldest carnival traditions. She won't break that until his knees collapse completely."

"Lovely," I said, and went back to peering through the gaps in the stalls' shutters and checking their wheel arches, keeping an eye out for wrens while I did so. But I suppose we were too far from the walls for any to reach us. I hoped that was the case, anyway, although I had a sneaking feeling that Ruiner was right, that there wasn't going to be one at all. That I was as trapped here as anyone else, in the suspended, popcorn-scented world of the carnival, where nothing ever changed and everything stayed the same, and the alternative was deadly.

The rest of the morning brought nothing new. We moved through the carnival, keeping up the pretence of training while searching for Jacqueline in any gap we could see. Jared tried to find her scent, but complained that the stink of damp alpaca wool, cooking meat from the canteen, axle grease, old popcorn, and his own unfamiliar body drowned out everything. The lack of Jacqueline lent my stomach a heavy, aching sickness, and all I could think of was the terriers, and how careless I'd been to lose her. I knew, at some level, that she could have hidden herself away anywhere in the carnival, that she was entirely capable and quite likely smarter than I was, that there were countless safe, secret places for a rat to hide, but the longer that passed, the more sure I was that I'd failed her, just as I was in danger of failing my brother.

When our hunt took us closer to the walls, I kept looking for wrens, but they were as elusive as Jacqueline. I did see a couple of ravens and some magpies, shuffling on the walls that adjoined the field but not coming any closer, their eyes bright and watchful. The ravens in particular seemed deeply interested in what we were doing. I tried to subtly wave at them, but they didn't respond, so maybe they were just hoping for some of Coltrane's jerky. I wondered if I could leave a note on the wall for them, something they could take back to Grace (if she even spoke to ravens and not just wrens — I had no idea how talking to birds worked. Were there different languages? Dialects? Accents?), but it was too risky. The odds of it blowing back into the carnival and being found by someone else was *way* too high.

At some point Starlight was going to realise I was missing, of course, if she hadn't already. Usually, I'd have assumed Petunia would be the first to notice, but if she was still deep in her front room rainforest then there was no counting on it. Starlight would guess immediately where I was, although what she did after that was a completely different question. Go to Theodore, probably, which wasn't going to get us anywhere. I doubted she was going to talk to Grace, somehow.

As the shadows slid around, beginning to grow again in the opposite direction, I headed to the canteen and loaded up on quinoa salad for Jared and a couple of used soup bones that Cheryl said would help Coltrane's gums. I took them to Jared's caravan and left them munching happily on their mismatched meals, then went back to the canteen, taking my pack with me. I'd decided it should stay with me at all times now. It was rapidly seeming like the only chance of finding Jacqueline was to draw her out. Besides, I had the uneasy feeling that when the time came, I wasn't going to have chance to go back and wrestle with Marvin before making a run for it.

Nobody seemed to have told Mike and Cheryl that I was no longer the camp's general dog's body, and the tables were cluttered with discarded glasses and dishes, so I collected a load on my way in and started washing up. I didn't mind bussing tables, and it was a good way to listen in on a few conversations. The debate regarding Nicki Minaj and Taylor Swift was ongoing, and had been expanded to include Olivia Rodrigo, and people were still speculating about new acts for opening night. No one was mentioning stray rats or Aubrey's plans for Ruiner, and I almost tuned out the conversation, sunk in my own thoughts.

But as I was clearing plates from an empty table toward the back of the room, I caught Lionel's name. It was the clowns, still looking nondescript in their everyday clothes, huddled together at the next table over with half-eaten plates of pasta and salad in front of them. I slowed my movements, shifting the plates around carefully and straining to catch the conversation.

"I reckon he was trying to get himself injured out," one of the clowns was saying, a gaunt man with hollow cheekbones and hangdog eyes. "Maybe he thought if he damaged himself enough, Aubrey would release him."

"Aubrey was never going to release him," a short, rotund man replied. "Aubrey doesn't release *anyone*. Not in a hundred years."

I wondered if that was a literal hundred years. It seemed quite possible.

"That's true enough," a woman put in. "I came here when I was thirteen. Joined up to get out of being married off to the next farm over. Wasn't even an adult, so the carnival contract shouldn't've held, but she wouldn't budge. Now I'm..." She thought about it, looking at her fingers as if she was going to start counting on them, then shook her head. "It was a long time ago anyway."

"Lionel knew that," another man said. He looked more like an accountant than a clown, right down to his button-down suit. "I don't understand why he took such a risk, messing around with strange cats."

"*Enchanted* cats," the woman said. "You don't mess around with enchanted cats."

"And one who's related to the town witch," the gaunt man said. "Should've never let them into his caravan. Fiona said it was like they put him in a trance, and she was too scared to say anything in case they turned her into a tadpole."

"Bloody witches," the accountant said. "Lucky she didn't kill us all."

"We should be hunting her down," the rotund man put in. "Make her pay."

"Well, her and the cat," the woman said. "Deal with them the proper way."

"Burn them both." The gaunt man raised his glass.

"Witches always burn," the rest said together, raising their own drinks.

A fork slipped out of my fingers, clattering off the plates and stabbing into the grass below. I crouched down to pick it up, cheeks burning, and the clowns watched me with flat, unfriendly gazes until I'd gathered everything and hurried away.

Witches always burn.

And carnivals always took their payment, one way or another.

~

I STAYED IN THE CANTEEN, clearing plates and glasses and collecting cutlery, dropping half of them as I did so, my fingers numb with fright. Everything seemed to have suddenly plunged underwater, the voices of the lingering lunchtime crowd indistinct and difficult to make out. The only words I could seem to listen for were *witch* and *burn*, and as much as I tried to remind myself that it was only a small contingent of clowns who had it in for me (and *clowns*. Of course they wanted to burn me at the stake, and probably pick the skin from my bones after, because clowns are terrifying), suddenly the whole place seemed full of suspicious eyes and unfriendly faces. It all felt violently unfair, too. I wasn't even a proper witch, and they still wanted to burn me for it. *Clowns.*

What was very clear, though, was that we couldn't waste any more time. We had to get out. But I had zero faith in my ability to get through the protective charms on my own, and even if that hadn't been the case, there was absolutely no way I was leaving Jacqueline behind. So it came back to our best chance being to clear Ruiner's name. No matter what Jared said about Aubrey, the carnival had laws. She'd said so herself. And that meant the people within it had to abide by them just as much as those outside. If I could find the real killer, she'd have to release Ruiner, and I still hadn't signed anything, so technically I *had* to be allowed to leave, right? Jared was probably just trying to scare me into helping him.

Although the clown saying she *wasn't even an adult, so the carnival contract shouldn't've held, but she wouldn't budge* was still clear in my mind. That was something we were going to have to deal with when it came to it, though. I didn't even know what the consequences were for breaking your contract. If it was just the ageing thing, two days weren't going to kill me. For now, I had to focus on getting Ruiner released, and making sure no one realised I was the supposed witch. The only lead I had was the missing crystal ball, and Fiona's lies about Ruiner and I getting all magic on Lionel. Did they all forget that outside magic didn't work inside the carnival? I supposed that was always the way of things, though. Truth was malleable when someone's guilt had already been decided.

I kept clearing tables and washing dishes, trying to look as un-witchy and non-combustible as possible, until Cheryl waved me away from the sink and held out a toasted sandwich, all thick slabs of softly browned bread and oozing cheese. My stomach turned over and I shook my head. It could be the best sandwich in the world and I still couldn't have eaten it. It was very slightly burned at the edges, just as a good toastie should be, but I didn't want to think about *anything* burning.

Cheryl examined me carefully, her eyebrows drawn together in concern. "Are you alright?" she asked. "Has something happened?"

"No," I said, wiping my hands on the tea towel. "Just not feeling great."

"You know you can come and talk to me any time."

I nodded, not quite looking at her. I was going to burst into tears and wail about clowns chewing on my femurs if I wasn't careful. "I think I'm just adjusting," I said aloud.

She gave me a disbelieving look, wrapped the sandwich in a sheet of wax paper, and pressed it into my hands. "Get yourself off and have a break," she said. "And if Gus or

Jared or *anyone* tell you to get back to work, you send them to me."

I risked a glance at her. She had both hands on her hips, feet planted widely, and she looked both as if I could throw her over my shoulder and run away with her, and also like the end of the world couldn't shake her grip on it. "Alright," I said. "Thank you."

She nodded at the sandwich, the heat seeping into my hands. "Make sure you eat that. You *have* to eat. You'll only feel worse otherwise."

I tried to imagine her cavorting wildly in the darkness while a stack of kindling went up in flame, eating its way to the stake — and me — in the middle, and I couldn't. The image was so ill-fitting it forced a smile out of me. "Yes, Mum," I said, and she flapped her tea towel at me.

"Get away before I change my mind." She handed me a large piece of brownie that was so dense it probably warped time and space, then glared at me until I picked up my backpack and left.

I didn't feel any more inclined to eat the toastie, which I'd tucked into my jacket pocket, but I took a large bite of the brownie as I left the tent, the rich dark flavour flooding my mouth. Not a balanced meal, sure, but it definitely felt like the sort of sugar hit that was magic in itself. I meandered my way toward Willow's caravan, but I had no desire to go in and speculate on the unhealthiness of the whole Ross/Rachel dynamic. Instead, I circled around, heading back toward the side shows. Fiona's trailer was still parked on the edge of them, ready for opening night, and she had a new banner on the side that sagged under the weight of all the sequins stuck to it. *The Famous & Fabulous Fiona, Fortune-teller Fantastique!* I thought she might've got a little carried away with the alliteration there, but I supposed it was all relative in this place.

I stood in the shadow of the chess stand, watching Fiona's caravan and eating my brownie, until I started to feel like a stalker. I mean, I *was* stalking her, but in this place, someone was going to spot me in no time. So I walked over and knocked on the door briskly.

Fiona opened it almost immediately, drawing back slightly as she saw me and her smile becoming slightly strained. "Hello Liz," she said. "Can I help you?"

"Hi," I said, smiling at her and trying to see past her into the caravan. "Aubrey sent me over. She wanted to know if you might've seen Lionel's crystal ball?"

She pulled the door a little closer to her, blocking my view inside. "No. Why would I?"

"I don't know," I said. "Maybe you took it to make sure it wasn't left in the caravan with that cat? And it must be good to have a spare, right? I don't imagine decent crystal balls are that cheap."

"They're *not*," she said. "The last one I bought was *ridiculous*. I mean, I realise there's inflation, but still."

I nodded sympathetically. "So a spare would come in handy, right?"

"Well, of course. But I wouldn't take Lionel's. It would've captured the whole moment of his death. It'd be very distressing."

"Oh. He had it when he died, did he?"

"Well, I'm sure I don't know," she said, and I could see her knuckles whitening on the door. "Sorry, why does Aubrey want it?"

"To see if it was there when he died. So she can be sure the cat's guilty."

"*Of course* the cat's guilty. Did you hear his sister's a witch? I saw them, you know. Dangerous sorts. She was basically *dripping* curses."

I supposed that could be a compliment, in a way. "But why would they want to kill Lionel?"

She shrugged. "Who knows why witches and enchanted beasts do anything. They can't be trusted."

I looked at the sign above her door, which read, *Enter and be sprinkled in magic!*, which sounded vaguely itchy. "Is it so different to fortune-telling?"

"Completely. I merely tell people what their future holds. Witches *break* futures."

Unless she meant the wreckage I was laying to my own future, I doubted that was something I was capable of, but I just nodded. "Sure. I'll tell Aubrey you haven't seen it, then?"

"Yes, thanks, dear," she said, and shut the door in my face.

I stared at it blankly for a moment, then headed off as if I was going to walk to Aubrey's trailer. Instead, I slipped into the rows of sideshows, and found a spot where I could watch Fiona's caravan without being seen myself. I had to get that crystal ball. Before, Fiona having it would've just pointed to her messing with the crime scene. Now it seemed like it was some sort of magical CCTV, proving without a doubt that Ruiner wasn't responsible. Fiona would have to go out at some point, and then I'd test my witchy breaking and entering skills. Or, more likely, just walk straight in, if the prisoner's quarters were anything to go by.

Maybe she'd already got rid of it, and this was going to come to nothing, but at least I was *doing* something. And that felt like hope in and of itself.

NINETEEN

A bit of a balls-up

I LOITERED around the sideshows watching the shadows growing longer, and polishing random bits of chrome or frowning at broken hinges if anyone walked past. I'd reached the point of reading the fine print on the *Beat the Strongman!* poster for the fifth time (*The guest accepts all risk of dislocations, hernias, aneurysms, embolisms, and broken bones. Neither the Masters of Mayhem nor their representatives accept any responsibility for injuries, or the side effects of any enchantments offered as treatment (including and not limited to extra bone growth, additional limbs and/or organs, or unexpected appetites))* when finally Fiona stepped out of her caravan. I pressed myself deeper into the shadows, and watched her pull the door closed behind her. She didn't lock it, so *finally* one thing was going my way.

I watched her walk away, readying myself to scurry forward and dive into her trailer, then frowned. She had a bin bag in one hand, swinging it casually. It looked almost empty, but also heavy, her shoulder slumping that way and her gait a little stilted. The bag formed a teardrop shape, pulled down by something solid and distinctly round.

"Dammit," I whispered, and eased myself out of hiding, following her as unobtrusively as I could.

Fiona walked briskly down the alley of shuttered food stalls, her head up and a faint smile on her lips. She hesitated next to a rubbish bin outside the pasta stand, then kept going. All the bins were empty, I knew, so it'd be obvious if she did dump it in there that it had happened after the carnival closed. She looked around occasionally, either checking if she were being observed or looking for other hiding places, then eventually she turned toward the big top. She took a glance behind her as she approached the main entrance, and I ducked out of sight, then hurried forward as she let herself inside.

I hesitated when I reached the heavy canvas flaps, hanging softly closed but with the ties loose. The day was still rich with afternoon light, so as soon as I opened the tent I'd be as good as announcing myself with trumpets and flashing lights. But I couldn't let Fiona just hide the ball and get away with it, either, so I slipped in after her, letting the canvas drop back into place behind me and peering around as my eyes adjusted to the dimness.

The blow came out of the darkness to the side of the door, and I barely had time to duck away, a glimpse of movement giving me just enough warning (which I had to thank my irritating brother for, as sneak attacks had been his favourite pastime as a kid). I dropped into a crouch with a yelp as the bag and its hefty cargo whistled through the space where my head had been a moment earlier, and scrambled away on all fours. I made it back to my feet just as Fiona charged, whirling the bag like an Olympic hammer thrower, and I sprinted down the aisle toward the ring, yelling, "Fiona, *don't!*"

She didn't reply, and the next moment the ball slammed into my shoulder, spinning me off balance and sending me crashing into the folding chairs. I flailed wildly, trying to get to my feet, and my hand closed over the smooth, rounded surface of the ball. The bag had broken, and the ball was trapped among the chairs. I clawed it toward me just as Fiona tackled me with a shriek.

"*Help!* I'm being attacked!" she screamed, and scrabbled for the ball.

"You attacked *me!*" I yelled back, trying to fend her off with one hand and keep hold of the ball with the other. She strained to get past me, and the crystal shivered under my palm, a red, hungry light abruptly swelling inside, turning my hand translucent and touching the fallen chairs with a fiery glow. We both stopped struggling to stare at it. The swirling, peacefully luminous colours that it had carried in Lionel's caravan were gone. Instead, there was a scorched look to the thing, as if a fire had been burning in its heart. The light built, spilling out in strangely striated shades of ochre and deep madder, twisting and spinning and casting the shadows of my fingers like angry ghosts across the big top.

"What's it doing?" I whispered.

"*You're* doing it," Fiona said, her voice catching.

We watched the shadows form shapes, projected unevenly onto the distant canvas. They slowly resolved into a distorted scene that I could just recognise as Lionel's caravan. He opened the door, and Fiona smiled in at him, waving vaguely. He nodded, saying something to her, but there was no sound to accompany the singed edges of the image. He put one hand on the ball, the perspective making it look as if his hand were closing over the top of us where we lay among the toppled chairs.

I ducked instinctively, and the whole scene shivered as he handed the thing over. The image changed, showing Fiona huddling over the ball in the privacy of her own quarters, face turned to a horror mask by the warped perspective as she carved scratches into its glossy skin. I felt the wounds the way the ball did, an affront and an injury that spread to an infection, turning it feverish by the time Lionel took it back.

"You sabotaged it," I said to her, as the images kept playing across the walls, a client walking out in disgust, Lionel examining the ball with a frown, someone else throwing a half-drunk smoothie at him, and each time the image grew darker at the edges as the ball sickened. "You killed him."

"I didn't mean to," she said, her voice trembling. "It was just meant to make his fortunes terrible. He was stealing my business."

"You're letting my brother take the blame," I said. "You know he's innocent, and you're doing *nothing*. You have to tell Aubrey."

She blinked at me. "Your brother. It *is* you!"

"No, wait—"

She grappled with me, trying to pin my arms in place. "Help! *Help! It's the witch!*"

I twisted, kicking her off me and scrambling to my feet. "The ball shows what happened! It *wasn't Ruiner!*"

Fiona lunged for the ball, and I tried to pull her back, but she lashed out at me, landing a clumsy slap on my face that was nevertheless enough to make me yelp and let her go. She snatched the ball up, and I threw myself into a tackle, wrapping both arms around her and taking her to the ground. She kept her prize clutched to her chest as she twisted and bucked wildly, still screaming, and I clung to her. I *had* to get that ball.

We rolled through another row of chairs, scattering them in our wake, and she managed to slam an elbow into my chin. I squawked, and she tore away from me, rolling to her knees and hurling the ball as hard as she could toward the bleachers.

"*No!*" I shouted, flailing for balance as I tried to get to my feet, but there was no way I was stopping it. The ball hit the corner of one of the rows of seating, and maybe if it hadn't already been so weakened it would've been alright, would've merely chipped itself or worn a crack like a scar, but whatever curse she'd put on it had all but destroyed it already. It exploded like glass dropped on tile floors, shrapnel flying in every direction, and light roared out of its heart, burnt browns and reds and sickly yellows, licking across the canvas and seats and sawdust, lighting the whole of the big top like a fever dream. I shielded my face with one arm, yelping as a stray shard of glass nicked my ear.

"*Eugene!*" Fiona screamed, and I dropped my arm to see the dwarf standing in the aisle. He must've heard our shouting and come to investigate, and as I watched, he tilted slowly forward, then crashed to the floor like he'd been hit with a tranquilliser dart.

Fiona and I both froze, then scrabbled wildly toward him, getting tangled up in each other and the chairs before finally making it to the aisle and rushing toward the motionless dwarf. I dropped to my knees next to him and hefted him over onto his back. His eyes were open, staring sightlessly at the ceiling, and where his beard hadn't protected him, glass sparkled on his cheeks, blood drifting in little rivulets from a myriad of tiny wounds. I poked his shoulder warily.

"Eugene?"

There were no major wounds I could see, no blood pooling under him, nothing more than those little shards shining on his cheeks, but still he stared blankly at nothing.

"He's dead," Fiona whispered. She had both hands up

to her face, the fingernails pulling at her cheeks as she stared at him. "It killed him."

"I don't know," I said, searching for a pulse on his wrist. "He might just be—"

"*You* killed him," she said, her gaze shifting to me. "It was you."

"*What?*" I dropped his wrist, staring at her. "You threw the bloody thing!"

"Witch," she said, her voice a little stronger.

"*No.* This is all you and that damn ball!"

"*Witch!*" She screamed it this time, and pointed at me, rather theatrically, considering there was no one there but her and I. Although that situation wasn't going to last long, not with the volume she was achieving.

I had a moment of perfect clarity, kneeling there next to the maybe-dead dwarf, with my ear still burning from the shattered crystal, and the afterimages of the ball's memories scorched into my brain. I'd just been as neatly framed for Eugene's murder as Ruiner had for Lionel's. Either we'd both burn, or I would and Ruiner would be kept as a sideshow attraction. And there had never been any other way it could go, no matter how hard I tried. The carnival took want it wanted and moved on, subject only to its own laws and desires. No one was coming to save us. No one *could* come to save us. And no one could stop the implacable momentum of the carnival.

I surged to my feet and took off at a sprint, evading Fiona easily and bursting through the big top's entrance with zero regard for anyone on the other side. I barely swerved around Franz, and he called, "Liz? Are you okay?"

I ignored him and pushed harder, not bothering to look back to see if anyone was following, or setting terriers or alligators on me, or getting out the throwing knives. I've never had the greatest turn of speed, but the prospect of being burned at the stake is surprisingly motivating.

I sprinted straight for Lionel's caravan, taking the long way around the big top that meant I didn't run straight past the canteen. I was sure people had probably already seen me anyway, but with any luck they'd just think I was late to feed Coltrane or something. I wouldn't have long, though, not with the way Fiona was carrying on.

I snatched the key off the hook under the trailer, my heart pounding too fast for even my unaccustomed sprint to justify.

"Ruiner!" I hissed as I struggled to get the key in the padlock. "Ruiner, *quick!*"

"What?" he demanded from behind the door. "How can I be quick when you're messing around?"

I ignored that as I finally got the key seated and ripped the padlock open, hauling the bolt back and opening the door. "We're going," I said. "We've to get out *now.*"

"About bloody time."

I shut the door, not bothering to replace the padlock, turned and sprinted for Jared's caravan.

Ruiner was already running for the wall, and I heard him yowl, "*Morgan, you divot!*"

Shouts were going up on the other side of the big top, and although I couldn't see the back door from here, I knew people would either be rushing to it, or already on their way out in pursuit of us. I skidded to a stop at Jared's door and threw it open, catching it as it rebounded.

"Let's go!" I shouted at them, and Coltrane leaped to all fours. Jared gave me a startled look from his bunk, and I said, "If you want half a chance at changing back, you've got to come with us. *Now!*"

"But my contract—" Jared started.

"Suit yourself." I took a step back, and Jared made his

mind up. He threw himself toward the door, and I turned and ran as Coltrane scampered past me, running on all fours like some sort of ape-man, ungraceful but surprisingly swift.

"*Move it!*" Ruiner yowled, mired on the grass halfway to the wall with the late afternoon light setting the ends of his soft grey fur alight. I sprinted toward him, taking my backpack off as I ran. More shouts were going up behind us, on this side of the big top now, our lead narrowing violently. I plunged my hand into the bag, hefting the grimoire out and whispering a silent apology to Jacqueline. Hopefully she could escape the carnival on her own. Surely it wouldn't hold a rat as jealously as it held people?

"*There they are!*" The shout behind us was laced with fury, and I almost stumbled.

Nearly at the wall, I abandoned the bag, grabbing the book in both hands, and opening it at random, all my attention on the barrier ahead of us. The pages fell open without hesitation, as if knowing exactly where I needed to be, and I shifted the grimoire to one hand, the spine resting along my forearm. I pressed my other hand toward the wall, palm out like some sort of magic cop ordering the charm to cease and desist. I had no reason to think I could unlock this any better than I had the door at the Cosy Cauldron, no reason to believe I wasn't just going to lock us in even more tightly, but we had no choice. There was no time to make a plan, to search for the right spell. I had to either trust the book and try, or wait to be dragged back and devoured.

I shouted the words, the cries of our pursuers closing fast, too much like baying for comfort, and the book hot and vibrant in my hand, both distasteful and intoxicating. The air shivered, an intake of startled breath, and something rang high and sharp on the edge of hearing.

Ruiner was standing next to a half-broken old stile, his wide blue eyes fixed on me, and I yelled, "*Go!*"

He never hesitated, just shot effortlessly up the stacked stones of the wall and threw himself over the top. My breath caught as I waited for him to be flung back, thrown into the arms of the carnival, but he just vanished into the field beyond.

"It worked! Morgan, *it worked!*"

I didn't bother to answer. I was already moving, the grimoire clutched in one hand as I scrabbled gracelessly up the rudimentary stile and jumped from the top to the grass below. To the scraggly, overgrown grass that smelt of manure and mud and wet earth, without a single whiff of popcorn or candy floss or anything more than the usual low-level magic of the world.

Not that I could pause to appreciate it. Coltrane and Jared were scrambling after us, panting wildly, and Ruiner shouted, "Morgan, move yourself!"

I moved myself, fast as I ever had, setting off in a hard sprint across the uneven ground as the carnival folk reached the wall behind us, shouting directions and instruction and invectives. The evening drew down low and dark and hungry, and the ravens watched with indifferent eyes, and the shouts took on a new tone as the hunt fell on our heels.

"*Get the witch! Burn her! Burn the witch!*"

TWENTY

Going to the dogs

WE DIDN'T MAKE IT.

Of course we didn't make it. How could we? Even adrenaline and panic could only lend me so much speed, and sprinting had never been my favoured pace. Even if the ground hadn't been rough and uneven, tussocks and holes and rocks rearing up in my path and making me swerve and stumble, I was no match for Mavis the knife-thrower. I kept looking back, knowing it was slowing me down yet unable not to watch the pursuit bearing down on us, and I saw her came over the wall in one smooth, leanly muscled movement, not wasting breath on shouts. She broke into a long-legged run with her head down and those two big knives still strapped to her thighs.

Gus was barely a pace behind her, pounding after us like an Olympic sprinter, his face twisted into a furious snarl. Behind them, a squabbling bottleneck formed at the wall as everyone tried to get over the stile at the same time, the clowns pushing the most fiercely to be the first over. A couple of the horse-riders took to their animals with an easy agility, bareback and without so much as a bridle. The horses spun obediently, lengthening into gallops that took them up and over the lowest point of the stone wall, adding the thunder of hooves to the howl of the chase. Two rangy mutts with too many teeth came flying over the wall, all snarls and wrinkled snouts, and I screamed at Ruiner to run faster. He didn't look back, his tail streaming behind him and his ears back.

The entire carnival was after us, and so, yes. There was no world in which we could've made it. I knew it, but I kept running, stumbling and catching myself, pushing on with panic like bile at the back of my throat, suddenly understanding how animals will destroy themselves in an effort to escape. I'd've run until my heart exploded, just to have the *chance* to not be hauled back.

Jared was barely ahead of me, his unfamiliar body still not quite under his control, and the dogs angled toward him, nipping at his flanks. He snarled, trying to push harder, but he kept getting his feet tangled up and tripping himself up. Behind me, Coltrane was trying to run on all fours, which wasn't going particularly well for him, either. The only person that could have made it was Ruiner, the fading light turning him into a sleek, swift shadow bulleting across the ground toward the next wall.

I had one moment to think that at least I wouldn't have to explain to our mum that the carnival ate my brother, then Mavis hit me from behind, the impact taking me off my feet and carrying both of us to the ground. I yelped as one knee hit a rock and my free hand skidded through the rain-soaked grass, the other still in a convulsively tight grip on the grimoire. I slid forward on my belly with the knife-thrower firmly attached to me, feeling like I was giving a badly executed piggyback ride to an overgrown toddler. To my astonishment, Ruiner spun back at my cry, his sprint barely slowing as he turned. He bolted toward us with his teeth bared and his ears flat.

"*Hands off,* you stab-happy muppet," he yowled at Mavis, and she hissed, rearing up onto her knees and keeping one hand on my back as she drew a knife with the other, slashing at Ruiner with it.

He hissed back, dancing away, and I shouted, "Ruiner, don't! Just go!"

He hesitated, looking at me with those un-cat-like eyes as Gus lunged for him, hands outstretched, and someone shouted, "Megs, Mace! *Sic 'em!*"

"*Ruiner, run!*"

He slid away from Gus with instinctive grace, then broke into a full cat sprint without another glance back. The dogs boiled after him, and the horses washed past us, snorting with excitement and kicking up clods of earth. My brother skidded one way then another, changing direction fluidly, a shadow among shadows. I caught a final glimpse of him as Mavis hauled me up, his slight form vanishing over the next wall and into the field beyond while the dogs tried to scrabble up after him. They made it after a couple of tries, disappearing in pursuit. The horses were just behind them, but they balked at the height of the wall, their riders urging them on as they circled away, galloping for the next gate. Franz ran past me, heading for the wall, digging in his pockets as he went.

I whispered Ruiner's name again, my eyes stinging. The dogs had been *so close* behind him, and yes, he was fast, but their legs were longer and their teeth looked so *sharp*. Even if he evaded them, they'd have his scent. They'd just keep tracking him, and how long could he run, really?

Mavis had the back of my jacket twisted in one hand, her knife still gripped in the other hand, the light running off its edge in a manner that suggested it was sharper than was required for target practice. I didn't even try to pull away, just stood there with my knee smarting and the grimoire still clutched to my chest, straining to hear a yelp or a yowl from beyond the wall. Gus had caught up to Coltrane and tackled him to the ground, but was having difficulty keeping hold of him as he rolled about, thrashing and snarling.

"Dammit, Jared!" Gus bellowed as Coltrane snapped at his face, teeth bared. "You're not going anywhere! Just settle down!"

Coltrane ignored him entirely, and Gus attempted to sit on him, which didn't work too well. Jared, meanwhile, was trying to do a proper lion roar, but it seemed that wasn't an instinctive thing, as the end result wasn't particularly impressive. The clowns had encircled him, all of them keeping a wary distance while he pranced and reared and shook his mane out, teeth and claws flashing.

Gus managed to get Coltrane pinned down with both arms twisted up behind his back. It looked painful, but Coltrane just growled steadily, his face pushed into the ground and his legs straining for purchase.

"Call that bloody beast off," Gus told him, and Coltrane's growl hiked into a snarl. "What the *hell*, mate?"

Accountant Clown jumped back as Jared made a run at him. "It's gone rabid!"

"He's just stressed," Franz said, jogging back to join us. "Coltrane, come on. Good kitty."

I doubted *good kitty* would've worked if it had actually been Coltrane in the lion's body, but Jared's heavy head swung towards the strongman, and I could almost see the bemusement in his face.

Franz made smooching noises and produced a hard-boiled egg from him pocket. "Treat for the good kitty?"

"They don't make strongmen with brains, do they?" the gaunt clown said, almost conversationally. Franz ignored him, waving the egg at Jared, who wrinkled his snout in disgust.

"Move," someone said, and I look around to see Aubrey striding towards us, the buckles on her boots ringing. She had a rifle in her hands, and it didn't look like it was for shooting paintballs.

"No!" I shouted at her. "No, you *can't!*"

"I can do whatever I need to if the carnival needs it," she said, and nodded at Coltrane. "What the hell's wrong with him?"

Coltrane was still growling, hiking up into a snarl now and then, Gus struggling to keep a grip on him despite how firmly his arms were secured. Mike left the circle surrounding Jared and went to help.

"No idea," Gus said. "He hasn't said a word."

Jared attempted another roar, and Aubrey shifted her attention back to him, half-raising the rifle. "Jared, you need to calm him down," she said to Coltrane's prone form. "If you don't, I'm putting that damn moth-eaten cat straight in the ground."

Jared didn't say anything, but he froze where he stood, staring at the gun with his eyes wide in fright.

"Jared," Aubrey said warningly, and pulled the bolt back, raising the gun to nestle the stock into her shoulder. "I'm not playing around here."

Jared stared back at her, mouth hanging open so that his fangs were exposed, looking like he was about to take someone's throat out. Or he would've looked like that, to anyone who didn't know he was a vegan in a lion's body.

Coltrane growled and thrashed, and Gus said, "You're going to dislocate your own damn shoulder. Calm *down*, mate."

"Coltrane, be a good kitty," Franz said, easing himself forward as if to stand between the lion and Aubrey, and she sighted along the barrel.

"*No*," I said again. "Don't. That's Jared."

Aubrey shifted her gaze to me. "What?"

"That's Jared," I said, pointing at the lion. "Don't you think he'd have taken someone's head off by now otherwise?"

Aubrey looked back at Jared, and he hung his head. "Damn it," he said, staring at the ground.

Everyone stared at him, then the rotund clown pointed at me and said, "*Witch*. You did this!"

"I did not," I snapped. "It happened when Lionel was killed."

"By you and your bloody feline familiar," the clown retorted.

"He's my *brother*."

"Ew," Mavis said. "That's gross."

I scowled at her. "He's *not* my familiar, and even if he was, familiars aren't gross."

"Maybe, but you do all that dancing around in the moonlight naked with your *brother?*"

"You've never met a witch before, have you?" I asked her.

She shrugged. "Everyone knows that's what you do."

"*Everyone's* a bit bloody mistaken."

"Enough," Aubrey said. She'd lowered the gun, pointing it at the ground, but she hadn't relaxed. "Is this true?" she asked Jared.

"Yes," he said. "We were in the big top when Lionel was messing around with the cat, and the next thing we'd swapped places. Let Coltrane up, can't you?" he added to Gus and Mike. "He can't exactly do much, and you're going to dislocate my arms if you keep that up."

Gus looked at Aubrey, and she considered it for a moment, then nodded. He eased his grip on Coltrane as Mike got up, then released him completely. Coltrane surged up to all fours, whimpering and trying to favour his arms, but not quite ready to go upright. He scrambled a few steps away, gaze darting from one person to another, and Franz made the same shushing noises at him as he had at Jared, holding the egg out. Jared looked unimpressed.

Aubrey looked between the two of them, then at me and said to the crowd in general, "Bring them in."

"Hang about," I protested. "I haven't done anything!"

"Of course you have," she said as the clowns pressed around Jared, evidently trying to figure out how to get hold of a lion. Mike and Gus were advancing on Coltrane again, and he growled at them. "Fiona saw you attack Eugene."

"She did that!"

"*Witch!*" Fiona yelled from the safety of the wall. "You killed Lionel, and you attacked Eugene, and you'd have killed me *and* him if I hadn't fended you off!" She waved wildly, evidently demonstrating her fending-off skills.

"Well done, Fi," a man next to her said, and patted her shoulder.

"*She* cursed Lionel's crystal ball and made it backfire," I said. "She was trying to get rid of it when I found her, and she smashed it to make sure no one could use it to see what really happened. *That's* what happened to Eugene — he got caught in the shrapnel."

"As if," Mavis said. "Fiona wouldn't hurt anyone."

"I wouldn't," she agreed, straightening her jumper.

"You probably didn't mean to," I said. "You didn't expect Lionel would use the ball for such a strong spell, and you didn't expect Eugene to be there when you smashed it. But you *did* it, and now you're going to let me…" I trailed off, and swallowed, then made myself continue. "You're going to let me and my brother *burn* for it?"

Fiona looked away, her face pale. "I didn't do anything," she said to no one in particular.

Aubrey gave Fiona an appraising look, then looked back at me. "The carnival doesn't tolerate violence against its crew. It will have its price."

"Even if it's from the wrong person?" I asked.

"It only demands payment. Not precision."

I met her gaze as steadily as I could, pretending I didn't feel like either throwing up or collapsing to the ground and screaming in fright and frustration. "Fine," I said finally. "But let my brother go."

Aubrey glanced toward the next field, where the horse-riders could be seen, circling restlessly. "I suppose that depends how fast he runs." She pointed at the grimoire, still pressed to my chest. "Let's see what the witch has."

Mavis grabbed the book, and I wrestled with her for a moment before she raised the knife into my line of sight. I released the grimoire with a sigh I could feel shuddering all the way to my core, and watched Mavis give a little shudder as it fell into her hand. She passed it to Aubrey hastily, and the ringwoman took it, staring at the cover with something like wonder.

She was silent for a long moment, then she smiled, and it was oddly warm, the smile of someone who knows everything's going to be alright. I don't think I was included in that, though. She looked up finally. "Take her back and lock her up," she said, then nodded at Jared and Coltrane. "These two as well."

"But—" Jared started, and she shook her head.

"You were helping them escape."

"They made me," he protested.

"Really? They *made* you run, did they? Dragged them along with them?"

Jared hung his head. "She said she could change me back. I had to go with them."

I scowled at him. Not that I'd expected much more from him. Ruiner had been right with his Cowardly Lion nickname. I stood on tiptoes, trying to see into the next field, but the horses were the only ones visible, walking slowly with their riders peering at the ground. Mavis grabbed my shoulder, pulling me back onto flat feet as if she thought I was going to take to the sky.

Aubrey shrugged. "The details don't matter. You know you don't get to leave the carnival. Your contract is still valid, and attempting to break it has consequences." She turned to the wall, the grimoire clutched in one hand and the rifle hanging easily in her other. "Don't worry too much about the cat. Just make sure he can't get back in."

"Come on, little witch," Mavis said, and pushed me back toward the carnival. There was no point resisting, and no way to escape, so I went obediently, ignoring Mavis' occasional push to keep me moving. Once I was back over the wall, she herded me to Lionel's old caravan and pointed me inside. I clambered in, and stood in the middle of the floor, feeling claustrophobic and panicky.

"What if I need the loo?" I asked, and she shrugged.

"Hold it." She shut the door and I listened to the bolt shoot across, and the hard click of the padlock. Only once I was sure she was gone did I sink to the floor, resting my elbows on my knees and burying my face in my hands, a sob fighting its way into my throat. I was trapped, I was alone, my brother was probably being torn apart by dogs, and the carnival wanted me to burn.

And I'd thought finding out I was a witch had been a bad day.

TWENTY-ONE

A vote of confidence

I DON'T KNOW how long I sat there on the caravan's hard floor, shivering slightly with a mix of fright and the aftermath of adrenaline, but when I looked up at the tiny windows it was fully dark, the lights of the carnival staining the sky. Even though it seemed like it should've been the furthest thing from my mind, I was hungry, and after a moment of considering this, I remembered the toastie in my jacket pocket. I took it out — cold and greasy and somewhat the worse for wear after all the wrestling with murderers and running from carnival heavies — and took a thoughtful bite, looking around the caravan. Ruiner hadn't been able to bust out, but I was a human, plus had an attention span of more than two minutes. Surely, I'd be able to work something out.

I ate half the sandwich then got up, dusting my hands off, and set out to prove the theory. I had no idea what I'd do if I *could* get out, of course, since without the grimoire there'd be no way for me to get through the charms, but it was something to do. I couldn't just sit there and *wait*.

Unfortunately, a thorough examination proved that I was no better equipped to bust out than Ruiner had been. The windows only opened enough to allow some airflow, and even if I'd been able to break the latches unnoticed and force them wide, my brother in his current form would've been better suited for sneaking through them than I was. I had visions of trying and being stuck Winne-the-Pooh-style, half in and half out. The door was old and solid, and I doubted I'd be able to kick it hard enough to even loosen the lock. I couldn't find any Willow-style trap doors sunk into the floor, with alligators or without, and there was no other gap that I could see, not even a vent in the ceiling. Unless I counted the chimney for the wood stove, of course, but I was even worse suited for clambering up that than I was for squeezing out the windows. I was stuck.

I sat back down on the floor, the chair feeling vaguely unappealing, as if to sit in it would be to pretend that everything was perfectly civilised and normal, when it was a million miles from that. I couldn't even pretend that at least I'd succeeded in my mission to get my brother out. Those dogs were trained to catch pests. How hard would it be for them to catch a cat? I pinched my nose to hold back the tears. I was getting a headache, which was helping no one. I pulled out the rest of the sandwich instead, and ate it glumly, the cheese sticky and the bread stodgy, which suited my mood.

I had finished the sandwich and was poking through the cupboards, looking for anything inspiring (I wasn't sure *how* it might be inspiring — something to use as a weapon, maybe, or a magical lock picking tool, or some chocolate. Chocolate would've been fine) when there was movement at the door, a scuffle of the lock being opened. I backed away toward the stove, as if the little stretch of space between me and whoever was coming in might give me the chance to escape or resist.

Aubrey opened the door and looked in at me. She had a tote bag hanging from one shoulder that read, *We bring the Mayhem!* I thought, somewhat bleakly, that they certainly did.

She climbed inside and pulled the door shut behind her. We stared at each other, then she said, "Sit down."

I hesitated, but there didn't seem to be much point in not doing so, so I sat in the armchair, feeling the ghost of Ruiner's presence.

Aubrey sat down on the little built-in sofa opposite, where my brother and I had sat only a few days before, hoping Lionel was going to free him. "How're you doing?" she asked me, sounding genuinely solicitous.

"Oh, great. Being imprisoned is *fabulous*."

She smiled slightly. "Less than ideal, of course. But unavoidable."

"It's entirely avoidable. I haven't done anything, and you've no reason to lock me up."

She made a *hmm* sound, then said, "Trying to break a prisoner out. Attacking a member of the carnival. Trying to kidnap two others."

"Unfairly imprisoned *cat*. She attacked me. And Jared came of his own free will."

She smiled slightly, not arguing. "You are a witch, though."

"Only barely."

"And yet you have an exceedingly powerful book." She patted the bag lightly. "I'm amazed I didn't realise it when you first arrived."

I shrugged. "Like I said, I'm not much of a witch. Maybe the book's not very active."

"Perhaps. It could need a stronger mistress."

"Possibly."

We looked at each other for a long time, her eyes dark and level, and eventually she spread her hands in front of her. "The carnival is fading. Not enough people are interested in them anymore, even in magical towns. The thrall has faded, the charm become tawdry."

"That's progress, I suppose," I said.

"It doesn't have to be. It's fading, not dead. It needs a little magic returning to it, something to lend it strength, to enable it to draw people the way it used to."

"So that you can kill them off?" I asked. "I heard about that."

"Everything has a price. And everything needs something to survive. Plants need sunlight, and water, and good soil. People need much the same. A carnival's no different."

"Not too many plants out there committing murder."

She smiled slightly. "You'd be surprised what things will do when it's their only way of surviving."

I waited, watching her warily.

"This grimoire could help us," she said. "*Save* us. With it, there's no telling what we can do."

"There's a nice thought."

"So I propose a deal. You relinquish your claim on the grimoire, and I let you go free. You and your brother both."

I swallowed hard, the next words sticking in my throat. "My brother? You have him?"

"Of course."

"And he's okay?"

"He can be, if you take the deal."

He can be. What did that mean? That he was okay, the

dogs hadn't touched him? Or he was hurt and she meant I'd need to get him out to save him? "Can I see him?"

"Not unless you take the deal.

I sighed, rubbing my hands on my knees. Part of me wanted desperately to take the deal, and not just for Ruiner's sake, or to get out. The temptation to be free of the unending pressure of protecting the grimoire had weight. If the book was taken away from me, I could even go back to my normal life. No one would expect me to do witchy things if I had no witchy book. And right now, I couldn't imagine anything better than being *normal*, even if that meant crappy jobs and worse apartments. It also meant no tussling with fortune-tellers in carnivorous carnivals, so it seemed like a good trade-off to me.

But I closed my eyes, digging my fingers into my knees, and said, "I can't give it to you."

"Why not? By your own admission, you're not even really a witch."

"It was given to me for safekeeping."

She looked at the bag. "That's gone well then."

Ouch. But fair. "The book's familiar chose me as its guardian. I'm not even sure I *can* just give it up, not without her."

Aubrey seemed to consider this, tapping her fingers on the outline of the book where it rested in her lap. "I could give you a little more incentive."

"Oh?"

"If you don't give me the book willingly, I'll take it. Do you know how that works?"

I tried to say something, but it got stuck in my suddenly dry mouth, and I swallowed. "Does it involve burning?"

"It does. And on top of that, I'd keep your brother. So you burn, I take the grimoire, and he's trapped here forever, spending every one of his lives being chased by Marvin for the entertainment of the hordes. How does that sound?"

I found a breath somewhere, and tried to keep my voice level as I said, "But even if I agree, you can't let us go, can you? I know about the whole one in, one out policy. You need someone to replace Lionel. Plus you need to take payment from the town, so someone's going to die. Why would you let us go when you've got both of those covered if you keep us?"

She shrugged. "Neither has to be you or your brother. I can find others."

"So I give you the grimoire, you power up the carnival, kill someone, kidnap someone, and we just waltz off?"

"Pretty much."

"That's *horrible*," I said.

"Maybe. But if you don't, you burn." She said it simply, her smile almost gentle. "How much do you value your brother, little witch? And your life? How strong are your principles, really?"

I wiped my mouth. "How would I even know I could trust you, if I took the deal?"

"You don't." She got up, shouldering the tote bag again, and I almost fancied I could feel the heat of the grimoire baking out of it toward me, begging to be unleashed. "I'll come by in the morning, see what decision you've made."

I sat there and watched her leave, my hands loose between my knees. I listened to the lock slide into place, and the padlock click shut, and wondered if she really did have Ruiner, or if that was as much a lie as the rest of it. Because I might not be much of a witch, but I'd spent ten years married to a practised liar. I knew what it tasted of.

I could hand the grimoire over, but I was never leaving the carnival. Not alive, anyway. And the only upside to that was that she wouldn't kill anyone else. I hoped.

Although I suppose that all depended on how hungry a powered-up carnival could be.

∼

I DIDN'T MOVE for a long time after Aubrey left, not until Gus opened the door and pointed me across to the communal toilet van. "You want it, you better do it now," he said.

"What happens if I need to go in the middle of the night?" I asked, padding down the steps to the ground.

"Hold it," he said, which was unhelpful. But I went obediently over to the van, used the loo and splashed water on my face. I'd've asked for a toothbrush, but I doubted that was the sort of courtesy that was usually extended to witches. So instead I just swilled a bit of water around my mouth, then went back out again. Gus pointed me back to Lionel's caravan without speaking, and I plodded back toward it. There wasn't anything else I could do. Even if I got away from Gus, there were people everywhere, all of them eyeing me with unfriendly intensity. The only exception was Franz, who was loitering next to one of the trucks doing bicep curls in a desultory sort of way, and Willow, who trotted up to meet us.

"Back off," Gus said to her, and she waved at him impatiently.

"Honestly, what d'you think she's going to do? Magic me? If she was going to do that, we'd all be alligators by now."

That put a new perspective on Marvin.

Gus grunted but didn't stop Willow when she turned to

me. She handed me a little gift box, and one of her gossip magazines. "There," she said. "Your hair is in *desperate* need of some deep conditioning. And something to read."

I looked at the items, then back at her. "Thanks?"

"What else is in the box?" Gus asked. "That can't just be conditioner."

Willow lifted her chin. "Women's things, Gus. Do I need to spell it out for you?"

He opened his mouth, shut it again, then shrugged and said, "Whatever."

She winked at me and patted my shoulder. "You were a very decent roomie, for a witch."

"Um, okay," I said, not sure whether that was a compliment or not.

Willow ran her hands through her beard and strolled off again, humming quietly to herself. I looked at the box, which had more heft to it than some tampons and a bit of hair serum should justify.

"In," Gus said, and I climbed back into the caravan, then stood there clutching my box and my magazine, listening to the bolt shoot across the door again. Then I put the light on and drew the curtains, and only after that did I sit down and open the box.

I don't know what I expected. Some bolt cutters and an invisibility cloak, perhaps? But instead the box contained a packet of off-brand wine gums; a disposable nail file with rounded ends, so I couldn't even stab anyone with it; a bottle with no label that smelled highly alcoholic when I opened it; some makeup wipes and some eyeliner and mascara. Willow evidently felt I might need to re-do my emo-goth look before it all got melted off me. I stared at it all for a moment, then opened the wine gums and the bottle and sat back in the chair, staring at the ceiling.

"Thanks, Willow," I said aloud. "Huge help." I popped

a couple of sweets in my mouth and picked up the magazine with a sigh. I supposed reading about celebrities I'd only ever heard of in passing, plus such thrilling stories as *I Bought an Alien in Aldi* and *My Husband Cooked Our Salamander!* was better than moping. I flipped through the pages, barely seeing them, and at some point I registered there were letters circled in various places. I sat forward, frowning, flipping backward and forward, then went to dig through Lionel's drawers in search of a pen.

It took me a while to find one, but it wasn't like I was in any sort of rush. Finally I sat back down and started writing down each letter I found, my heart beating a little too fast, wondering what the message was going to be. An escape plan, perhaps. A promise that Theodore had been called, that someone was coming to my rescue. A vow that they wouldn't let me burn. I scanned each page carefully, being sure not to miss any letters, and wrote down page numbers and article titles too, just in case it was all some code that I'd need to crack. But I soon realised that was a step of subterfuge too far, and Willow had in fact, even circled punctuation and spaces, just to be sure I didn't miss anything.

WE dOn'T alL thInk You're gUilTy.

I looked at it for a little, then laughed softly and opened the bottle, taking a swig then almost expiring from an instant coughing fit. It tasted like she'd given me paint stripper.

"A vote of confidence," I said to the empty caravan. "How completely unhelpful."

Because while it was very nice to know not everyone thought I was a murderer, it didn't mean anything. People would have to actually do something for it to make any sort of difference, and I had a feeling no one was going to be too keen on that. Not in a carnival that could devour you if it so chose.

But at least I'd have the comfort of knowing not everyone thought I should burn, even as I did so. Such a comfort. I leaned my head back in the chair, closed my eyes, and hoped Ruiner was alright. Hoped that I hadn't failed completely.

TWENTY-TWO

Wine gums & desperation

I SAT in my comfortable chair in my cosy, lamplit prison, sipping a little more paint thinner and smothering the taste with wine gums. I flicked through the magazine a couple of times, then found a crossword puzzle that seemed to mostly involve questions about Friends. It wasn't nearly taxing enough to stop me thinking, but it was annoying enough to distract me, and if I could stomach enough of the nasty booze, I might even be able to get some sleep. I was aware that I should probably be keeping a clear head, but *why?* All I had to think about was how badly things had already gone wrong, and how much worse they were going to get tomorrow.

I also kept thinking of Ben's story, the one about the girl whose village had defied the carnival. How every single one of them had been devoured, leaving nothing behind but empty plates and running taps. How had it happened? Had the carnival called them to itself, the siren song deeper and more intense than the one that had drawn us into the street earlier in the week? Or had it gone creeping on sweeping canvas skirts toward the village itself, swallowing everyone in its path? It made me think of those jellyfish that turn themselves inside out over their prey, fold them up and drift off again, absorbing them as they go. Maybe that's exactly how a powered-up carnival worked, the one-a-show rations only a stopgap, not enough to truly sustain it. Maybe, like crocodiles, they had to eat a full meal once every so often and could survive on that for years afterwards.

It was a horrible thought, and the image of the big top slinking down Hollowbeck's strange streets, with their mishmash of shops and houses, farms and cafes, was so vivid I could barely breathe for it. But what could I do to stop it? Give up the grimoire, and Aubrey could do anything she wanted. Or she'd burn me and do whatever she wanted anyway. If the carnival was that hungry, the book itself wasn't going to be enough.

I buried my face in my hands. I couldn't think of a single way out of this, no matter how many wine gums and nail files I was provided with (and honestly, the nail file was a little rude. My nails were *fine*. I mean, nibbled short, but fine). I wondered where Ruiner was, if he'd made it to town or if Aubrey really had him. Or if the dogs had been quicker and fiercer than he'd been able to contend with. If maybe there hadn't been anything left for Audrey *to* get. I swallowed a sob, pressing it back with my hands against my mouth. Crying wasn't going to help. I had to *think*. What about, I didn't know, though. I was marooned on an island of alligators and popcorn, with no way in or out.

～

I WAS STILL SITTING THERE with my head in my hands half an hour or an hour or two hours later, wondering if I should put more effort into trying to drink the paint thinners, when I heard scuffling in the wood stove. Or not the wood stove itself, but in the chimney. I looked at it, frowning. The scuffling came again, accompanied by some scraping, then a screech that started at the roof and raced all the way to the stove itself, sounding an awful lot like fingernails on metal. It ended in a *thud* inside the burner, followed by an expectant silence as I stared at the blackened glass. A wren, perhaps? But how would it have got through the charms? And surely any sensible creature would've come to the window.

Something scratched behind the wood stove door, creating little lines in the soot inside the glass. I cleared my throat, less so that I could speak and more to announce to any chimney monsters that I was here.

The scratching intensified, and was accompanied by an imperious squeak.

I threw myself out of the chair and crashed to my knees in front of the stove, scattering wine gums all over the floor. I fumbled with the handle and jerked the door open, my heart going far too fast.

A mound of soot and ash with a set of bright dark eyes glared out at me and gave a reproving squeak before climbing out onto the hearth and shaking herself off.

"Jacqueline," I whispered, glancing at the door as if Gus — or whoever was on guard duty, as I assumed someone was — might charge in and grab her. "Where did you come from?"

She squeaked at me again, and tried for another shake, then pawed at her filthy fur unhappily.

"I found her." The voice drifted from inside the chimney, and I had to swallow a yelp. The words were spoken in a hiss that echoed and bounced, the distance distorting them until it felt like talking to a captured ghost.

"Ruiner?" I said, keeping my voice low. I wanted to yell

228

his name, make him promise it was really him, and I could feel tears threatening again, but good ones this time.

"Yeah, I can't get in. The vent's too small," he said. "And that woman with all the knives is hanging about and looking stabby, so I don't fancy trying the windows."

"No, fair enough. Are you alright?" I asked him.

"Relatively speaking. I hid in a rabbit burrow and those bloody horses just pranced right past. Got kicked twice by a rabbit, though. Vicious thing."

I closed my eyes, thankful to whoever looked after cats and annoying brothers that he hadn't been torn apart, stomped on, or shoved in a cage by Aubrey. "How did you get away from the dogs? I thought for sure they'd get you."

"Yeah, bit weird, that. They got all distracted once they were over the wall. Found something dead to roll in, maybe."

"Maybe," I said doubtfully. "Where did you go, then? Did you get Theodore?"

"Was that the plan? I didn't realise we had a plan."

"Well, no, but having the police involved might be good. Or, you know, *anyone* other than carnival folk."

He growled softly, the sound bouncing and rolling in the chimney. "I sneaked back in while you were all yammering away in the field still. Figured it was my only chance before the charms went up again."

I took a deep breath and reminded myself that he could've just left and never come back. "I get your thinking, but that means we're both trapped. And no one's coming to help us."

His snort carried much more clearly than his growl. "No one was coming anyway. You know Toothy Ted and Isabella weren't going to help. They did *nothing* when I was grabbed."

"That's not fair. Theodore was going to look into it," I

said, perfectly aware how ineffectual that sounded. "He'd definitely come and help if he knew what was going on."

"Right, because no one's guessed where you might've run off to?"

I stuck my tongue out at the chimney.

"I know what you're doing."

I rearranged my face and picked up a water bottle Gus had thrown in to me earlier, soaking the corner of a bandana I'd found during my pen hunt and using it to clean Jacqueline's little snout and paws. "So no one knows what's happening here still?"

"Look, I found the bloody rat, didn't I? I can't do *everything*. Besides, you and your new bestie Grace were meant to be swapping sparrows or something, weren't you?"

This time I put two fingers up at the chimney, just for variety, and said, "How are you going with breaking me out, then?"

There was a pause, then he said, "Admittedly, I'm still working out some details. This whole rescue lark is tougher than it looks. But you've got a familiar now. That's got to help, right?"

I offered Jacqueline a wine gum and she took it daintily. I moved on to cleaning the rest of her off as well as I could. "It does help." In terms of morale, if nothing else. "How did you find her?"

"I've spent enough time around that rat enough to know what she smells like. I did a bit of scouting and found her in this cage, all buried in a heap of costumes. I couldn't get her out, of course, but I just hung about and eventually one of those freaky ghost triplets turned up."

I thought about it for a moment. "The trapeze artists?"

"I guess. All pale and waif-y."

"Why did they have Jacqueline?"

"No idea," he replied. "Anyway, I told this one I'd kill them off just as I did Lionel—"

"Oh, that's helpful."

"We're not getting any less guilty as far as Empress Aubrey goes, are we?"

"Fair point." I found a cleaner spot on the bandana and gave Jacqueline another wine gum.

"Anyhow, the scary cat act worked, and Ghosty got all in a knot, saying I couldn't say anything to their buddies about them having a rat. Not the done thing, apparently."

I thought of Art. He'd never actually denied seeing a rat, just said the dogs weren't doing their job if there was one. "They wanted a pet?"

"Or a snack, given those teeth. I didn't hang around for details. Just said the rat was with us and they'd do well to keep their mouth shut, else it was game over."

I imagined being menaced by an overly fluffy, foul-mouthed grey cat with a weird attachment to a well-mannered rat. Oddly enough, I could see my brother making it work. Bluffing was one thing he'd always been good at. Or lying, as it was more commonly known. "Was it Art?"

"Again, wasn't waiting on details. Jackie and I made ourselves scarce and went grimoire hunting."

Jacqueline chittered at me.

"Yeah, I know," I said. I didn't need to be able to speak rat to know that I'd managed to exceed even her lowest expectations of my ability to look after the grimoire. "Any luck?" I added to Ruiner.

"Not really. Jackie there—"

Jacqueline hissed.

"I think she prefers you call her Jacqueline."

"I claimed her from the Milky Bar Kid, who looked

like he was fattening her up for breakfast. I'll call her Ratty Sinclair if I want."

Jacqueline looked at the stove as if she were thinking of making her way back up it, and I bundled her in the bandana while she gave an outraged squeal.

"Jacqueline did what?" I asked Ruiner.

"Tracked it to some caravan with a bloody great crocodile underneath."

"That's Marvin. He's an alligator."

"That makes it so much better. Anyhow, he charged us and we had to leg it, and then we ended up trailing all over the place without finding anything. I don't think she's that good at tracking."

I had to squish Jacqueline against me to stop her wriggling free this time, and I said, "The alligator lives under the caravan I was staying in. The grimoire *was* there, but I think Aubrey's probably keeping it on her. And even if you find it, you're not exactly equipped to run off with it."

"True," he admitted. "What's your plan, then?"

"Tomorrow I'm going to be burned."

He was silent for a long moment, then he said, "What?"

"Aubrey wants me to hand over the grimoire, but I can't. She's going to use it to supercharge the carnival and then I think it'll eat Hollowbeck."

There was another pause, then Ruiner said, "Is that really our problem? I mean, if you can just hand it over then walk away…"

I swallowed a yelp as Jacqueline bit me. "Stop it," I hissed at her, then said to the chimney, "There's no way she'll let me walk away. And even if she did, we can't let that happen to Hollowbeck, let alone whatever else she'll end up doing with the grimoire. We need a plan."

"Alright. What's yours?"

I petted Jacqueline, who'd stopped biting me but still looked unimpressed. "I was mostly getting drunk and eating wine gums."

"Good start." He was silent, and I heard the tick of his claws as he circled the chimney then settled again. "When d'you think this whole burning thing will happen?"

"Before the carnival leaves, so I guess before the show on Saturday."

"It's not Saturday anymore. I heard the crew talking — Aubrey's brought it forward. It's tomorrow night now."

That was hardly surprising. Aubrey would want this done as soon as possible. I narrowed my eyes at the floor, popping a wine gum in my mouth automatically. Jacqueline chittered and held her paws out, so I gave her another. A little sugar rush couldn't hurt.

"Ruiner, you said Lionel needed to be in the big top just before the show started, right? When the anticipation was the highest, it meant the magic was strongest?"

"Yeah?"

"So it'd make sense for her to do it then, wouldn't it? If she's trying to kill me and break my claim on the grimoire, she's going to need some power from the big top. And it also means the crowd will feed it up, make sure it's got enough magic to do the job."

"*Feed it up?*"

"It's a thing. Apparently it's fading because it hasn't had a good dose of magic in ages."

"Oh, diddums to the scary tent."

I snorted. "Yeah, but it makes sense, right? So we've got all tomorrow to come up with a plan. Plus the carnival will be open, so they'll have to lift the charms. You'll be able to get out and find Theo."

"Will that help, though? Remember, Aubrey threw him out."

"She threw me out, too."

"Yes, but you were invited back in."

It was a good point. "Grace, then," I said. "*Anyone.*"

There was another long pause, then he said, "That's it? That's our plan? Hope someone can help?"

"Do you have a better one?"

"No," he admitted.

"Then it's what we've got. You keep yourself hidden and get out as fast as you can. I'll … I don't know. Try not to get burned alive before you come back with the cavalry."

He didn't answer right away, and I listened to him circle the chimney again. Finally he said, "What if I can get Jared and Coltrane free? Maybe they can make themselves useful."

"Maybe. I'm not sure I trust Jared, though. He's going to want to be back in Aubrey's good books."

"Fair point," he said. "Hiding it is." I waited to hear his soft paws pad across the roof, but there was just silence, then he said, "Are you all right, Morgs?"

I huffed. "Not really. I'm scheduled to be burned at the stake. It's not exactly conducive to my best mood ever."

He gave a little snort. "I get that. I'm sorry. I shouldn't have rushed in thinking Lionel was going to solve everything."

"It's not your fault. I thought it was a decent idea, at least. And he might've even been able to help you if Fiona hadn't sabotaged the crystal ball."

He sighed, heavily enough that it drifted down to me in a whisper, amplified by the chimney. "We'll figure this out. Theodore's *got* to do something if he thinks you're about to be burned at stake."

"I'd hope so," I said. "Doesn't say much for our friendship otherwise."

Ruiner gave his little cat huff of laughter. "Alright, Morgs. Chin up."

This time I did hear the soft pad of his paws across the roof, quick and sure, then nothing but silence.

Jacqueline and I looked at each other. She'd eaten her third wine gum and was looking around for more, and I picked up the water bottle again, then hesitated.

"Are you staying, then?" I asked her.

She looked from the chimney to me and raised one paw. The claws were still caked with soot.

"Good call," I told her, and went back to cleaning her off. If nothing else, it stopped me thinking about the day to come, even if the ash and muck was a little too on the nose. Was it going to be a literal burning? Were they going to tie me to a pyre in the middle of the big top? Was it going to look like part of the show, somehow, harnessing all the power of the crowd's excitement? Or would I simply be out the back somewhere, burning from the inside out due to a spell, or a poison, or — I shot an uneasy glance at the flask. That stuff was *definitely* flammable, and I tucked it back into the box, safely out of reach. There was no point doing their work for them.

However it was going to work though, I did know one thing. I was going to end up one dead witch.

TWENTY-THREE

In the spotlight

I DECIDED that sleeping was probably a good option, so I curled up onto the small sofa bunk under the window, pulling a heavy blanket over me that smelled of pipe smoke and menthol. Jacqueline prowled the caravan, investigating, but although I opened the window, she didn't seem inclined to squeeze out. I suppose being lost in a carnival, held prisoner by a sharp-toothed trapeze artist, and chased by an alligator would kind of put one off exploring for a bit. She ate more wine gums instead, until I reclaimed the bag and explained the concept of a balanced diet to her, which she seemed as impressed by as the rest of the world.

After that, she settled down next to me and we did sleep a little, fitful and uneasy. Jacqueline sneezed and coughed as she groomed herself, while I was restless with worry and fright and half-formed nightmares that weren't much scarier than the actual situation we were in. It was almost a relief to hear the fairground waking up outside, before dawn even started to stain the sky. The carnival might not be a fan of witches and their familiars, but in the long stretches of deep night, it had started to feel as though we'd been cast adrift in the caravan, lost to a silent void.

Things gained momentum rapidly outside, the sense of anticipation shivering through the caravans and trucks and tents, lending urgency to every movement and raising the hair on my arms. People shouted warnings and exhortations, equipment was dragged out of trucks and horses were roused, crates clattered into stalls, and lights and sound systems were tested, the whole place alive with hurrying steps and swirling costumes, while above it all the Ferris wheel creaked through a few cautious revolutions, trying the day on for size. The wedge of sky I could see from the windows was clear as the dawn bloomed across it, but there were clouds building up on the horizon, heavy and angry looking. The scent of frying bacon and fresh bread underlined it all like a promise, making my stomach rumble.

I stayed kneeling on the little bunk, peering out like some Victorian child shut up in the attic for their own safety, even though it was quite the opposite. Jacqueline sat on my lap, lifting herself just enough that she could see out but hopefully not be spotted, still shedding soot and ash everywhere despite my best efforts. She really needed a proper bath.

Speaking of which, I needed a proper bath myself, but I somehow doubted anyone was going to let me freshen up before they got down to the burning. There didn't seem to be much point. I'd have to make do with the toilet break offered to me by Gus, who looked more irritated than ever when he opened the door.

"Bloody babysitting duty," he muttered, as I padded down the steps. "Got better things to be doing, you know."

"I'm sure you can leave me locked up," I said. "Not like I can climb out the chimney."

He gave me a suspicious look, and I hoped I wasn't smeared in too much ash. He didn't say anything else, though, so I hurried into the loos to wash my face and rinse my mouth — and promise my reflection that I really would get some decent conditioner once I got out of here.

I'd gone past hungry and into famished by the time Aubrey opened the door, bringing a thermos mug of coffee and a bacon sandwich with her. She set both on the little built-in side table next to the bunk and looked at me, eyebrows raised. Jacqueline had made herself scarce, but I didn't need my little ratty conscience to tell me what the right choice was. Right, but not realistic. Even with her and Ruiner to help, I knew we didn't have much of a chance. But there *was* a chance. If we could get the grimoire, if Theodore could get in, if Grace helped, if, if, if. If wishes were fishes and horses could fly and all that, but this was Hollowbeck. If we could achieve the impossible anywhere, it was going to be here.

"Well?" Aubrey asked.

"No," I said simply. "The grimoire was entrusted to me, and it's got … stuff." I waved vaguely, meaning all the deals I still had to work out, as well as its own innate power. "I can't give it up."

She nodded, looking neither surprised nor disappointed. "That's fine. Not ideal, and it'll be a bit messy, but we'll work with what we've got." She didn't bother arguing or trying to persuade me, just left, locking the door behind her.

It was so anti-climactic that I just sat there staring blankly at the painted wood for a bit, until I remembered the coffee. I retrieved it and returned to my perch under the window, cradling the insulated mug in both hands. The contents were still scalding hot, but I gulped down a couple of mouthfuls anyway, then broke into violent coughing, almost spilling the rest.

"Oh, come *on*," I muttered, once I'd recovered. I sniffed the mug rather more cautiously, then sighed and set it back on the little table. It had been generously laced with whatever vicious spirit Willow had given me last night, so either I had allies who were trying to make sure I was too sozzled to notice I was being burned alive, or I had enemies who were trying to make sure I was too sozzled to resist. Either way, I couldn't risk drinking it, which was a *crime*. If only Aubrey had known how readily I'd've traded the grimoire for one of James' coffees right then, we could have avoided a lot of messiness.

I picked up the sandwich instead, inspecting it for rum-soaked bacon or brandy butter, then pulled a couple of crusts off the heavy slabs of homemade bread. I set them down on the magazine and placed them in front of Jacqueline, who inspected them with every evidence of approval, and clutched one piece in her front paws to nibble on.

"It's good to see you," I told her. "I was worried."

She gave me a sideways look and kept chewing on her bread. I wasn't quite sure if she'd also been worried about me, or mostly about the grimoire. But since she couldn't say either way, I decided to believe it was both.

I took a huge bite of my bacon butty, spilling ketchup down my chin. I mumbled distress around my mouthful and picked up the napkin that had been tucked underneath the sandwich, wiping my face without any particular grace. There was no one here but Jacqueline to see me, after all.

It wasn't until I lowered the napkin that I noticed the ink, shadows, and indentations bleeding through from the other side of the paper. I stared at it for a long time, chewing mechanically, then set my sandwich down and unfolded the napkin with exaggerated care. Was *this* going to be a promise of rescue? Cheryl swearing she'd save me? A smuggled message from Theodore?

I pressed it to the bed carefully, and read it once, then again, then a third time just to be sure. It didn't take long. It was only three words. Then I scrunched the paper up and hurled it across the caravan, wishing it were heavy enough to smash into the wall, to send splinters of wood flying everywhere, to at least make a *noise*, not just drift to the ground and languish there, fragile and useless.

Although that suited the message, really.

All it had said was, *We're so sorry*.

As if that mattered. I'd rather not have known, to be honest. Because what did *we're so sorry* mean, other than *we're not going to help?*

Absolutely nothing at all.

I LOST my appetite after that. I considered throwing the rest of the paint stripper into the coffee and drinking the lot, but being either hungover or still drunk by that afternoon wasn't going to help us execute our audacious and, to be honest, pretty much non-existent plan. Instead, I fed Jacqueline some more bread, ate a few wine gums on the theory that the sugar was good for my energy levels, then settled down to wait.

Somewhere around lunchtime I banged on the door and demanded to be taken to the toilet, and Franz let me out, his face drawn with worry and unaccustomed lines dividing his forehead. Stepping out into the fairground was like emerging from a cocoon, the sense of anticipation and anxious excitement pouncing on me like a physical thing. People rushed about everywhere, in costume and out.

Horses pranced as headdresses and flashy bridles were fitted, and goats bleated in excitement, trying to clamber on top of each other, the caravans, and anyone who stood still long enough. And everywhere I looked, people either avoided looking back at me, or glared at me with a flat hostility that had an edge of excitement to it. I had a feeling the anticipation in the air wasn't just due to the show.

"You know I didn't kill Lionel," I said to Franz, as he escorted me back to the caravan.

He looked at his feet, encased in knee-high lace-up boots. His leopard skin-print leotard stopped mid-thigh, and his legs looked cold, despite the big puffer jacket he was wearing over the top. "You're a witch, though," he said.

"That's not a crime," I replied.

He didn't answer, just walked back to the caravan without lifting his eyes from the ground. It wasn't until I climbed back up the steps that he said, "I wish you'd escaped."

"So do I. But I didn't. And now I'm going to burn unless someone helps me, aren't I?"

"I can't, " he said, his voice almost a whisper. "The carnival won't allow it."

"The carnival? Or Aubrey?"

"It's all the same," he said. "There'd be consequences. Maybe not right away, but there would be. I'd pay."

I nodded. "I guess you'll just have to live with it, then." I closed the door before he could do it. There was a pause, then he shot the lock across, and I sighed. Whatever crisis of conscience he was having, it evidently wasn't enough. Just like everyone else.

～

I PASSED the rest of the day on the little sofa, wishing I had a book or a better magazine. I'd even have gone for a DVD of bloody *Friends*, but all I had was the constantly shifting view outside, both impossible to look away from and full of rising dread. As the afternoon grew deeper and the clouds swelled toward us, the stalls groaned into life and music started to seep across the grounds, tinny and unsettlingly distant, as if heard through a door between worlds.

The first shrill shouts went up just as afternoon tipped into dusk, the sky murky with orange light. The cries were joyful, overflowing with excitement, and it'd be kids on the merry-go-round, or swimming across the ball pit, or playing the duck races, any one of those lovely wholesome things, while back here it crept closer and closer to the moment they set me on fire. Ruiner hadn't returned, and I hoped he was alright. It'd be a lot harder for him to sneak around in the daylight than it had been last night, and I just hoped he stayed well out of sight until he could get out and find Theodore. I doubted Hollowbeck's police force would be far from the gates, even if he couldn't get in.

By the time Aubrey came for me, the scattered shouts had risen to a chorus, mingling with the laughter of adults, and the crash of rides, and the bellows of the sideshow crews, dragging the punters in. Jacqueline vanished as the ringwoman opened the door and looked at me. She was dressed in her top hat and waistcoat, a cane gripped in one hand, her long hair tumbling over her shoulders and her makeup dramatic, rendering her vaguely unreal.

"Last chance," she said, and I shook my head silently, getting up and clumping down the stairs to join her. She didn't say anything else, just put one hand on my shoulder and guided me toward the big top, more as if she felt I needed the support than as if she were afraid I'd bolt. The canvas doors to the backstage area were pinned back, the interior flooded with mellow light, and the scent of sawdust and hard-working bodies washed around us as we headed in. The only people inside were the clowns, and they watched us pass with greedy eyes, their faces white with paint and streaked with reds and yellows in patterns that seemed to bleed into different shapes.

Aubrey walked past them without speaking, steering me into the big top itself and straight to the centre of the ring. Only the faintest lights were on, and I couldn't tell if half the carnival crew were gathered in here, or none at all. Given the noises from outside, louder in here than they had been from the caravan, I guessed most of them would be busy. That had to be in our favour, right?

"Kneel." Aubrey pressed on my shoulder, and I stared at her.

"Abso-bloody-lutely not. If you want to burn me, you can burn me standing."

She sighed, and whipped her cane around, fast and hard. It caught me behind the knees and I went down with a howl of pain, legs folding of their own accord.

"Lights!" Aubrey shouted, and a spotlight came on directly above me, burning down into the sawdust. It painted a circle of arcane symbols around me, nothing I recognised even from the book, but I could feel the weight of them from here. The circle was big enough I could've held my arms out and my fingertips wouldn't have touched the borders, but I didn't want to try it, somehow. I hugged my arms around myself instead, ignoring my smarting legs and hoping Jacqueline had got out of the caravan okay. I'd left the window open for her, so she should've. Although how I expected a rat to help me was a whole other question.

Aubrey reached into her coat and removed the

grimoire from the tote bag, hanging hidden at her side. She stood just outside the circle, looking in at me, and I glared back, trying to seem defiant but mostly feeling tired and alone and as close to defeated as it was possible to be when the final round hadn't yet been played.

"Relinquish your claim," she said. There was an undercurrent of power in her voice, and I was suddenly grateful I'd resisted the spiked coffee and the paint thinners, tempting as it had been. I didn't think I'd have been able to deny her otherwise, not standing here in the centre of the carnival's power, old and resilient and terrible.

But I shook my head and found my voice somewhere. "No. You'll have to take it if you want it."

"Suit yourself." She turned away, stepping into the shadows to pick up Jared's lion-taming stool, and set it between her and me, at the edge of the circle. She placed the grimoire on it and stepped back again, then started talking in a low voice. It was simple and undramatic, a whisper to a friend, the words inaudible, but I felt the atmosphere change in the big top, a stretching and uncurling as of a sleeping beast awakening. Her voice rose slightly, and the air over the spotlighted symbols began to shimmer. Heat rose off them, and the scent of scorched wood shavings, and I staggered to my feet, hugging my arms still more tightly around myself.

My face was already damp with sweat, and it was blossoming all over my shoulders and back as I shouted, "It's *my* book. I claim it!"

She paused her chant to shake her head, almost indulgently. "It's not going to help you in there."

I ignored her, stepping as close to the edge of the circle as I dared. The heat from the symbols was raging, blowing my hair back like I was standing in the draft of some great fire roaring down a hallway toward me, focused and ferocious and full of destruction.

"I won't let you take it," I said, barely hearing myself over the rush of hot air.

"You don't have a choice." She waved her hand, muttering something, and the circle constricted abruptly, the scorching edges of the spotlight beam closing in on me. I stumbled back, smelling singeing hair, the arms of my jacket smouldering. I ripped it off hurriedly, throwing it at the edge of the circle as if it'd smother the symbols, but simply went up with a hungry *whomp*, flaming to ash as the symbols painted themselves over it.

I stared at it, then took another step back as the heat on my face grew unbearable. Even as I did, I felt the matching heat on my back, taunting and hungry, the circle growing ever smaller. I looked around wildly, squinting to try and see past the blazing spotlight.

"Ruiner!" I shouted. "*Ruiner!*"

But there was no sign of him, no sign of Jacqueline, or Theodore, or Isabella, or *anyone*. There was just Aubrey, watching me with some mix of sorrow and delight, and the looming, ravenous big top, waiting for its chance to gulp down the power of the grimoire. No one was coming to help. No one could. She was going to burn me right here, sending me up like a candle in the middle of the ring, while the crowd pushed and surged and laughed outside, and delight ran like terror around and around the tent. I had the sudden thought that maybe there wouldn't even be anything left of me. That the spotlight would get tighter and tighter until it turned into some sort of space laser out of a cartoon that would zap me to nothing, leaving just a charred pile of ash and bone, waiting to be trodden into the sawdust as the show started.

Aubrey's chanting intensified, and I dropped to my

knees, trying to make myself into the smallest target possible and stay as far from the ever-closing edges of the light as I could. I could smell my hair burning, and I had the sudden, absurd thought that not even Willow's conditioner could fix this sort of damage. I cried out as the edge of the light touched one shoulder, and when I jerked instinctively away I burned the other one, too.

"*Ruiner!*" I screamed, although I didn't really want my brother to see me burn. And that was about all he'd be able to do. Nothing was getting through those runes.

"And now," Aubrey said, raising one hand. The light slid off of the gloss of her hair and the slick of sweat on her face. Her expression was solemn, less triumphant than satisfied, someone who's taken on a difficult task and almost achieved it. "The carnival will live on."

I covered my head with both hands and screamed again, wordlessly this time, in equal parts rage and frustration and pain, and wished the same could be said for me.

TWENTY-FOUR

Bring on the ferrets

EVERYTHING WAS HEAT, the near-blinding spotlight burning down into the sawdust, scorching its way toward me. The searing pain on both shoulders where it had already touched me, the savage prickle of heat on my back and head, the stink of burning sawdust and charred cloth, and the steady soundtrack of Aubrey's chant, barely heard over the rush of blood in my ears. I had the desperate thought that I just wanted this to be *over*, that I couldn't take the ever-advancing heat anymore, the looming threat of the burning to come, that I just wanted it to be *done*, yet still I huddled myself smaller and smaller, eking out every last second before that final moment came.

The weight and threat of the light was so overwhelming that it took me a moment to register that someone was yelling. Not yelling, *yowling.* I jerked my head up, squinting past the light to see Ruiner sprinting out of the shadows, tail up and ears back, screeching an unending litany of insults that involved animals, other people's family members, and some anatomically improbable and likely illegal acts. Aubrey swung around to face him, but she'd evidently been as engrossed in the whole *burn the witch* thing as I'd been, because she was too late to sidestep him. He flung himself at her, swarming up her clothing like she was his very own cat tree. Judging by her yelp, it was with the assistance of every tooth and claw he could put to work, too.

"Bloody *animal!*" she shouted, trying to fend him off, then her gaze darted past him and she added something that Ruiner was no doubt going to add to his repertoire. I peered into the shadows and spotted Marvin scuttling with deceptive speed across the ring, jaws agape and collar flashing. He went straight for Aubrey, evidently in hot pursuit of Ruiner, and she kicked out at him with a shout of fright. He promptly closed his jaws on the offending leg, and she screamed.

Ruiner leaped clear as Aubrey fell to the floor, Marvin still attached to her leg. The alligator didn't seem to notice him — evidently he was happy just to be able to bite *someone.*

"The light!" I shouted to my brother. "Get the light!"

He looked from me up into the far reaches of the tent. "*Where?* Where's it controlled?"

"I don't know! Just *hurry!*" The light was still closing on me, more slowly now that Aubrey was distracted with beating Marvin around the head with her cane, but it hadn't stopped entirely.

Ruiner ran for the closest pole, evidently planning to scale it and dislodge the light from above, and I cried out as the beam caught my shoulder again. There was nowhere for me to go to avoid it.

"*Hurry!*" I yelled again, and Aubrey surged to her feet, aiming a final blow at Marvin. He backed away with his jaws wide and his tail thrashing like a huge, dangerously disgruntled cat.

"*Burn!*" she shouted at me, then lunged forward to grab the grimoire as the light snapped into a tight beam, drenching me in heat. I heard Ruiner shout something, but I was too busy screaming to be able to tell what. Dimly, though, I saw Jacqueline flow across the ground and onto the stool, burying her teeth in Aubrey's hand.

Aubrey yelped and jerked back, blood scattering from her fingers, and Franz came pounding across the ring, a clown still clinging to one arm as she tried to hold him back, and another rolling away across the sawdust. He snatched up the stool, sending Jacqueline and the grimoire flying across the ring, took half a step back, and hurled it straight up into the circle of light.

If anyone else had done it, there was no way it could've worked. It'd have been a nice gesture, but the most it would've accomplished was bopping me on the head when it came down. Instead, the stool whirled straight up, effortless as a thrown ball, and we all heard the *twang* as it hit the cables above. The spotlight bounced wildly and whirled off target, ending up aimed at the side of the tent. The scent of burning cloth, with an uneasy undertone that was too much like cooking meat, washed over us, and I collapsed into the sawdust, trying not to cry.

"*No!*" Aubrey screamed, and I scrambled up, staring at her. She held my gaze for a moment, then we both lunged into the shadows, in the direction Jacqueline and the grimoire had vanished. Behind us, Marvin hissed, and Ruiner came tumbling back down the pole with a yelp of alarm.

Aubrey shouted to the clowns to grab me, and Franz roared, opening his arms wide and charging toward them, catching Accountant and Burly around the waists and driving them back toward the backstage entrance.

"Morgan! Morgan, let's *go!*" Ruiner yelled, but I was

still hunting for the grimoire and Jacqueline. Aubrey caught up to me, grabbing my arm, and I cried out as she tore the burned skin. I spun around and managed to land a clumsy slap on her face, and she responded by swinging the cane at me. She was using her left arm, though, and wasn't as quick as she had been before. I grabbed it, trying to push her back and away, and Ruiner shouted again.

"*Morgan!* This bloody reptile's going to eat me! *Come on!*"

I shoved, hard, and kicked at Aubrey's injured leg at the same time. She went down with a scream, and I wrenched the cane off her. "The book!" I shouted at my brother.

"*Sod the book, you muppet! Run!*"

I wanted to argue, but Franz was going down in a pile of clowns, roaring like Goliath, and Aubrey was already rolling to her feet. I was solidly against a repeat of the whole burn-the-witch thing, so I whacked her leg with the cane to send her back to the ground and sprinted for the main entrance, Ruiner flying off the bleachers where he'd taken shelter from Marvin and racing to join me.

We bolted up the aisle, Marvin galloping after us and Aubrey's shouts following us, faint carnival light outlining the door ahead, promising some fleeting safety in the crowd outside. They couldn't burn us in front of the whole town, could they? I ran harder, the scent of fresh cold air drifting to join us, and we were going to make it, we'd get out and get Theodore and come back for Jacqueline, and—

The canvas was thrown back just as I reached it, and Gus and Mike grabbed me, one on each arm before I could even protest. Mavis stepped past them, dropping a sack over Marvin, who froze mid-run, flattening himself to the floor, and behind us Aubrey called, "Cut it fine enough? It's almost showtime. Move!"

I was propelled back down the aisle, my arms screaming with pain but my own words dead in my throat, the chance of escape retreating with the scent of popcorn and candy floss and the outside world.

"Put her in the centre and sort out that bloody light," Aubrey said. "Who's got the cat?"

No one answered, and Mavis said, "I got Marvin."

"Marvin I'm not worried about. The cat's an issue."

"I can look for him," Mavis offered, and Aubrey sighed.

"Forget it. There's no time. Let's just get set up."

Mike and Gus pushed me into the centre of the ring. Franz and the clowns had vanished, and I wondered if he'd escaped them or if they'd dragged him off.

"You don't have the book," I said to Aubrey. "What's burning me going to do?"

"It still releases your claim," she said. "And that grimoire won't get out of this tent. The big top's had a taste of it now."

I shivered, and glanced up as the light swung back toward me. There was a scorched patch on the canvas where it had been shining, but I fancied I could already see it healing. The light settled over me again, back to its original width. I couldn't feel any heat coming off it, but it wouldn't be long. "So, what, you're just going to burn me while half the town watches?"

"The whole town," she said. "It'll look like part of the act. It'll be *exciting*, and then the carnival will feed."

"Feed on what?" I asked.

"All the rest," she said, and grinned, wide and wolfish.

"Do we need to do that?" someone asked, and Aubrey turned to look toward the main entrance. Willow stood there, Marvin at her heels. His mouth was partly open, and she'd attached a leash to his collar. "If it has the grimoire, maybe it doesn't need anything else."

"Do you want to try and stop it, Willow?" Aubrey asked. "Because if so, be my guest. See how that goes for you."

She didn't answer, and Aubrey looked over the assembled crew. The clowns had emerged from backstage, sporting some ripped costumes and a couple of black eyes and swollen noses that weren't due to makeup.

"The carnival is dying," she said. "*Starving.* A soul here and there is barely enough to keep it alive. Lionel's death woke it, and now it *must* feed. Maybe the witch will satiate it, but I doubt it. It'll take us all unless we let it eat its fill."

No one spoke, and I reached a cautious hand out, testing the edge of the circle. It was like pressing my fingers to a hot stove, and I snatched them back, tucking my fingers into my armpit protectively.

"Does anyone really want to stand in its way?" Aubrey asked.

More silence, and I understood it, I *did*, who wants to be eaten by a sentient canvas shack, but they were condemning a whole *town* to it, and not even trying. Not even challenging its ringwoman.

"Then places." She picked her hat up from the ground and dusted it off. "The show begins!"

THE BIG TOP filled up fast, the carnival workers running to take their positions, some opening the doors, other shouting outside to call the townsfolk in. The clowns began to tumble and run across the ring, swarming up the poles and swinging from the trapezes, spinning themselves around my circular prison in cartwheels or somersaults or on unicycles, and I stood in the centre and yelled at the crowd to get out. No one gave the slightest indication they heard me, even though I could hear the laughter and mutters as they found seats, the *oohs* and *ahhhs* of excitement as they watched the clowns cavort. I resorted to sign language, jumping up and down wildly and pointing back at the doors, and the clowns imitated me, until we were jumping and waving in unison, like a really terrible new TikTok dance.

And all the while the tension in the tent grew, until I couldn't understand how the crowd couldn't feel it. The air was thick with excitement, the canvas trembling, and I almost fancied I could see the sawdust shivering. Did they *honestly* think this was just the fun of the carnival? It was making my stomach turn in lazy rolls, and I wondering briefly if the clowns would copy me if I threw up.

The tent was still filling up, and Aubrey was right — it really was the whole town this time, cramming into the seats, shoulder to shoulder. The anticipation grew, the whole place vibrating with it, and Aubrey strode around the edge of the ring, barely limping, as the clowns' efforts intensified. She pointed at the light, and it began to narrow. It was moving faster now, ceremony crumbling in the face of the tent's hunger, and my already burned shoulders stung with the heat.

"*Stop this!*" I shouted, but still no one reacted.

The trapeze act started, the clowns melting away as the pale forms of the trapeze artists swung through the dark air, lit by shifting spotlights, drawing more gasps from the audience. I could barely breathe between the heat and the pressure of the tent, and I watched Aubrey spin toward Gus as he ran down the aisle. He had a book in one hand, and a motionless scrap of fur in the other.

"*Jacqueline!*" I screamed.

Aubrey snatched the book from Gus and raised it in one hand like a trophy, turning to look at me as the lights swirled across the crowd and the trapeze artists swung and spun and leaped, and the big top groaned somewhere on the edge of hearing. She started toward the centre of the ring, book still raised, and the heat of the spotlight bore down on me, and the first ripple of unease ran through the crowd, a collective shiver like a pack of cats running across a whole town's worth of graves. Somewhere, a child started crying, and another joined in, and a couple of people stood up, looking uncertain.

"*Get out!*" I yelled, even though I knew they couldn't hear me. "Get out, please, *please* get out!"

In Gus's hand, Jacqueline unfolded with startling speed and buried her teeth in his wrist. He screamed and dropped her, and she shot across the ring, heading for Aubrey.

"Is that a *rat?*" someone yelled, and someone else screamed, even as the gaunt clown raced out of the darkness, taking great stomping strides in his oversized shoes. Jacqueline swerved him and shot into the front row. The audience there surged to their feet, everyone shouting and pushing to get out of the way, and Aubrey shouted, "Everyone, please be calm, this is part of the act!"

Which maybe, possibly, might've worked, except a flood of furry forms came plunging down the aisles, swarming the bleachers and scampering through the chairs, and more people started screaming. Suddenly the spell was broken, and everyone started pushing and shoving, trying to get past each other and run for the exit as ferrets darted and clambered and nipped at exposed ankles.

I cheered, but my triumph was short-lived as Aubrey

yelled, "*Seal the doors!*" and spun to point at the light. I braced itself for it to snap down to that terrible, burning beam again as power surged around me. The crowd crushed together at the exit, screams and shouts taking on a new, even more panicked note.

Then a slight body came swinging out of the darkness, almost languidly graceful on the end of the trapeze. They let go, flipped twice, and smashed into Aubrey, both of them crashing to the ground. She shrieked as she fell, the grimoire flying out of her outstretched hand and sliding across the floor. The spotlight winked out and I threw myself forward, scrambling to the grimoire and snatching it up. Aubrey was already on her feet, screaming at the trapeze artist, who I supposed was Art.

"I'll let it eat you too," she yelled at him. "Useless bloody son of a ghost!"

He didn't respond, just sitting on the floor with one arm hugged close to him and a worried look on his face, and she spun to face me, holding a hand out. "Give it to me."

I didn't answer. There were clowns at the backstage door, the shouting crowd still crushed at the main entrance, and no other way out. The air still shivered with power, and Jacqueline came scooting out of the thicket of fallen chairs. I crouched to pick her up, not taking my eyes off Aubrey.

"Give it to me," she repeated. "I'll let you go."

Jacqueline squeaked at me, and I looked down at her. She had one paw on the grimoire, and the other one patted at my hand. I hugged both her and the book, and raised my voice to be heard over the chaos in the aisles. "You have to stop this."

"I can't," she said. "It has to feed."

I glanced up the aisle. Kids and adults all tangled

together, pushing and shouting and crying, and I was sure it wasn't just the ferrets. They could feel it now, feel the threat. "Let them go, and I'll give you the grimoire."

Jacqueline hissed, then gave me a very unnecessary nip.

"It's too late," Aubrey said.

I'd thought it was just my burns, but the grimoire was hot in my hand and actually seemed to be getting more so as we spoke. Jacqueline chittered again, pushing at my fingers with her paws and snout. I looked at her, and she pushed again. I opened my hand and the grimoire fell to the floor, the pages fanning wildly then falling open, just as it had at the wall. Jacqueline jumped after it, and Aubrey started forward.

"Stay back," I shouted at her, crouching down.

She ignored me, snatching up her cane as she came. *"Give it me."*

Jacqueline squeaked, and I scooped her and the book up, taking a step back as Aubrey advanced. I didn't have time to read what the spell was, didn't have time to prepare. Not that it would've helped. It was either going to work or it wasn't, and in the absence of a witchier witch, I was the one that was going to have to do it.

I started reading aloud, forming the words as well as I could, unfamiliar and clunky. The air shivered, a new shudder, and I felt the attention of the big top shifting toward me.

"Stop it," Aubrey said, raising the cane over her shoulder as she advanced. "I said, *stop it.*"

I ignored her, still reading, the weight of Jacqueline against me the only thing real in the whole place. The big top was tightening down, almost as it had when Aubrey kicked us out a thousand years ago, but this was worse. It was folding in on us, the air tight and claustrophobic, as if it were unable to escape, pressure building as if we were in a diving bell plunging into some eternally dark ocean trench. I raised my voice, trying to be heard over the screams of the crowd as they intensified. Aubrey was almost to me, and I couldn't seem to move to escape her, my limbs too heavy. All I could do was keep reading and hope I could finish before the cane came down.

She pulled it back, her whole body twisting like she was going to take my head off with the blow, and Ruiner came screeching across the ring, all claws and teeth as he flung himself at her. She ignored him, the element of surprise lost, but even as she leaned into the swing and I threw myself to the floor, trying to keep reading at the same time, Jared burst from the backstage door. The cane whistled over my head, and I kept my eyes fixed on the book. He was on her in two bounds, carrying her to the ground, and I reached the end of the spell.

Audrey screamed, and the entire carnival convulsed. Jacqueline tugged urgently on my hand, and Ruiner shouted, "Morgan, keep going!"

"It's finished! That's the whole spell," I shouted back, checking over the page while Aubrey and Jared rolled across the ring, him growling and her shrieking abuse.

"Then do it again!"

"I can't! I'm not a witch, I don't know how to do this!" I was almost crying, because if the book had chosen the spell, it should've worked, everyone should be out, but the carnivals' terrible consciousness was still bearing down on me, pressing the air from my lungs, and the whole town was still trapped inside and *why wasn't anyone coming to help me?*

Ruiner skidded to a stop next to me, looking up at me with those familiar blue eyes. "You can," he insisted. "It's only bloody words. You were always into them. Read the damn words!"

At the entrance, someone shouted, "It's coming down! The tent's coming down!"

I looked up, seeing the massive poles swaying about us, and Ruiner shouted, "Read the words, Morgan!"

I forced myself to look back at the page, and it swam in front of my eyes. Maybe it was due to the pain of the burns, or the suffocating heat, or the impossible pressure of the tent, but it hardly mattered. I couldn't read the spell. I couldn't make it stick.

The carnival was going to win.

TWENTY-FIVE

Out of the tent into the fire

I SQUEEZED MY EYES SHUT, and when I opened them again someone was walking across the ring, moving quick and light, utterly calm amid the chaos. They knelt down in front of me and I met Grace's warm, amused eyes.

"Need some help?"

"Yes," I said softly.

"Give me the book." She held a hand out, the fingers long and elegant, and I just stared at it for a moment, the shouts and screams of the carnival drawing distant. Jacqueline shifted against me, and I looked down at her. She returned my gaze with sharp eyes, and tipped her head just slightly. Maybe it meant nothing — she was a *rat*, after all, she could've been scratching an itch, but it filled me with a sudden, exhausted fury. She'd given me the bloody book, and now she was just, *oh, whatever?* Just because Grace was all nice hair and long legs and dimples and, okay, proper witchiness? Who was the one that had sneaked into a carnival, and busted out Ruiner, and brought down the charms, and fought off an egomaniacal ringwoman? It hadn't been sodding *Grace.* Alright, fine, she probably wouldn't've ended up in the situation in the first place, but *I'd done it*. And leaving jobs half-done was Ruiner's thing, not mine.

"No, you're alright," I said to Grace, and got to my feet, glancing around the big top. The lights were swinging wildly as the tent convulsed, sides heaving like labouring lungs, and the carnival folk had vanished. Some of the crowd had rushed across the ring, looking for a way out, but the backstage doors were sealed too, now, and I wondered how Grace had got in.

Only Aubrey remained, still pinned in place by Jared, and she screamed at me, "You're not witch enough to do this!"

"Try me," I said, and started reading. The words made more sense this time around, easier to shape, and they rang in my ears rather than feeling sticky and distant. It was a banishment spell, I realised somewhere around the third line, and I focused on that, focused on the sense of balling up the whole mess and flinging it as far from Hollowbeck as I could. The pressure of the air eased, the canvas heaving and wobbling ever more wildly, and when I finished the second round I started a third without pausing, my voice louder, almost shouting now.

Aubrey screamed again, a wordless wail of grief and loss as the first shriek of tearing canvas filled the tent. Grace turned and ran up the aisle, and I dimly heard her shouting for everyone to spread out, stop pushing, be ready.

Another ripping sound, loud as a thunderstorm overhead, and light from the stalls and sideshows flooded into the big top. Aubrey cried out again, all pain and desolation, and Jared hefted himself to all fours, backing away from her with his heavy snout furrowed. She curled in on herself, hands digging into the sawdust. I kept reading.

More shouting at the entrance and toward backstage too. More light pouring in as the entrances burst open and people surged out, all of them running, lifting kids up and pushing each other on. The lights inside were snapping off with the pops of exploding bulbs, raining shards of glass on us, and Ruiner stared up at me, his ears back.

"Morgan, you've done it. We need to go."

I shook my head, going back to start the spell again, because I could still feel it. *It*, the spirit or soul or consciousness of the carnival pushing back against me, clinging to the edges of the world. I felt like I was playing some sort of wildly arcane whack-a-mole, bits of carnival spirit popping up every time turned my back. People wouldn't be out of the grounds yet, and at the very least, if I couldn't banish it entirely, I had to hold it down until everyone could get out.

I glanced up at another shriek of ripping canvas above us. I glimpsed the night sky through gaps in the roof as the seams shredded and great swathes of material unfurled toward the floor, as if the very fabric of the world was parting.

Jared was padding in an anxious circle, and I shouted at him, "Get out! Hurry!"

He didn't hesitate, running for the main entrance with his mane flowing softly. Then there was just Ruiner, Jacqueline and myself huddled together in the centre of the ring, and Aubrey still lying on the floor in front of us. Sawdust blew around us in strange little eddies of wind, spiralling into whirlwinds and twisters.

Aubrey turned her head to me, and I could see tears on her cheeks. "You're killing it," she whispered.

I read the final line and stopped, feeling the spell still ricocheting around us. The crowd had vanished, and I could imagine them pouring through the fairground, racing for the gates, abandoning the sideshows and food stalls, emptying the merry-go-round and the Ferris wheel, fleeing in panic through the heavy wooden gate and into the safety of Hollowbeck's old lanes, running for home and locked doors and familiar places.

"You were going to kill everyone," I said to Aubrey.

"It was dying," she said. "All those years, all those towns, all those shows, and it was *dying*." She closed her eyes, turning her face to the ceiling. "How could I let that happen? You and your book were a gift."

"But you tried to take the whole town," I said, while the tent convulsed and crumbled around us.

"It was so hungry. It's a living thing, after all."

I could feel that, feel its death throes in the shaking floor and tearing canvas, and I pressed a hand to my head. I was trembling.

"Morgan, we have to go," Ruiner said. The fur was up on his back, his snout wrinkled against the twisting winds. "The whole thing's going to come down."

"You've all but killed it," Aubrey said, her voice so low I could barely hear her. "Just leave, can't you? Let it go in peace."

I looked at the grimoire, then around the tent again. "I can't just leave. What if you go off and devour another town?"

She laughed, a little hiccoughing sound, and turned her head to look at me. There was sawdust in the thick mass of her hair, and tears had worn tracks in her makeup. "We can't devour a town now. We can't devour anything. It'll be all we can do to survive, especially these days. No one cares for carnivals anymore."

We stared at each other, and I thought of Isabella saying, *the carnival always persists*. It was both heartbreaking and horrifying, the thought that it would limp on and on, with its crew in tow, bound to it even as it shrank and faded and became little more than myth, relegated to smaller fields and more remote towns, ever battling the advance of a modern world that it couldn't comprehend. But still it would persist.

I closed the grimoire. "You'll leave," I said. "You won't attack any towns. You won't take any payment. And you'll let anyone leave who wants to."

"We'll die," she said.

I held the grimoire up. "It's that or I'll keep saying this spell until I burn this place to the ground." I didn't know if I meant it, didn't know if that was even possible, but she examined me for a moment, then nodded. "Tell me you agree," I said. "And I *promise* I'll bloody well hunt you down if you go back on it."

She smiled at that, and gave a little bark of laughter. "I knew you looked like you could do the work. Fine. I agree. Just leave. Let me salvage what I can."

I hesitated, still holding her gaze, and thought again of that whack-a-mole sensation, and the awful, crushing hunger of the carnival. Something was niggling me. "You said the book and I were a gift. But how did you know I'd come?"

She laughed softly. "Because an enchanted male is always going to look for a male magic worker to solve his problems."

"You set it up? You *killed* Lionel?"

"Some prices have to be paid. He told me Fiona cursed his crystal ball, so I said I'd fix it for him. I did, in a manner of speaking."

I stared at her. "But how did you even know about Ruiner? About me?"

Before she could answer, the big top gave an agonising convulsion, the last of the lights exploding like meteors.

One of the main poles snapped, the noise just about shattering my eardrums, and it plunged down into the bleachers, bringing the roof with it. I yelped, ducking as the canvas crushed down around us, wedging us into a little pocket that heaved and swelled like the fibrillating heart of a dying beast.

"Morgan, *move!*" Ruiner shouted.

"But she—"

"*Now!*" Something was groaning above us, and I looked up to see the final pole wobbling side to side, splits appearing in its length.

I turned to run for the backstage area, Ruiner racing ahead of me, and Aubrey called, "Here!"

I glanced at her, not intending to go back, but she was holding a scrap of paper out toward me.

"Take it, little witch."

I didn't have time to consider it too much. I swerved toward her, snatching the paper from her hand and shoving it into a pocket, then plunged after my brother into the tangle of discarded props and clothing strewn across the backstage space, clutching Jacqueline and the grimoire tight. I dodged through the debris like some sort of assault course, then burst out the other side into darkness lit with multicoloured lights, and filled with screams and commotion.

I barely made it out before the big top collapsed in on itself with a shattering of wood and tearing of canvas that sounded like screaming. I turned to watch, hugging the grimoire still closer as I backed away, unable to look away from its slow destruction. Jacqueline struggled out of my grip and climbed to my shoulder, and Ruiner padded up to me. He was panting, and there was sawdust in his fur.

"She's still in there," I said.

"Good," Ruiner said. "You know, considering she was going to burn you alive and eat the town and all."

I shook my head. "She didn't deserve this."

Ruiner made a little frustrated sound, but before he could say anything someone grabbed my arm, spinning me around. I cried out, both from the pain that shot through my burns and the unexpectedness of it.

Gus glared at me, his face contorted with fury. "*Witch*," he hissed. "What did you *do?*"

I pulled away from him and took a step back, but bumped into someone else and whirled around. I was trapped in a circle of carnival folk, their faces cold and flat and furious.

"She was going to kill everyone," I said, turning back to Gus. "She was going to destroy the entire town."

He shoved me in the shoulder, making me stagger. "You've destroyed *us*."

"Witches always burn," the female clown said, her face ghastly with running paint and her hair lank and stained with sweat. A murmur went around the group, and I searched for friendlier faces, for Franz or Art or Willow, but they weren't there. Maybe they'd taken their chance and run when the big top fell, or maybe they knew they'd be too outnumbered to help, that they'd only be dragged down with me. I clutched the grimoire tighter. Whatever strength it had lent me earlier, it seemed to be gone. Shouts and screams were still rising from the other side of the big top, but I couldn't see anyone. We were hidden from the road by the circle of accommodation trailers, so even if anyone was looking, we were as good as invisible, lost in the carnival once more. I don't know why I'd every though it'd let us go.

"I couldn't let her do it," I pleaded, looking from the clowns' smeared faces to Mavis' cold stare to all the others, their expressions a homogenous mass of hostility. "Don't you understand? Wouldn't you have done the same, to save your town?"

Gus pointed at the big top. "We were too slow. You've already destroyed ours. So I guess we'll just have to make you pay for it."

"No—" I started, but the circle closed too fast for me to finish the sentence, let alone fight back. Half a dozen different hands grabbed hold of me, wrenching the grimoire away despite Jacqueline's hisses, then she was gone too. I couldn't even keep my feet, lifted bodily and hauled across the fairground while I bucked and twisted, yelling for help. Someone slapped me, and I yelped, then kept yelling, because it wasn't like things could get any worse.

"Witches burn!" the female clown shouted. "*Witches burn!*"

"*Witches burn!*" the crown shouted back, drowning my cries, the fury rising in a choking tide. "*Witches burn!*"

"*Ruiner, run!*" I yelled, trying to be heard over them, hoping that he'd been smart enough to get out, that my brother's unfailing instinct for self-preservation wouldn't falter now. I couldn't see him, at least, so that was something.

The crowd parted as we arrived at Lionel's caravan, and I was bundled inside. I tried to catch the doorframe, to brace myself against it, but Mike pushed me in so hard I fell to the floor and skidded across it, fetching up against the chair with a yelp. The door slammed, and as I rushed back to it I heard the bolt slam across. I ran to the windows instead, pounding on one, and as I did I saw a couple of the horse riders lugging red jugs toward us.

"No," I whispered, and stopped banging my fists on the widow. I grabbed the chair instead and used that as I caught the first whiff of gasoline. The chair was heavy, and I wrenched my shoulder as I lifted it, but it merely bent the plastic of the window rather than breaking it. I dropped it and went back to my fists, screaming for someone to let me out.

The smell of the gasoline was intensifying, then there was a sudden *whoomph* as someone put a light to it. I froze, both fists pressed to the window, and stared out at the crowd. A circle around the caravan were cheering, but Cheryl stood further back, one hand over her mouth. Art was next to her, his arm still cradled in his other hand, looking even paler than normal, and Fiona was already walking away. And I hated them, *hated* them for not trying, but at the same time I understood it. They'd be in here with me otherwise.

The sides of the caravan were catching now, flame flickering up to the window, and I stepped back from it. Smoke started to fill the space, and I pulled my shirt up to cover my nose then dropped to my knees, trying to get under it, to scrape out an extra minute or two. The caravan was filling up so quickly that it was virtually impossible, though. The hot air tore at my chest, and I curled myself as small as I could, as if that would somehow make the fire less likely to reach me. I closed my eyes, and started to giggle. I'd escaped burning and destroyed an entire sentient carnival, only to burn to death in a dead wizard's caravan. This had not been on my list of possible deaths.

The giggles turned into coughs, tearing at my throat, and I thought vaguely, *well, at least I got my bloody brother out.*

Then the back door was ripped open and two strong, cold hands grabbed me, all but throwing me outside. I collapsed onto the ground, hacking and wheezing, and when I finally managed to look up through streaming eyes I found Ruiner peering back at me anxiously.

"*Hhhh?*" I managed.

"You're welcome," he said, and I would've hit him if I hadn't just about died. Instead I grabbed him and hugged him, looking around to see Theodore clutching a clown by the back of the neck and with another in an armlock, his hair smouldering and a furious expression on his face that made his cheekbones look even more devastating, although the way his fangs were hanging out was a bit off-putting. I blinked around.

Hollowbeck hadn't run. Hollowbeck had invaded the carnival.

Scuffles were breaking out everywhere, townsfolk giving chase while the carnival crew alternating between hiding and fighting back. I spotted Petunia laying into Mavis with an umbrella, her aversion to the carnival apparently overcome if she got to beat it up. Tanya was loping through the crowd with her teeth bared, Jared trotting after her looking as adoring as a lion can. James and Mike were engaged in some ineffectual-looking fisticuffs, while just beyond them Jurgen and Ruby were apparently trying to take down the remaining three clowns *and* Gus all at once, aided by about three murders of crows, and Ben was standing in the middle of it all clutching a collection of handcuffs and shouting, "Theodore, do you need these yet?"

Theodore snarled and threw a clown at one of the sideshow workers, and Ben said, "Maybe not."

"The book," I managed, my voice wheezy. "The grimoire."

Next to us, the caravan groaned, then collapsed on its axles, belching heat, and both Ruiner and I yelped. I rolled unsteadily to all fours and started to crawl away, then encountered a pair of large boots. I looked up, past some bare knees and a leopard skin leotard, and Franz grabbed me by the back of the shirt, hefting me up effortlessly and propelling me a few more meters from the burning caravan before letting me puddle to the ground again.

"Thanks," I said.

He crouched in front of me, knees cracking loudly. He winced, and pulled the grimoire from where it had been tucked into his belt, then extracted Jacqueline from inside his leotard. She squeaked, managing to look mortally offended. I didn't blame her.

"Sorry," he said. "Aubrey's banishment charm was still in place. It took a bit before it broke and I could invite your police officer in."

"That's okay," I managed, and we both watched Theodore rampaging across the fairground. His method of arrest seemed to involve throwing people at each other, then letting Ben cuff them while they were still stunned. Ben looked like he was about to cry from the stress of it, not helped by Isabella following him and shouting instructions. I thought of something. "If her banishment broke…"

He nodded, straightening up. "She's gone." And before I could apologise, or explain, or do anything at all other than feel the tears at the back of my throat, he smiled and said, "We're free." Then he turned away, hurrying back into the crowd, and Ruiner, Jacqueline, and I looked at each other. Jacqueline squeaked.

"Yeah," Ruiner said. "In his *leotard*. You're going to need a bath."

She hissed at him, and I wheezed laughter, catching a sudden whiff of tea tree oil and incense as someone crouched down next to me. Starlight handed me a bottle of water, the top already off, and I grabbed it, gulping greedily.

"I told you the ferrets would come in handy," she said

conversationally, while Hollowbeck and the carnival shouted and tussled around the corpse of the big top, and freed horses charged through the chaos and the caravan burned and the stars looked on, and I laughed so much I spat water over Ruiner, and he spat back at me, and Starlight patted my hair, and that was okay. It was more than okay.

We'd made it. And that was more than I'd dared hope for.

TWENTY-SIX

And breathe

THREE DAYS LATER, we regrouped on the roof terrace of Tanya's bar. The weather was back to Hollowbeck normal, the sky a high dome of stars above a perfectly crisp autumn night. There'd be frost tonight, I could feel it, but Petunia had moved out of her indoor jungle and got rid of all the paddling pools, so I knew it'd be the sort of frost that painted abstract art on the windows and held the dawn in crystal clarity.

Apparently being able to thrash a handful of carnival workers had helped her get over her aversion to them to the extent that Franz and Art were currently my fellow guesthouse residents. Unlike the other mysterious guests, I actually saw them, as Franz spent all his time in the kitchen eating Petunia's lemon drizzle cake, and Art had taken to gardening with a glee that didn't match his expertise. Petunia had been trying to explain the difference between onions and tulip bulbs when I'd left that evening, and the table had been heaped with them.

I inspected my drink and had a sip. It was loaded with honey and thyme and something punchy that both nipped my throat and soothed it. With any luck it might help me get over sounding like a thirty-year, pack-a-day smoker. Ruiner sprawled next to me, his snout stuck in a large bowl of something that had a strong whiff of fish, and Starlight sat next to me clutching a giant glass studded with fruit and at least three little umbrellas in both hands. Howard — or I thought it was Howard — and Jacqueline watched each other from our respective shoulders warily.

"I think I'd like to go to the seaside," Starlight said, slurping at a straw. "This makes me think of the Caribbean."

"I'm not sure Blackpool's going to cut it, then," I said. "Not quite the same."

"No," she admitted. "But you have to take a *plane* to the Caribbean."

"Well, yes. Don't you like planes?"

"I've never been on one," she said cheerfully, and plucked a bit of pineapple out of her drink.

"What, never?" Fine, she was a bit younger than me, but the golden age of budget airlines and package holidays wasn't that long ago. I didn't know anyone who hadn't at least bounced across to Spain for a boozy all-inclusive.

"No. I'm a witch."

I stared at her. "Witches can't fly?"

"It just seems…" She trailed off, thinking about it. "*Un-witchy*. Also, it's really bad for the environment, and that's *definitely* un-witchy."

"Right," I said, and looked at Ruiner. He was staring at Starlight, and shifted his gaze to me, pupils round in the low light. He started to say something, and I nodded across the terrace hurriedly. "Look, it's Theodore and Isabella."

"Well, yes," Starlight said. "They did say they'd meet us here."

"I just mean they've arrived."

She gave me a puzzled look, and fished more fruit out of her drink, while Ruiner narrowed his eyes at me.

Isabella floated across the terrace, greeting the other drinkers on her way and pausing to chat to a couple in the corner, but Theodore walked straight over and sat down opposite us, his usual red drink in one hand. Tanya had put a thermos sleeve around it, presumably to stop it cooling down too quickly.

He greeted us, his teeth thankfully back to usual size, although the fire seemed to have intensified the effects of the fake tan. He was all but glowing. "Are you healing up alright, Morgan?" he asked.

"Not too bad," I said, touching my new, much shorter hair. Getting rid of all the singed bits had also got rid of most of the greens and blues, but I wasn't convinced Starlight's hairdressing skills were up to much. She refused to let me go to Hollowbeck's actual hairdresser, though, as she was convinced they kept samples of everyone's hair for nefarious purposes, and after the last week I'd been too tired to argue. As for the rest, the strange herbal salves the Hollowbeck GP had gifted me were doing an astonishing job of healing up the burns, and other than the nightmares, I was feeling almost myself again.

"What happened to the carnival?" I asked Theodore, as Isabella joined us, leaning over to sniff my drink.

"Oh, very nice, Morgan," she said, before he could answer. "Citrus?"

"I think so," I said, and she fluttered her hands over my cheek, cool even in the night air.

"It's good to see you out."

"Thanks." I smiled at her. I'd mostly forgiven her for not helping Ruiner straight away. It couldn't be easy, balancing the needs of the town against the needs of the individual, but I thought I understood it a little better now.

She was welcome to mayoring. I certainly wouldn't want to do it.

"To answer your question," Theodore said, "The big top was unsalvageable, I believe. The poles were dust, and only a few scraps of canvas were left. Gus banned me from the grounds as soon as he could, of course, so I wasn't able to inspect it properly, but there was little left."

"And Aubrey? Was she really ... gone?" I couldn't bring myself to say *dead*.

"As far as I know, they didn't find her," he replied, his voice gentle. "She was the ringwoman, as much as part of the carnival as the big top was. I doubt one could survive without the other. They were born of the same cloth."

I sighed, rubbing my forehead, and Isabella said, "You did what was right, Morgan. More than anyone else could. You freed those who were trapped, and stopped the town being devoured."

"I still killed her. And the carnival, whatever it was. It was alive."

She nodded, exchanging a glance with Theodore. "Such choices are not easy. It takes a smart witch make them."

I snorted, waiting for Ruiner to say something rude, but he just said, "What'll the rest of them do, then? The ones that didn't leave the carnival?"

"I imagine they'll fade," Theodore said. "Become more of a fun fair and keep traveling, trying to recover what magic they can. It won't be easy, but they'll survive it."

"Who left, then?" Starlight asked.

"Art and Franz are at Petunia's," I told her. "Jacqueline hides every time she sees his leotard."

"He should get some trousers anyway. He's going to get cold," Starlight observed.

I snorted, and Isabella said, "Willow has also stayed in

town. Others have left the carnival but not stayed in Hollowbeck — not everyone here is happy to have them."

"Makes sense," Ruiner said. "You know, what with them trying to feed us all to the carnival."

"Franz helped," I said.

"*Barely.*"

"He did," I insisted. "He helped you get away from the dogs."

"He chucked his emergency protein balls at them. It's hardly *helping,* is it?"

"You would've been doggy chow if he hadn't. *And* he stopped me getting burned up."

"That he did anything at all is astonishing," Isabella said. "And your trapeze artist as well. The carnival demands complete loyalty. The punishments are severe."

"I never did find out what the punishment was," I said, and she shook her head gently.

"I wouldn't ask them. Let's say your burning would have been merciful."

I shivered, and Ruiner said, "Well, whatever. They only stepped in when we'd already done the hard work, so, you know. Unimpressed."

"Are cats ever impressed?" Starlight asked, offering Howard a piece of melon.

"*I'm not a cat.*"

"What about Jared and Coltrane?" I asked, before Ruiner could get in a huff.

"Still in the wrong bodies," Theodore said, frowning down at his shirt. It was a delicate pink, and now had a blotch of crimson on the chest. "Grace attempted to help, but couldn't manage it. They went back to the carnival and are hoping to find someone who can help in the next town, or the one after. Such things are not easily undone."

Ruiner and I gave matching sighs, and he said, "We know."

"So, you didn't actually lock anyone up?" I asked Theodore.

He shook his head. "I could have arrested the whole carnival, I suppose, but Hollowbeck doesn't really have a jail."

I stared at him. "But what happens when you arrest people?"

He waved vaguely. "I don't really arrest anyone. I might detain someone for a little, but usually they've just had one too many at one of the *other* pubs." He said it with a little sniff of disapproval for the poor standards of such places. "Or they've had a little argument with a neighbour and cursed their goldfish, or potatoes. I have a couple of cells, but once people cool down I just let them go."

"But what if they do something really bad?"

"Like Edith?" he reminded me. "She was banished for killing Norma. That is how we usually deal with serious crimes. We have very few of them, and most people don't seem to like to upset me." He grinned, and I tried not to look at his teeth, but that meant I was looking at his cheekbones, and I turned my attention to my drink instead.

"So you just let the whole murdery lot off?" Ruiner asked.

"Well, no one from town was murdered," Theodore said. "And the carnival is essentially destroyed, plus we got Morgan — and you — back. That felt like enough."

None of us said anything for a while, just sat there sipping our drinks while Isabella hummed to herself softly, hands folded in her lap and one cushion vanishing into her back in a disconcerting manner.

"Is Petunia still doing okay?" Starlight asked me.

"Yeah, she seems to be fine since she got to beat up the carnival folk."

"I thought so. The weather's been good again."

"Very sensitive to changes in the atmosphere, Petunia," Theodore observed. "I assume that's what comes from being a weather witch."

"How many different sorts of witches are there?" I asked.

"As many as there are witches," Isabella said. "Every one of you has their own way of being. You're people, after all."

I sighed. "That's unhelpful. I thought maybe I was trying to be the wrong sort of witch, and that's why everything keeps going pear-shaped."

"You're an excellent witch," she said. "You saved Hollowbeck."

"I really didn't," I said, and gave Jacqueline a nut from the plate on the table. "It was mostly her. And I wouldn't have even got into the carnival without Grace."

"*Grace*," Ruiner and Starlight both started, and I shushed them. As if summoned, Grace was striding across the terrace to join us, her hair flowing loose over her shoulders and her legs somehow looking even longer in loose jeans and boots. She sat down next to Theodore and grinned at us, flashing those dimples. I immediately remembered I had a coffee stain on my shirt and tugged my jacket a bit tighter.

"Feeling better?" she asked me.

"Not too bad," I replied. "I was just saying I wouldn't have been able to get into the carnival without you."

She waved dismissively. "I told you, you can do a lot with two smart witches."

"Sure," Ruiner said. "Nice words. What about all those

messages you were meant to be swapping when you stuck my sister in the carnival?"

I noticed he kept a decent distance from her while he said that, his muscles coiled tightly in preparation to flee.

She shrugged. "Birds, you know. They can be very unreliable. *Birdbrain*'s a term for a reason."

"You knew that before I went in?" I demanded.

"Well, sure. But the important thing was that it gave you the confidence to go in, right?"

We all stared at her, and I said, "So you had no idea what was going on in there?"

"A magpie told me you washed a lot of dishes."

"I did wash a lot of dishes," I said. "I also almost got burned at the stake."

"Sure, but we were there by then, right?" She patted Theodore's arm. "Theo here was keeping an eye on things, after all."

"Theodore," he said stiffly. "And yes, it was rather obvious Morgan had gone into the carnival, despite our explicit instructions not to."

"Your explicit instructions were *do nothing*, which wasn't happening." I said. "No one gets to kill my brother but me."

"And I merely offered a little support to get you in," Grace said. "And was there to help if you needed it in the big top, too."

Ruiner huffed. "*Help.* Get your hands on the grimoire, more like."

She raised an eyebrow at him. "Being a cat has not improved your disposition, Ruiner."

"All these witches sneaking around the place make me jumpy."

"Why? Did you upset one?"

He narrowed his eyes at her and she grinned, then looked at me.

"I hope this has earned me a bit of trust, Morgan," she said. "We can help each other."

Both Starlight and Ruiner gave surprisingly matching huffs, and Starlight said, "She's already got help."

Grace smiled at her. "Of course. But have you never heard of a coven?" She looked at her watch, then got up without waiting for an answer. "Must go. I'm meeting someone. See you all soon."

She strolled off, and we watched her pause at the door that led the stairs just as James came through. He looked around and spotted us, waving, and she kissed him quickly on the cheek then led the way to a corner table. He gave us an apologetic shrug and followed her.

None of us said anything for a moment, all carefully not looking at Starlight, and eventually she sniffed and said, "He really has no taste."

Ruiner opened his mouth, then shut it again without me even needing to poke him.

"I mean since he broke up with me," Starlight added, then continued hurriedly, "I broke up with *him*."

I nodded and said, "Anyway, genius move with the ferrets. That was impressive."

"For sure," Ruiner agreed. "Routed the whole crowd perfectly. They would've all still been sitting there staring at clowns and dribbling while the carnival ate their souls otherwise."

"I heard it was a great success," Theodore said solemnly.

Starlight straightened the front of her jumper. "Ferrets are very underrated."

I laughed and leaned back among the cushions as talk turned to ways to re-home the excess of ferrets, as, useful or not, we couldn't keep them all in the shop. The cold air was soothing on the last of my burns, and the deep wild night beyond the soft lights held peace and silence and beauty as much as it held carnivals and chaos. And right here, sitting with my brother the cat and my rat familiar, plus a witch, a ghost, and a vampire, it seemed that the beauty was a lot closer than I had found it anywhere else. Maybe because I'd fought so hard to keep it.

I touched my pocket, where the note Aubrey had given me lived. I didn't dare leave it out in case my brother found it, and I wasn't ready to share it yet. Wasn't ready to show him how the paper and the print matched the others I had received when we first arrived so exactly. We'd survived the carnival. We didn't need to be looking for other threats yet.

But I did need to figure out who was sending them, who had told Aubrey to set a trap for us. Because there'd be more to come. The note promised that. *You're no witch*, it read. *But you'll still burn.*

And I almost had.

But right now Starlight was protesting that she actually had *very good control* over the ferrets, thank you very much, and the whole thing where they'd got out and broken into the pet shop and destroyed an entire box of bouncing balls was the pet shop's fault for leaving a window open, and Isabella was laughing, and Theodore was suggesting that if he could put drunk people in cells, perhaps ferrets should be treated the same way. I watched them, smiling slightly, and my brother put a paw on my arm.

"What?" I asked him.

"Alright?"

"Pretty good, actually."

"Me too," he said, and took a deep breath as he stared up at me with wide eyes.

I thought for a moment he was going to tell me how

much it meant, that I'd gone to the carnival after him, and if he did that I was going to tell him what it meant to me that he'd never backed down, not once, in all the chaos, and that Grace was wrong about being a cat not improving his disposition.

Then he whispered, "I think there was *catnip* in my drink," and promptly rolled off the seating onto the floor and attacked the laces of my trainers. I jerked my feet away with a yelp and burst out laughing as he bolted off into the shadows with his tail up.

Starlight put an arm around me and hugged me, laughing as well, and I was suddenly quite sure that things were going to be okay. Coven or not, threats or not, when you have friends that stand by you, how can it not be?

The End

What To Read Next

When Morgan get a cryptic message from her ex-husband Jason, she knows that whatever trouble he's in, it's her fault. Over Ruiner's protests, she heads back to the normal world to find him. She and Ruiner face treachery, dangerous deals, and soul-stealing coffee as they search for Jason and try to save Darrowdale and Hollowbeck while they're at it.

Get Life's A Witch Today

About the Authors

Amelia Ash likes the quiet life. During the week, she works at the tea shop inside a friend's quirky bookstore, and on the weekends, she combs the countryside for estate sales, collecting trinkets, old furniture, and, in one memorable case, a clawfoot tub. In the evenings, she likes to binge-watch HGTV with her life companion: a barely domesticated cat named Lizard, who she suspects might possibly kill her if he could double his size and operate a can opener.

~

Kim M. Watt: Originally from New Zealand, Kim (she/her) now inhabits a slightly different world, crafting funny fantasies and off-beat cosy (or cozy) mysteries in which tea-drinking dragons collude with resourceful ladies of a certain age, baking-obsessed reapers run petting cafes for baby ghouls, and cats always bring the snark.

Kim's stories blend myth and reality in small and spectacular ways, where the Apocalypse comes on a Vespa, and the healing magic of tea and a really good lemon drizzle cake is unquestioned. But most of all, her tales are about friendship, loyalty, and people of all species looking out for one another. Because these, above all things, are magic.